THE LOST VOYAGE OF JOHN CABOT

Also by the Author

Moondog
Room 13
Tartabull's Throw

THE LOST VOYAGE OF JOHN CABOT

A NOVEL BY *Henry Garfield*

A Richard Jackson Book
Atheneum Books for Young Readers
NEW YORK   LONDON   TORONTO   SYDNEY

Atheneum Books for Young Readers
An imprint of Simon & Schuster Children's Publishing Division
1230 Avenue of the Americas, New York, New York 10020
Book design by Kristin Smith
The text for this book is set in Hadriano.
Manufactured in the United States of America
First Edition
2 4 6 8 10 9 7 5 3 1
Library of Congress Cataloging-in-Publication Data
Garfield, Henry.
The lost voyage of John Cabot / Henry Garfield.— 1st ed.
p. cm.
"A Richard Jackson Book."
Summary: A fictionalized account of the voyages of explorer John Cabot,
particularly his 1498 journey to the New World from which he and two
of his sons never returned, inspiring his middle son Sebastian to eventually
make his own voyages of exploration looking for the northwest passage to
Asia and for some trace of his long lost father and brothers.
ISBN 0-689-85173-1
1. Cabot, John, d. 1498?—Juvenile fiction. 2. Cabot, Sebastian, 1474
(ca.)–1557—Juvenile fiction. [1. Cabot, John, d. 1498?—Fiction. 2. Cabot,
Sebastian, 1474 (ca.)–1557—Fiction. 3. Explorers—Fiction. 4. America—
Discovery and exploration—English—Fiction.] I. Title. PZ7.G17939Lo 2004
[Fic]—dc21
2003007429

To my parents

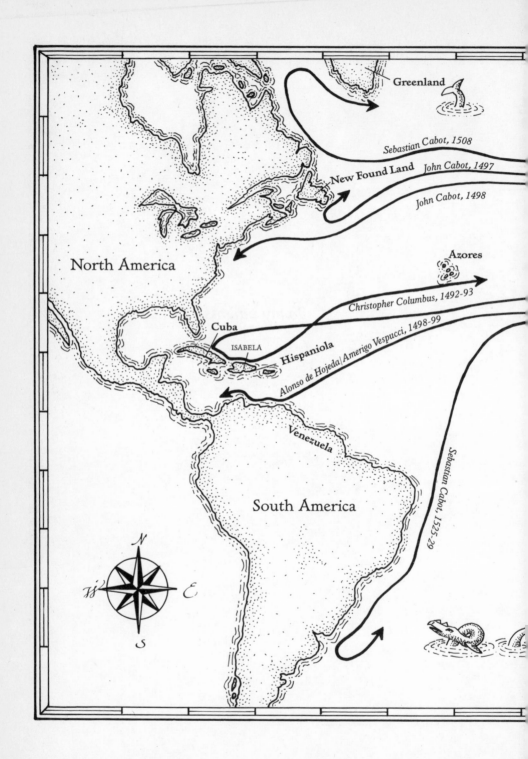

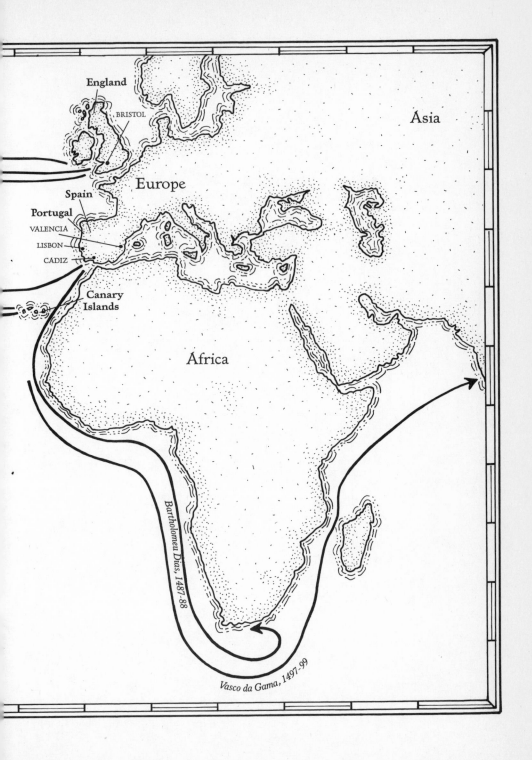

England

BRISTOL

Asia

Europe

Spain

Portugal

VALENCIA

LISBON

CADIZ

Canary
Islands

Africa

Bartholomeu Dias, 1487-88

Vasco da Gama, 1497-99

CHAPTER 1

31 May 1498

Dear Sebastian,

Thank God I am still alive to write these words. I have never seen such a storm, and I hope to never see its like again.

I wonder if Ludovico still lives. I fear for him, and for all those on the other ships. There is no sign of any of them on this rolling sea.

The sky is only now beginning to clear, after five days of hell, during which the only difference between night and day was that in the day you could see the angry gray-green waves a moment before they pounded the ship. Father has ordered sail rigged on our two remaining masts. The mainmast snapped like a toothpick on the third day of the storm.

You have never seen such waves, Sebastian. Walls of green water half the height of the mast that is now gone!

Many of the men were praying. Others cursed Father for bringing them on this voyage. Never mind that they owe him their lives. For three days and nights he remained on deck, without food or sleep, keeping our stern to the tremendous seas. At the height of the tempest, he lashed himself to the tiller, and even as I huddled below, expecting each wave to crack our ship open like an egg, I could hear him shouting defiant curses into the wind. One man was lost, swept overboard with the mainmast and rigging while cutting it away. But it was Father, and only Father, who saved the rest of us. He is a great man, Sebastian.

We do not know where we are. Father thinks we must be closer to the New Found Land than to England, for the storm came out of the northeast, and we have been driven before it for many days. With only the two smaller masts remaining, there is little we can do but remain before the wind, which continues from the northeast, though it is diminishing. At midday the sun was but a bright fuzzy spot behind the gray, and Father said it would be impossible to take a sight. "Perhaps tonight we will see the Pole Star," he said. "The sky is clearing in the west."

I know you are angry, Sebastian, at being left behind. I know you resent me. It pains you that Ludovico stands third-in-command on Father's old ship, and that I am crew

on his new one, while you, the middle son, must remain
behind and not see the New Found Land, nor, perhaps,
the riches of Asia beyond. But I tell you honestly that we
are lucky to have survived. During the storm, I would have
traded places with you in a heartbeat.

And that is why I am writing this, though your eyes may
never see it—because every day on this vast and uncharted
ocean is a day spent face-to-face with Death. When we
return, these letters will serve as a record of our voyage, and
I will hand them to you when next we meet. It is a comfort
to know that you and Mother are safe and well in England.

Your loving brother,

Sancio

4 June 1498

Dear Sebastian,

We continue to the west in rolling seas churned up by
the storm. No sign of Ludovico and the Matthew, or the
other ships. Of course, it is hard to see any distance,
because when the mainmast was swept away we lost our
crow's nest and our highest vantage point. Father has sent
me and some of the smaller men into the rigging on the
forward mast, but there has been no sight of land, or any
other vessel. Nothing but green waves.

Today we passed through a school of fish so thick that men were lowering baskets over the side and hauling them up full, one after the other. They are the same stockfish we see piled high on the docks in Bristol. Surely Bristol is home to the greatest and most daring sailors in the world. Father has done well to pick a crew from among such men. Most Englishmen think the bounty of fish from the Bristol fleet comes from Icelandic waters, and the fishermen have been happy to have them think so. But one of the older men told me that the Bristol fleet has been gathering its catch from waters to the south and west of Iceland, and that Father's New Found Land has been known to them for some time.

The cow and the pigs and all but three of our chickens were lost to the storm, but our supply of dry food is intact. So long as the sea remains abundant with fish we will not starve. But we do need to make repairs. We must reach a shore soon. We cannot sail to Asia without our mainmast and its sails and rigging. Sails we can construct from canvas we carry on board, but we must find a landfall where there is timber.

Sebastian, our father knows he did not reach the tip of Asia last summer, in spite of all the speeches and prizes. But he knows also that Columbus has not seen Asia either, nor come near it. Father told King Henry exactly what he wanted to hear: that the New Found Land was the

4

northeast promontory of the Asian mainland, and that to reach the riches of Cathay and the court of the Great Khan, his fleet need only follow the land as it falls away to the southwest. "Because I am sailing across the shoulder of the world, my route will be shorter than the route of Columbus, who is sailing across its belly," he said.

My brother, I have tried to forget the look of bitterness on your face, or the last words you spoke to me. I knew you wished to be in my place. We must return, if for no other reason than for you and I to put things right between us.

Your loving brother,
Sancio

7 June 1498

Dear Sebastian,

Two nights ago the seas were finally calm enough and the sky clear enough for Father to take a fix on Polaris. He placed it forty-five degrees above the horizon, which means that we are already south of Bristol's latitude, and south of last year's landfall on the New Found Land.

From Dursey Head, Father set a course to the northwest, explaining to the crew that it would save both time and distance over the usual method of following the parallel. Farther north we were more likely to find easterly winds, he said—a prediction that came terribly true. By sailing first north and then south of true west, we would describe a course closer to a "great circle," which is the shortest path across any section of the surface of a sphere. Many of the men looked at one another and frowned when Father said this, for surely such a concept is beyond the understanding of most seamen. I am not sure I understand it myself.

There is still a great abundance of fish, indicating, Father says, that we are near land. Yesterday, the lead line found bottom at just over sixty fathoms. This caused great excitement among the crew, and Father ordered me to the top of the foremast, but there was no land in sight. We stood off during the night, lest we come upon a shore in the dark, but in the morning there was still no land to be seen, and no bottom under the lead. Father seemed puzzled, saying we must have passed over some underwater bank, and he ordered a course set due west, and sent me into the rigging twice more, but there was still nothing to see but ocean.

No ship broke the horizon either. Father has not spoken Ludovico's name. He is not a man to voice his troubles to others, as you well know, and his immediate attention is to this ship and her crew, but I can tell you that it is a comfort to him that you, at least, are on terra firma.

The abatement of the storm has returned things more

or less to normal aboard ship; we are back on regular watches and regular meal times. Last night I had the evening watch and the morning dogwatch; the weather has been fair and movements of the ship steady and predictable, so as to lull one to sleep on the forward boards, with the sound of the sea on the other side of the hull. Tonight I must be on deck at midnight. The spirits of the men are much improved with hot stew in their bellies and the day's ration of beer. Father Cartwright has resumed the morning and evening prayers and the recitation of psalms, and although Father has little use for these rituals, most of the men observe them. I have found most sailors to be religious men, though to me it seems their faith is as one with their superstition—that is, they do not want to risk offending anything, real or not, that might influence their safe return to port.

At fourteen, I am the youngest of the thirty-five (now thirty-four) men aboard, though Peter Firstbrook and William Hennessey are your age, Sebastian, and have become my best friends among the crew. I am often teased and made the butt of jokes for being the captain's son. Some of the men look at me strangely when they see me writing these letters or reading from one of my books, for most of them have never learned to read or write. At times I read aloud to William and Peter from The Travels of Marco Polo, *and we whisper among ourselves of what it will be like to arrive in Asia.*

It is nearly time for my watch. I remain, as always,

Your loving brother,

Sancio

11 June 1498

Dear Sebastian,

These past three days and nights found us surrounded by a thick, moist fog. Father dares not simply plow westward, for fear of running into an unseen shore. So we jog on and off, throwing the lead, hour after hour. The men are in a sour mood. There is no horizon and no sky. It is like sailing on the surface of an immense bowl of broth with the steam rising off of it, only this steam is cold and clammy and offers no comfort.

Father said the fog was a sure indication that land was close, for such fogs do not form in mid-ocean. And still the lead came back without finding bottom, and the men grumbled all the more.

We are now thirty-one days out of Bristol—nearly the time it took Father to reach the New Found Land last summer. He thinks we have sailed a greater distance, for the storm pushed us south of our intended path, and the

*land tends to the southwest. Soon, God and wind willing,
we will stand upon it.*

Your loving brother,
Sancio

12 June 1498

Dear Sebastian,

*Land! Glorious, solid, unmoving land! We have done it,
Sebastian. Battered, dismasted, separated from the other
ships in the fleet—we have nonetheless crossed the Western
Ocean and come to safe harbor.*

*William saw it first, near the end of the morning watch.
Within minutes the green outline of the hills was visible to
every man on deck, and a great cheer went up. Father
ordered sail shortened, and we began a series of tacks, for
the wind, what there was of it, came very nearly from the
direction of the land, and we were many hours working
toward it. As we approached we could see that we had
closed with a rocky shore, replete with small islands and
half-submerged ledges. Father proceeded with caution,
standing off and ordering frequent soundings, so that it was
nearly dusk when the anchor was cast over the side for the
first time since we left Bristol.*

We lie in a small bay with trees all around and low hills

behind. There is protection from every wind direction but southeast. The trees are tall and straight, and one among them is sure to be perfect for fashioning a new mainmast. The shoreline is rock, with the exception of a flat landing area near the innermost part of the bay. As it was nearly dark, only Father and the priest and two of the sailors went ashore, the sailors armed with crossbows. Father planted the flags and erected a cross and claimed the land in the name of King Henry VII of England, and then, as dark was drawing on, the men returned to the ship. They saw no natives. Tomorrow we shall all go ashore and scout the area.

Tonight, pairs of guards will watch the shore for fires or other signs of human company. It looks like a good land, and Father cannot imagine its being uninhabited. It is possible, he said, that this is an extension of the New Found Land he coasted last summer.

Father ordered an extra ration of beer, and there is much merriment. We must make repairs, and the fleet is scattered, our older brother out there somewhere, if he is not at the bottom of the sea. Tomorrow we will face these things. But tonight, all that matters is that we are here.

Your loving brother,
Sancio

CHAPTER 2

"**Y**OU WANT TO TAKE HER IN, SEBASTIAN?" Sebastian Cabot snapped out of his daydream and looked at the longboat's owner and helmsman. Richard Ryerson was his father's friend, and in the days since the departure of the fleet, Sebastian had taken to riding out to King's Road and back with him almost daily, just to get a glimpse of the sea. Ryerson never charged him.

"Sure. Yes," the boy said, and moved toward the stern to take the tiller.

"The current's easing a bit," Ryerson said, trading seats with Sebastian. "That's the beauty of Bristol, this current. No other place like it."

Sebastian settled in at the tiller and steered the boat around a bend, and the city of Bristol came into view. The four oarsmen, not many years older than he, pulled the boat through the water with strong, smooth strokes.

Indeed, the tides made Bristol what it was. You could drift out on the ebb and run back on the flood, and you could do this daily, no matter what the wind or weather. Seven miles up a river, protected by a steep gorge through which the tidal waters surged twice daily, Bristol was the best port in the British Isles.

But if the concept was beautiful, Sebastian thought, the city itself was not. The English lacked the Mediterranean sense of style. Bristol was stolidly utilitarian. The docks were built out onto the mudflats, where ships sat uselessly eight hours out of every twelve, while most of the city's ten thousand or so people lived crammed together along narrow streets that climbed the steep hillside. Dominating the approach was the old castle and fort, which had guarded the city for some six hundred years. Sebastian knew from his lessons and his father's tales that Bristol had twice been sacked by Vikings, despite the protection of both the difficult approach and its man-made fortifications.

This afternoon the boat had only three passengers besides himself: a young couple and an old sailor off a Basque fishing ship. Sebastian liked taking the boat down to King's Road, where he could look out the channel toward the open sea and watch for ships returning from trading missions to the Mediterranean, or from the fishing grounds, far to the west, where his father and his two brothers had gone.

Sometimes large merchant ships would be waiting at King's Road to be guided up the river, as it was a treacherous passage for a captain who had never visited Bristol before, between the rushing tides and the numerous shoals they covered. For nearly four years Sebastian had watched the great ships make their way through the gorge and round the twists and turns in the river, dependent upon pilot boats a fraction of their size.

Sebastian recalled last year's triumphant return of the *Matthew*. Crowds had gathered around the docks as his father's ship was led in, news of the discovery of the New Found Land having already traveled upriver to the city. Within weeks his father had returned from an audience with the king himself, in possession of a contract to outfit a new expedition—five ships, to sail the following spring. He remembered the months of preparation, the shuffling of favored positions within the harbor so his father's ships could enjoy the most convenient moorings, the constant stream of visitors, the knots of men who moved with him around the docks, consulting over ship specifications and crew and provisions. And he remembered most keenly his own bitter disappointment that he, his father's second son and next in line to assume a position of responsibility on the deck of one of his father's ships, or so he supposed, would instead remain behind in Bristol while his two brothers went along to share in their father's glory. His father had explained his reasons, and Sebastian had argued, right up until the day the fleet floated down the channel. But who was he, a boy of fifteen, to argue with the great John Cabot, whom the entire city of Bristol treated as if he had walked, Christ-like, rather than sailed, to the New Found Land?

Three weeks had passed since the fleet had sailed. His father had suggested that Sebastian accompany him on the *Pandora* as far as King's Road and ride back with Richard Ryerson, but so sharp was Sebastian's disappointment that he had refused to take part in the departure, or even wish his father and brothers Godspeed. Instead, he had turned from the docks and walked high into the hills behind the city, where he could look down at the river from afar and watch the ships work toward the sea.

It had been his turn—that was the plain and simple truth of it, and he hadn't wanted to listen to his father's reasons for leaving him behind: that seafaring in unknown waters is a dangerous undertaking from which men sometimes do not return, and that Sebastian's mother might bear the loss of a husband and one or two sons but not the entire family. Why could Ludovico not have stayed, then? Barely twenty, Ludovico had shipped out on the *Matthew* the previous summer and now strode her decks as second officer of the second boat in the fleet. The Bristol men called him "Lewis," and they obeyed him, for his authority came directly from his father, and his father's authority came directly from the king. Ludovico cut an impressive figure on ship. Taller than their father, darkly complected in the way of southern Europeans, Sebastian's older brother commanded respect by his mere appearance, and the Cabot name only added to his reputation with the sailors. He would make a fine captain one day. Sebastian knew that his father envisioned his oldest son as commander of a fleet of trading ships along the western route to Asia that they would pioneer. He had heard his father boast that someday the Cabots would live among the wealthy merchant families along Redcliffe Street, overlooking the harbor and its mighty fleet of ships. Sebastian would also sail to foreign ports, and bring home his share of wealth to the family empire. All this his father dreamed of, and spoke of around the dinner table when he was home, and Sebastian believed it would happen.

No, he did not begrudge Ludovico his standing, for

oldest sons were expected to follow fathers in their businesses—and their father's was exploration and trade. That was why the family had come to Bristol. What Sebastian could not forgive was his father's decision to take his younger brother Sancio, a child of fourteen, as a ship's boy on board the newly constructed flagship, the *Pandora*. Why Sancio, who regularly ditched his lessons to explore the waterfront and backwaters of Bristol, yet could always seem to talk his way out of trouble?

Perhaps it was trouble their father had on his mind, and he had taken young Sancio along on the voyage to keep him out of it. Only last year, the boy had loosed a tender from one of the great trading ships and floated clear out to Hung Road on the ebbing tide. There he ran the boat up on some rocks, cracking two of the planks, and had been rescued by a fishing boat. The fishermen had made much of Sancio and given him huge quantities of fish to take home to his family. Their father, then preparing for the sailing of the *Matthew,* had been more curious about Sancio's adventure and its unexpected ending than angry at the theft, although he had to pay for the damage. Ludovico had fearlessness, but Sancio had something else, Sebastian thought, something like a cat's innate ability to land on its feet.

And what did that leave him? Sebastian would never be as tall or strong as Ludovico nor as lucky as Sancio. He had no special qualities, although he applied himself to his lessons and was useful around a boat. He could do his geometry problems, but they bored him; he could speak English but thought it a crude language, full of harsh sounds, lacking the poetry of Castilian or his native Genoese. Sancio faked his way through Euclid, and the English he had picked up came more from his prowlings about the harbor than any concentrated effort to learn; you could pick up bits and pieces of several languages just by hanging around the Bristol waterfront. Sancio still had a child's ear for language, Sebastian reasoned—which explained why he could assimilate new words and phrases so quickly and seemingly without effort. As for Ludovico, he was such a strong physical presence he barely had to speak at all.

Sebastian knew the truth of it—that his father considered him the dullest of his three sons. "I must rely on you to look after your mother and our house in my absence," he had said, days before the fleet's departure. But was not "reliable" another word for "predictable"? He could just as easily be a reliable hand aboard ship, while Sancio looked after things. But he knew what his father would say to

17

that objection. Sancio was a boy still, unsuited by years or temperament to doing a man's work or taking on a man's responsibilities. But that was only his father's spoken reason. How many times had he heard his father laugh when Sancio brought back some colorful bit of conversation from the docks to the dinner table? Sancio was his father's favorite. That was the real reason he was out on the Western Ocean aboard the *Pandora* while Sebastian remained in Bristol.

Above the busy waterfront Bristol presented layers of stone upon stone, row houses crammed together along narrow streets that wound up the steep banks of two converging rivers, the Avon and the Frome. The most notable buildings, aside from the castle itself, were the churches. Sebastian picked out the simple but elegant spire of St. Nicholas, where he and his mother attended services, just down the street from their rented house. Off to starboard stood the magnificent St. Mary's of Redcliffe Cathedral, with its square bell tower and quadruple spires. Nearby, spread out along Redcliffe Hill, were the grand houses of Bristol's wealthy merchants, the owners of the great trading vessels—and of three of the five ships in his father's fleet. Sebastian had been in a few of those houses. Such meals they enjoyed! Venison stew with red currant jelly, pheasant, boar's head! And all served on fine china and flavored with spices from Asia, purchased, Sebastian knew, at a high price from Arab middlemen. When he looked around in those houses, Sebastian saw colorful tapestries imported from who knew where, fine tables of dark, polished wood, figurines carved out of walrus tusks. He had never seen such wealth, not even in Venice. He found it a bit appalling, considering how the majority of Bristol's people lived.

The waterfront stank. It wasn't so bad at high tide, when the mudflats were covered, but exposed, they reeked with the excrement of ten thousand people. Everything ran into the channel, including spillage from barges, the remains of fish, animal carcasses, sometimes even human bodies. The waterfront was long, and divided into two sections: the key, along the bank of the smaller Frome and closer to the channel, and the back, around another bend in the Avon, with Redcliffe Hill on one side and St. Nicholas Bank on the other.

Here Sebastian steered the longboat, as the starboard rowers held their oars and the two men on the port side pulled the boat around the bend in the river. The tide was nearly slack now, the water flat, and the boat glided swiftly through it. Then another bend, in the other direction, and they were underneath Redcliffe Gate and the great cathedral, then past it. Sebastian called out directions to the oarsmen and steered the boat to a smooth landing at the dock on St. Nicholas Bank.

"Well done, lad," Ryerson said as Sebastian and the bow man secured the lines. "My offer is still open, you know."

"Yes, sir, and thank you," Sebastian said. "I will discuss it with my mother."

Though it was late afternoon and the dockside markets were closed for the day, the waterfront was still busy, as several boats had come in on the high tide for outfitting or to off-load cargo. Sebastian walked along the river toward his mother's church and the bridge, which was the farthest oceangoing ships could go. He and his family had crossed that bridge to attend dinners on Redcliffe Hill, and Sebastian's father had remarked afterward that the bridge was the only link between Bristol's social classes.

At the church Sebastian turned left and headed up St. Nicholas Street toward his house. The smell of cooking meat from several of the tightly bunched houses reached his nostrils as he made his way with long strides up the hill. The Cabots lived well, in a two-story dwelling they rented from one of the Redcliffe Hill merchants. Farther back from the waterfront, poorer families sometimes lived in one cramped story of a five-story building, but Sebastian and his mother had all the room they needed. The house, in fact, felt empty with the absence of his brothers. He did not mind his father's absence so much, for it was nothing unusual. His father had been leaving on and returning from trips ever since Sebastian could remember.

His mother greeted him as he walked in the door. "Sit down and I'll serve you some stew," she said. "Mutton and vegetables." There were farms on the land behind Bristol, but most of the city's goods came by river, for transport by water was easier than travel over England's primitive roads. When his father had gone to see the king after last summer's journey to the New Found Land, he had been absent from Bristol for more than a week, even though the distance between Bristol and London was less than that between the mouth of the River Avon and Dursey Head in Ireland, which could be reached in two days with a fair wind.

The long wooden table, made of the same Wye Forest oak that had gone into the construction of the *Matthew* and the *Pandora,* had always seemed large even with a full family around it. Sebastian's mother took a seat opposite him, and said, "We could have a seven-course meal, you and I, like the rich do, and still not fill this table."

"Perhaps we should cut it in half, and make two tables," Sebastian said as he began to eat.

His mother laughed easily. Mattea Cabot was a handsome woman, dark-haired and dark-eyed, shorter than her husband and three sons, sturdy yet small, not round in the way of so many older women. She was forty-five; the years had etched lines around her eyes and the corners of her mouth, and there were strands of white in her dark hair, which she wore in a bun at the nape of her neck. She had set up house in Venice, Valencia, and now Bristol, and in every house she had endured her husband's long absences. As her sons grew older she turned to them increasingly for conversation, so that by Sebastian's fifteenth birthday they had fallen into something that resembled friendship, and Sebastian found that he could talk to his mother easily about all matter of things. With his father it was different. Sebastian's father had crossed the ocean; now the king of England had placed him in command of five commissioned vessels. He was becoming a legend. But John Cabot had always been something of a stranger in his own house. Sebastian often thought he knew the legend better than the man.

"Mr. Ryerson has said I can have a job if I want it," he

told his mother, wiping up the remains of his stew with a thick piece of bread. "As helmsman on one of his river boats."

"There is plenty of money, Sebastian," his mother said.

"Father's money," Sebastian replied. "Meant to pay for this house and our food in his absence. I'm old enough to earn my own. Mr. Ryerson says I know the river and the currents as well as anyone. And I have taken some turns at the helm already."

Mattea sighed. "You are your father's son," she said. "Always wanting to be going somewhere. I'm sure you know the river—you are on it often enough."

"Mother, I can't just do nothing."

"There are your lessons."

Sebastian pushed his empty bowl away. "Lessons! Euclid and his angles! What difference do they make while I am stuck here in Bristol?" He rose from the table and walked over to a small stand, on top of which stood his father's homemade globes, one the size of a grapefruit, the other larger than a man's head. He picked up the larger one and pretended to study it. "The only way to learn those things," he said, "is out there, in practice, not in theory. The way Sancio is."

His mother fell silent, anticipating that Sebastian was trying to start an argument, which he was. He disliked his twice-weekly math and Latin lessons almost as much as the Sunday Mass his mother forced him to attend. His teacher was a small, wizened old man from Marseilles named Frederick Vigneron, who seemed to think that the theorems and formulae were beautiful things in and of themselves, and saw no reason to sully them by association with the physical world. He did not care to discuss the dimensions of the world or the extent of the Western Ocean or the latitude of the island of Cipangu and the kingdoms of China, his father's destinations. Sebastian found the lessons boring and often let his mind wander.

A job would not get him out of going to church on Sunday with his mother, but it might discourage Mr. Vigneron, for if he was never home during the day, when would the old teacher find time to come to the house? His father had no doubt paid the man to keep up with the lessons, but his father was somewhere across the sea.

Sebastian turned the globe in his hand. His father had constructed it using layers of paper and glue, one hemisphere at a time, and then glued the two hemispheres together, so that it was lightweight and hollow, with only a slight bulge at the equator. Then he had painted on the lands and ocean. The familiar lands of Europe and the Near East were rendered with fair accuracy, as was India and the outline of Africa, which the Portuguese had shown could be rounded to the south, well below the equator. Much of the southern hemisphere had been hastily painted, for it held little interest for Sebastian's father and even less for the English king. He had placed a large white landmass at the southern pole and drawn fanciful pictures of sea serpents all around it, but in truth no one knew what lay in the far south, because no one had ever been there. The bulk of his father's artistic efforts had been devoted to the north, especially to those reaches of the Western Ocean into which the men of Bristol had been sailing for generations. Iceland was there, and Greenland too, a thumb sticking down from the frozen wastes of the north, also painted white. The great mass of Asia extended halfway around the globe, and off its far coast his father had placed scattered islands, dotting that part of the Western Ocean into which Columbus had sailed. But Sebastian's father had drawn an even greater extension of Asia in its northern reaches, so that it nearly touched the large islands he had placed to the south and west of Greenland, at a distance comparable to that between Lisbon and the Azores. Find a way beyond those islands, he had told Henry VII, and you will have your western route to Asia.

"Guesswork," Sebastian said. He scowled down at the globe in his hand, turning it until the uncharted but much speculated-upon islands in the Western Ocean were in front of his face.

His mother came up beside him and laid a hand lightly on his shoulder. "When you are old, Sebastian, it will be guesswork no longer," she told him. "Yours will be the generation to map the world. How lucky you are."

Sebastian turned the globe again, pretending to study it, hiding his irritation. He loved his mother and believed she would do anything for him, but sometimes she said the most incredibly annoying things. Everyone knew Sancio was the lucky one.

They had come to Bristol by sea, of course, nearly four years before, passengers on a Genoese merchant ship captained by a man who had known his father, and his father's father. Sebastian was continually surprised at the number of men his father knew from ports all over Europe. In Valencia there had been a steady stream of visitors. In Bristol, too, though it was a new country for Sebastian and his brothers, Giovanni Caboto—or John Cabot, as they called him here—enjoyed the company of other seafaring men. Sebastian had often heard his father regale visitors with tales of his travels to Arabia and the ports of the eastern Mediterranean; the Bristol sailors reciprocated by telling of their own adventures in Scandinavia and out on the Great Western Ocean. Sebastian had heard and seen more of the world than most boys his age. But he had heard enough and wanted to see more.

Sebastian remembered the journey from Valencia to Bristol, and their father's unwavering certainty that the family's future lay in England and not Spain. Sebastian had stood on the foredeck in the rain as the ship passed through the Strait of Gibraltar. He had felt the long, undulating swells of the open sea for the first time. At Lisbon he had observed the rise and fall of the tide, more pronounced than in the Mediterranean, though nothing like the spectacular tides of Bristol. Across the mouth of the Bay of Biscay, the ship had steered out of sight of land completely, and for the first time in his life Sebastian had been surrounded by an expanse of moving blue water. He had watched with awe as the captain brought them upon Land's End in Britain using nothing more than the sun and a magnetized needle floating on a card in water. His father told him later that with more reliable timepieces one could, in theory at least, circle the world with nothing but an astrolabe and a compass.

The house in Bristol had been waiting for them, for his father had not come here as a stranger, and was held in some regard by the men who owned the merchant ships and who, through their control of goods and money, effectively owned the town. Sebastian and his mother and his brothers had been the strangers, and four years had not eased that feeling.

In those four years, Sebastian's father had put to sea three times, while Sebastian had not been farther than the mouth of the River Severn, which emptied into the Bristol Channel, which led to the open sea. He had learned to speak and read English reasonably well, and how to handle a small boat on the River Avon's tricky currents; he had studied his father's charts and learned the constellations. He was ready for adventure. One day, he promised himself, he, too, would sail over the western horizon.

Sebastian set down the globe and turned to his mother. "I'm going to take the job," he said to her. "I like being on the river, and the money will help too."

His mother's expression did not change. "Your father would say that your lessons are more important," she said. "And his pension is quite adequate."

"My father would not be opposed to the making of money," Sebastian said. "He has chased after money all his life."

"That is true enough," his mother acknowledged.

"Besides," Sebastian added, "I cannot live in my father's shadow forever."

CHAPTER 3

GIOVANNI CABOTO WAS BORN IN GENOA, in what would eventually become the country of Italy, in 1450. His father, Egidius, was a trader in imported goods and the owner of two shops in the busy port city. Young Giovanni would often pass time with other boys around the docks, watching the ships sail in and out, listening to the talk of the sailors. Among the crowd was a tall, red-haired boy a year younger than Giovanni named Cristoforo Colombo, who would become known to the world as Christopher Columbus.

Once, in the centuries before the Black Death, Genoa had ruled the Mediterranean. Its ships had carried the soldiers of the Crusades to the Holy Land and returned laden with silks and spices from the mysterious Far East. By the time of Giovanni's birth, however, Genoa had been supplanted by Venice, on the opposite side of the

Italian peninsula, as the world's preeminent naval power.

As a child, Giovanni saw that many of the stylish hillside houses stood empty, the families of their owners having either died in the plague or moved on in the face of hard times. Giovanni's family struggled too, although he and his brother and three sisters never went hungry or without new clothes. But a shadow hung over the family, as it hung over the whole city, and that shadow only deepened with the news that Constantinople had fallen to the Ottoman Turks—news that sent shock waves through Europe in 1453, when Giovanni was three years old.

At first, daily life changed little. But fear hung in the air, in the shops, on the docks where the ships came in. The Turks were said to be barbarians intent on subjugating all of Europe to the sword of Islam. They would not be satisfied until there were mosques in every city around the Mediterranean and the Papacy itself surrendered.

Egidius dismissed such talk as nonsense. "Venice will always be Venice," he said. "Its banks control the commerce of the world, and even infidels need money to live." But the Turks now controlled all major trade routes to Asia. The spices and silks on which Venice and Genoa had grown rich now had to pass through the hands of Islamic middlemen, sworn enemies of Christian Europe.

In the summer of 1460, when Giovanni was ten, the Caboto family left Genoa and moved to Venice. Egidius sold his two shops and hired himself out as a buyer and seller for a large Venetian mercantile firm. It meant less independence but more money, and young Giovanni eventually became an apprentice for the same company.

Venice's look and feel were different from Genoa's. Whereas Genoa was built like a fortress on steep hillsides surrounding its harbor, Venice seemed part of the sea itself. Low, flat, and half-drowned, Venice seeped out into the Adriatic, and its influence spread over the known world like ink over water.

In his teens and early twenties, Giovanni traveled on Venetian sailing ships throughout the Mediterranean and as far as the Madeira Islands, off the coast of Portugal in the Great Western Ocean. He became a keen observer of wind and weather and an adept mariner. He learned how to use an astrolabe and a compass, and he picked up the art of "dead reckoning," which involved estimating a ship's speed through the water and predicting the next landfall. He learned how to pilot large trading vessels into and out of tricky harbor approaches, and he picked up bits and pieces of several languages he needed to negotiate with businessmen who came from as far away as Alexandria and Lisbon.

In Lisbon he ran into his childhood friend from the docks of Genoa, Christopher Columbus, and the two sometimes traded stories of their adventures. Columbus had been shipwrecked in Portugal and settled there after apprenticing himself to a mapmaker. Portuguese sailors, in tough seagoing ships called caravels, were pushing outward and expanding the horizons of trade. Lisbon's docks were stacked with Baltic timber, Icelandic codfish, Madeira wine. There were also captive groups of near-naked dark-skinned Africans, captured and brought back to Portugal to work in the vineyards and sugarcane plantations as slaves.

It was in Lisbon that Giovanni met the rough northern sailors from Bristol for the first time, and heard their tales of the fabled Isle of Brasil and other lands far out in the unmapped Western Ocean. And it was at one Lisbon tavern or another that the talk around the tables first turned toward a possible western route to Asia.

Though Caboto traveled widely, he found his life's companion in his home port. Mattea Soncino, daughter of a successful Venetian merchant with whom Giovanni did business, was hesitant at first. But Giovanni Caboto charmed her, brought her gifts of perfume and Persian silks, and talked of distant places. In 1478 they were married, though Caboto continued to travel. Soon there was a son, Ludovico, followed three years later by Sebastian and a year after that by Sancio.

Barely a year after Sancio was born, Giovanni's father collapsed in his waterfront office in Venice and died. As the eldest son, Giovanni was required to look after his father's business interests and provide for his aging mother. He invested profitably in a saltworks and several pieces of farmland, and the family lived well.

Throughout Sebastian's youth, his father came and went, and his returns from abroad were scenes of great joy. Caboto was generous with gifts for his sons. Sebastian and Ludovico played chess regularly (and Sebastian lost regularly) with a set from India made of teak and balsa wood. Their father spoke of the Turks' push into Greece, and of the efforts of the Spanish, newly united under Ferdinand of Aragon and Isabella of Castile, to beat back the Islamic Moors on the western side of the Mediterranean. He admired the Portuguese ships and their ventures out into the Western Ocean. And he related tales he'd overheard about Basque and British fishermen and the trade wars with their Scandinavian counterparts, and the search for new fishing grounds even farther out toward the edge of the Earth.

Sebastian knew that talk of "the edge of the Earth" was nonsense. One needed only to watch a ship, or an island, come up over the horizon, and observe that the top of the object appeared first, to deduce that the surface of the world was curved. This was so obvious that he could not remember ever having had a discussion about it. If one traveled over the surface of a sphere, one could literally go around the world and return eventually to the starting point. That no one had ever done it did not mean that it could not be done.

But in Sebastian's world, the land ended at the Western Ocean, and this was true at all latitudes. Marco Polo, Venice's most famous son, had walked all the way to the court of the Great Khan two centuries before, and brought back tales of fabulous lands and great riches. But he had walked east, through deserts and across mountains and over vast tablelands. One could not walk west—not from Iberia or Africa or any of the kingdoms of northern Europe—for always the Western Ocean stood in the way. But if one could *sail* west, would not one reach the eventual end of Asia, from the other direction? Sebastian's father reported that there was much talk of this idea among the traders and travelers of Christian Europe, and not just late at night in Lisbon bars. Sooner or later, someone was bound to try it.

• • •

One day when Sebastian was six, his father came home with a handsome, leather-bound volume and plunked it onto the table. "This," he declared, "is going to change the world."

His wife and three young sons looked at him. Finally Ludovico said, "A book. What of it?" The family owned several books, including a Bible in which Sebastian's grandmother had inscribed his and his brothers' dates of birth and baptism.

"Not just any book," his father said, picking it up and thumbing the pages open, displaying them. "A *printed* book." When his wife and sons stared back at him blankly, he continued. "There is a new printing house here in Venice, and they are using a new method, invented by the Germans. The letters and words are cast in metal, and can be moved, and set in whatever arrangement the printer desires. Once a page is set, it can be inked and printed hundreds of times. Think of it! Hundreds of copies can be made in the same time and at the same cost it once took to make a dozen. Do you know what this means?"

"More books?" Sebastian ventured.

"More books!" his father cried. "Books for everyone, even the poorest peasant, the lowliest dock laborer! And do you know what *that* means? It means the secrets of the ages can no longer be hidden away and guarded by monks in stone towers while the rest of the people struggle in ignorance. Do you know, my sons, that most houses in Venice have no books at all? That most people cannot read? How is a man to better himself if he cannot have access to the experiences of his ancestors and the lessons they have learned? Or to the sights and sounds and customs of faraway places he has never visited? Printed books will bring those things to the masses. We are entering a new age—the age of information!"

The book Sebastian's father brought home that day was *The Travels of Marco Polo,* which would eventually go to sea in the hands of his brother Sancio. In Venice, the book sold nearly as many copies as the Bible. Marco Polo was the closest thing the business-minded Venetians had to a national hero. Everybody knew at least the outline of his remarkable story.

In 1271, the seventeen-year-old Marco and his two uncles sailed to the eastern shore of the Mediterranean, then traveled overland through Persia and Afghanistan and across high mountain passes and the Gobi Desert, finally arriving at the court of Kublai Khan at Shangdu in 1275. For the next seventeen years, Marco traveled to many parts of China as part of Kublai Khan's diplomatic service and kept a journal of his impressions. The Polos were finally allowed to leave China in 1292 in order to escort a princess to her arranged marriage in Persia. They traveled by sea, with stops at the islands of Sumatra and Ceylon and along the coast of India before arriving at Hormuz on the Persian Gulf. They then proceeded overland through Turkey and Greece, and returned to Venice (where many of their relatives had given them up for dead) in 1295. Their tales, and the silks and gems they managed to keep out of the hands of bandits on their return trip, captured the imaginations of their countrymen.

In 1298, Marco was taken prisoner during a sea battle between Venetian and Genoese forces, and was imprisoned in Genoa for more than a year. While in jail he dictated his *Travels* to a fellow prisoner. Hand-copied editions of the book circulated in the courts of Europe, and his name remained a legend always on the lips of Venetians. The advent of printing, a century and a half after his death, would make him immortal.

But now the overland route to the East had been sealed by the Turks, making Marco's descriptions of China and the eastern kingdoms all the more tantalizing because those places were again out of reach.

With Constantinople in the hands of the infidels, Alexandria, in Egypt, became the conduit for trade with the East. But the Arabs with whom the Venetians dealt had become more troublesome over the passing years, and the silks and spices and dyes and coffee so prized in Europe had become rare and expensive. The businessmen who employed Sebastian's father were worried. Trade was their lifeblood. If the Turks could not be defeated in battle, which seemed certain, then the overland route would remain closed. The Arabs were hardly friendlier. Venice's elite were becoming convinced that a way needed to be found to circumvent the Muslim stranglehold on commerce with Asia.

And so it was that Giovanni Caboto came home one day in the summer of 1489 and announced to his family that he was being dispatched on a journey to Arabia.

"Isn't it dangerous?" Mattea asked. "The Arabs are known to be unfriendly to foreigners."

"I have undertaken dangerous missions before," Sebastian's father said.

"But not to hostile territories."

"I will take Lorenzo de Mille and Alexia Silvio with me. Both speak Arabic well, and I know a little Arabic myself. We will disguise ourselves as Arab pilgrims."

"If you are discovered, you will be stoned to death—after they cut out your eyes and tongues," Mattea said. Such lurid tales of the barbarism of non-Christians were common in the markets of Venice.

"No such thing will happen," Caboto assured his wife. "Arabia is reputed to be a savage place, but the Arabs know the value of money. They will trade with us if it is in their interest to do so."

"And they will kill you if they find that it is in their interest."

But such arguments had never deterred Sebastian's father before, and in the evening he spread a map out on the table and showed his sons the size of the Arabian peninsula and its strategic importance. He traced a finger down the Red Sea and out into the Indian Ocean. "The Arabs have no great ships like ours, but they have been sailing to the near coast of India for centuries," he said. "It is unfortunate that there is no water route between the Red Sea and the Mediterranean. From Alexandria to the Red Sea it is no great distance, but one cannot sail a ship across a desert. The Arabs are there, and we must deal with them."

And so Giovanni Caboto sailed once more from Venice, bound for Alexandria, as his wife and three sons stood on the dock and watched his ship shrink into the distance until it was out of sight. He would be gone for nearly a year. In his absence, his aging mother would die, and news would reach Venice that the Portuguese sailor Bartholomeu Dias had rounded the southern tip of Africa, proving the existence of a sea route between western Europe and the Indian Ocean. The news would shake the business community of Venice to its watery under-pinnings. And Giovanni Caboto, discouraged by his experiences with the quarrelsome Arabs, would turn his eyes to the west.

CHAPTER 4

19 June 1498

Dear Sebastian,

To repair a ship in a harbor such as Bristol is a simple matter compared with what Father must now attempt here.

The tidal drop is around eight vertical feet—plenty of space to work with. Had we a dock, it would be a simple matter to run the ship alongside at high water and let her ground out. Father is considering building one.

We have seen no natives. If this is an island, it may be uninhabited, though Father thinks this unlikely. There are signs that men have been here before us, and recently. We have found piles of shells heaped up on land far from where any storm tide could have deposited them, and charred remains of a cooking fire.

We continue to watch for any of our other ships. Two red pennants, which can be spotted from a distance against the green of the forest, fly from the tops of the Pandora's *masts. Father's first order of business is to repair the ship we have, but each day he dispatches a group of men to the headland at the bay's entrance to scan the ocean for sails. Each day the ocean remains empty. I can tell he is thinking of Ludovico.*

It is a true wilderness—the sea on one hand, the forest on the other. The land seems to be wooded all over, like the forests of Wye and Dean near Bristol. There is enough timber here to construct a fleet of ships. The trees grow straight and tall. We have felled several of them already, and the men have constructed a large open shelter in which as many as want to can sleep ashore. A tree has been selected from which to fashion the new mainmast. Father returns to the ship each night, as I do. It is roomier now with fewer men aboard. He has posted watches both on shore and on ship, for this is an unknown land and the intentions of whatever inhabitants there may be remain unknown as well. Perhaps we are being watched from a distance.

We would be hard to miss in any case, for each night there are large bonfires on the beach. Father takes care to limit each day's supply of beer and spirits, but the men are much relieved at surviving the storm, and Father knows the importance of keeping them in good cheer.

On our second day ashore, several of the men brought down a deer, which was gutted and roasted over the fire, and we all enjoyed the taste of fresh meat after weeks of salted pork and mutton.

Would that we had a man among the crew skilled in the classification of plants and animals! There are beasts in the forests not seen in Europe, including a ravenous, badgerlike creature with black patches around the eyes and a bushy, ringed tail. Any food left out is soon discovered by these foragers and carried off. There is also abundant bird life—not only the gulls and terns seen in all northern ports, but great long-legged and long-necked birds that feed at the water's edge at low tide, and magnificent soaring hawks, all black save for white feathers at the head and tail.

There are many shellfish to be found along the shore when the tide goes out, including beds of mussels, and lobsters with large foreclaws, which can be caught by turning over rocks and poking around in the seaweed at low tide. They are good eating when boiled, though a few of the men disdain them as "cockroaches of the sea." Still, we will not starve in this place, no matter how long it takes to repair the ship.

For the present, the men have been occupied in hunting and constructing the shelter and thanking God for their survival. But Father knows they will soon grow restless.

While many have nothing in England to return to save lives of crime and poverty, nonetheless they are in a strange land, and the new is always more frightening than the familiar, he says. Besides, they are sailors, and will soon grow anxious to sail.

On Sunday, Father Cartwright conducted Mass on shore. Most of the men attended. Father used this as an opportunity to explore the land to the west of the bay on foot, and he took me with him, as well as Stephen Conant, one of the less religious among the sailors, who armed himself with a crossbow. Father has been reluctant to journey far from the encampment, though his caution seems strange for one who has passed among the Arabs in their own country. Yet he is mindful of what happened to the men Columbus left on his newly discovered island. When he returned a year later, they were all gone, killed by his so-called Indians. We have only the one ship, in the absence of the rest of the fleet, and it is our only lifeline back to Bristol.

We hiked over a rise and down through a wooded valley, cutting blazes on the trees as we went so that we could retrace our trail. A high outcropping, bare of trees at the top, stood a short ways inland, and we made for this. It was not really that high—certainly much lower than the hills near Valencia—but after weeks at sea my land legs are still wobbly. From the summit we could look back to the bay where the Pandora lay at anchor, and we could also follow the coast as it fell away to the west. It is a jagged coast, much like Ireland, only not so bold. If one were to follow the coastline on foot, one would walk much farther than the straight line described by a ship coasting offshore, or a bird flying overhead.

Father remarked that our landing place offered ample shelter, an abundance of timber, and deep water near the shore. "The Egyptians built the pyramids with nothing more than ropes and the sweat of many men," he said. "Surely we can build a wharf."

It was encouraging to hear him express optimism, but I noticed that he kept looking out to sea, at the unbroken blue horizon. He has not given up thinking about Ludovico and the other ships, though he has not once mentioned our brother's name within my hearing.

In the other direction, away from the sea, are more hills, some bare, some wooded. I could see several small lakes, as well as marshes and scattered open areas, and not far in the distance, a small river wound its way seaward between the trees.

"A good land," Father said.

"With much wildlife, I'm sure," said Conant as he described small circles around the summit, peering into the woods, his bow ready. "Men could live well here. Strange that we have not seen any."

But just as he said this, my eyes picked up something in the distance, beyond the inland hills. I stood. It was a plume of smoke, thin and on the edge of visibility, rising vertically from the green landscape. A fire. People.

Father and Conant didn't see it at first, even after I pointed it out. But finally they did.

"Well," Father said, "we knew such a land could not be uninhabited. We have seen the signs. We had best be ready for company."

We must meet them soon, for we cannot sail away from here until we have replaced the mainmast, and that will take some days. What will such a meeting be like? Will they be friendly, or hostile? Will we be able to speak with them? Will they know the way to Asia? Many questions ran through my mind as we hiked back to the camp. Father met with several of his men after that, but I do not know what was said, for he sent me back to the ship as soon as we returned. And now that I have told Peter and William of what we saw, and related all this to you, I am bone-tired, for I am not used to overland travel.

Your loving brother,
Sancio

Dear Sebastian,

We did not have to wait long.

They appeared not from the woods but from around the headland to the west, in two long, low boats made from the bark of birch trees with wooden rails and crosspieces for reinforcement. Two natives sat in each boat, fore and aft, and they propelled them with paddles. The craft looked flimsy, but they moved swiftly across the water. The men took notice of the Pandora, *but they kept their distance, circling the ship and exchanging stares with the sailors on board. Most of us were at that time on shore, it being the middle of the morning, and busy in the construction of the dock Father has ordered built. It is backbreaking work, requiring the moving of a large number of heavy rocks to hold the timbers in place. I believe that most of the men were grateful for the interruption.*

The natives beached their strange boats a short distance from the great pile of rocks we had begun, and for a few awkward moments we stared at one another. They were leather-skinned and dark-eyed. Their hair was black and braided down beyond their shoulders, with the exception of one man, who had his hair cropped short so that it stuck up from the top of his head like bristles. They were dressed in skins from the waist down and naked from the waist up, and I noticed that their bodies and faces were nearly hairless. In physical stature they were not much different from Europeans; that is, they were of different heights but not notably taller or shorter than our crew.

Father had brought ashore a small chest filled with Venetian trinkets—earrings and pendants and small spoons and knives—for the purpose of making gifts to any people we might meet, and he now ordered this brought out as our two parties continued to look each other over across the small stretch of beach. I could see that the natives were fond of adornments, for two of them wore necklaces made of shells, and the short-haired man had a shark's tooth dangling against his chest on a strip of leather. One of them had thrust a long white feather into the braid at the back of his neck. But the most striking feature of their appearance was that they had streaked their faces and chests with some sort of reddish material. What purpose this served, if any, I do not know.

The priest, who happened to be on shore at the time, started toward the group of natives, but Father held him back, saying, "I am the leader of this expedition, and I will represent our people." Picking out several pieces of jewelry, he approached the four men.

"Welcome," he said in English. "We have come from across the ocean."

I don't believe Father expected to be understood, but somebody had to speak first, after all, and I think he hoped to convey by the sound of his voice that our intentions were peaceful. He held out the gifts in his hand, and one of the natives—the man with the feather, who seemed to be the leader—bent to examine them. Then he did a surprising thing. He placed his hands on Father's face and began to feel his skin all over—his forehead, nose, eyebrows. One hand traveled to Father's hair; the other rubbed his beard, which Father has neither shaved nor trimmed in the weeks since we left Bristol. The native's hands worked their way down to Father's shoulders, his arms, chest, and ribs. Father stood still for this somehow. Remember, Sebastian, that our father has seen many different places and customs, and where a man less experienced in the world might have taken offense at such touching, to Father it was something to be observed and noted. Surely we must have seemed as strange to these people as they did to us.

Father placed a hand on his chest and said, "Caboto." The native responded with some words in his own language. It sounded like no language I had ever heard—but then, why should I expect to hear a familiar tongue halfway around the world, when one can hear a dozen different languages in one small part of Europe?

Father next tried some words in Arabic, which the

natives seemed to understand no more than they had understood his initial greeting in English. Finally the man accepted the trinkets that Father held out to him, and the four men passed them among themselves, making admiring noises and exchanging words that were unintelligible to all of us there on the shore. One of the natives gestured to the Pandora, riding at anchor, and then to their own small boats, and Father pointed to the east, to the horizon. The leader of the natives said something to the man with short hair, who went to one of the boats and brought out a package wrapped in soft tree bark. This he laid at Father's feet. The package proved to be several large fish, recently caught, their scales still gleaming. Clearly the man intended for Father to have them, in exchange for the pieces of jewelry. Thus our first trade in this place was completed.

"They seem friendly enough," I said to Peter Firstbrook as we stood watching this exchange.

"But what strange-looking people," he said. "And how strangely they dress. I would have expected Asians to be decked out in silk and finery, like in that book of yours."

"They are not Asians," I said. I have tried to explain to Peter and William what Father has explained to you and me and Ludovico, that this New Found Land is an island, and that Asia lies beyond it, perhaps as far from here as we are already from Bristol.

The natives returned to their boats and pushed them back out into the water. We watched as they cautiously approached the Pandora. *Their boats looked quite tiny next to our ocean-crossing vessel. Father watched from the shore, concerned, for should the natives have wished to see the ship, he'd have wanted to be on board. But finally the leader of the natives gave a signal, and the two boats headed off, not in the direction from which they had come, but eastward along the coast, as though they had been on an expedition that our encounter had only briefly interrupted.*

When they had gone out of sight, there was much talk among our men. Who are they? Where is their village? Where are their women and children? What do they think of us? Work resumed on the dock, but the men buzzed with questions, and I noticed a few of them glancing frequently out to sea, or into the trees, on guard for another appearance.

Father was wary too, although the natives showed no sign of hostility. At dinnertime we cooked the fish they brought, and the men talked about the unfamiliar visitors as they ate.

"They'll be back," Father predicted as he and I sat out on the afterdeck that evening. "This language that they speak—it is unlike any that I have heard before. We must

try to communicate with them. What is their idea of their world? How far have they traveled? They could tell us much."

"They could not have traveled far, in boats such as theirs," I said.

"Perhaps they have other boats," Father replied.

"If so, would we not have seen them? Would they not have sought out distant lands, even as we are doing? Would not their ships have appeared in England?"

Father laughed at this, and rubbed my head like he used to do when I was small. I pulled away from him, for I am not a child any longer, but this made him laugh all the more.

"You ask good questions, my son," he said.

The questions kept me awake long after the sun's glow had disappeared from behind the tall trees on shore, and long after Vega had begun to descend from its position at the zenith in the hours after sunset. Peter, William, and I have selected a sleeping area out near the bow, for the nights are pleasantly warm, the stars are familiar friends, and the insects prefer to remain among the trees on shore. I wondered if the natives of this place use the stars to navigate as we do, if they mark the passing of the night by the movement of Kolchab round the Pole Star. Do they use the same constellations we do, or do they see different pictures, derived *from different legends? What names do these people have for them? I could hear Peter's soft snoring as I turned these things over and over in my mind. I finally drifted off, and woke to the blazing sun sitting low on the water, and Father's foot nudging my ribs, his voice ordering me to rise.*

Your loving brother,
Sancio

24 June 1498

Dear Sebastian,

Today is St. John the Baptist Day. Father Cartwright celebrated an extended Mass in the morning. It was exactly one year ago that the Matthew *made landfall in the New Found Land.*

Work on the dock has been proceeding swiftly during the long hours of daylight, but this being a holiday, Father allowed the work to stop in the afternoon, and tables were laid out and a holiday feast prepared. It was a poor feast compared to what we would have had in England, but our unappetizing shipboard fare was augmented by another deer the men had shot, and there were fish and boiled mussels as well. The tables were hewn from tree parts not usable in the construction of the dock, and we sat in rows atop logs rolled into place for that purpose.

*We had not seen any natives since our first encounter
with them, several days ago. But as we were eating, a fleet
of their slim, swift boats appeared in the bay. Eliot Morison
saw them first, and nearly choked on the piece of meat
between his teeth. Everyone was on shore for the feast;
it was one of the few times the* Pandora *was unmanned
and unguarded. Father stood, fearing for his ship, but the
natives headed straight for our tables and the smoke of our
fire. I counted eight boats. In a few moments they were all
on shore.*

*This time there were several women among them, and
two boys who appeared to be about my age. One of the
women carried a small child on her back in a bundle made
of sticks and skins. A few of the men carried bows fashioned
of flexible wood and containers filled with arrows.
And they brought food: smoked fish, some sort of bread,
sweet-smelling red berries, and wooden bowls filled with a
kind of porridge. They also brought decorative gifts,
including a long necklace of shells and beads and feathers,
which their leader draped around Father's neck. There was
nothing to do but make room for them and their gifts at
the tables.*

*Father Cartwright was flabbergasted. "How did they
know today was the Feast of Saint John?" he said in great
excitement. "We must be in Asia after all, for surely there*

have been Christian missionaries among their people!" He wanted to celebrate another Mass right then and there, in the middle of the meal, and he would have, had not Father been there to stop him.

"I do not think our Saint John is the reason for their visit," he said. "I think they are simply welcoming us to their land."

Their food was better than ours, though some of our men shied away from the porridge. The natives sampled our fare without much enthusiasm. But when Father poured wine for their leader, seated next to him, the man smelled it and screwed up his face. He took a small, tentative sip, then turned and spat it out on the ground. Several of our sailors found this hilarious.

Communication was awkward and difficult. Father desperately wanted to ask the natives about their land. Did they travel to the west, and what did they find there? Were there villages, cities, other people with whom they traded goods and stories? Where was the horizon of their world, and what relation did it have to Asia? He tried several languages, and the native leader attempted to respond, but they talked past each other, and though Father maintained a smile and a friendly posture, I could sense his frustration.

The attention of most of our men, however, focused on

the four women, for we had been several weeks at sea and had not seen a human female since leaving the docks of Bristol. The women were shy, and did not meet the open stares of our men except in occasional, quick glances. Like the native men, they were dressed in clothes made from animal skins, which covered more of their bodies than the men's did. Like the men, they adorned themselves with strings of shells, beads, and feathers. The baby slept through most of the meal in its carrying case, leaned up against the table. But when it stirred and began to complain, its mother took some of the porridge on her fingers and let the child suck it into its mouth.

After the meal, one of the native men tied a hollow gourd to a low tree branch with a leather thong. The leader of the natives motioned for Father to watch as he picked up a bow and some arrows and paced off a distance, which he marked with a stone in the grass. Bringing the bow to his shoulder, he took aim and let an arrow fly. It pierced the gourd very near the center.

Soon several of the men were engaged in a spirited contest. Stephen Conant produced his crossbow, and grazed the side of the gourd with his first shot. Men of both races clamored to participate. Conant took a turn with a native bow, and several of the natives tried the crossbow. Their marksmen were as good as ours.

The contest came to an abrupt end when Eliot Morison brought forth one of our muskets and, with all the natives watching, shattered the gourd with a single shot. At the gun's report, one of the women screamed, and the native men who had been involved in the contest recoiled and retreated toward the trees, chattering in their strange language and pointing at Morison. "Put that thing away!" Father ordered him, striding up quickly to see what was the matter. "There is no need to frighten these people, when they have come among us in friendship." It was plain that the natives had not seen such a thing as a musket before. One of them went up to the shattered gourd, picked up a piece from the ground, and turned it over and over in his hand, staring at it in disbelief.

Soon after this, several of the native men gathered around Father, and by means of pointing and hand gestures indicated the Pandora, lying at anchor. "It seems they wish to see our ship," Father said. "I see no reason not to accommodate them. We shall give them a tour."

Aboard the Pandora, Father struggled to maintain order. The natives were all over the place, into everything, and not just looking, either—they picked up every loose object they could get their hands on. Father instructed several of his men to keep watch over the natives as they peered into every corner of the ship, including his cabin, *and he made sure that the muskets and crossbows were safely locked away, for the natives seemed to think that everything aboard our vessel was theirs for the taking.*

Metal objects had a particular fascination for them. They were curious about the astrolabe, and their leader seemed a little disappointed when Father refused to give it to them. We have more than one aboard, of course, but Father balked at giving it away, and with good reason, for we shall have to get back across the ocean at some point, and will need to navigate. He gave the leader a silver coin and two small knives, which seemed to please him.

Father Cartwright insisted on giving the man a small silver cross and a Bible. The shiny cross fascinated him, but he did not know what to do with the Bible. Father Cartwright opened it and read something from the Book of Psalms, his index finger running along the lines as he read. The native leader peered at the page indifferently. When the priest handed him the Bible, the native leader riffled the pages without looking at them. I wonder if they have reading and writing in their culture.

When the natives had finally been persuaded to leave the ship, taking away several souvenirs apiece, Father took me aside on the afterdeck. "If we could learn some of their language," he said, "we could discover much about this land of theirs, and where it is in the world. Your ear is much

better than mine, Sancio. You must spend time with them,
if you can."

"How long do you suppose we will be here, Father?"
I asked him.

"I don't know," he said. "But west from here, we are
likely to meet other natives who speak similar languages.
It would serve us well to be able to communicate with them."

I agreed that I would try to pick up as much of the
native tongue as I could. It seems that I will get the chance,
for they are encamped not far from our dock site, around a
roaring fire like our own, their boats drawn up on shore and
overturned. As the tide went out in the evening, I observed
several of them gathering mussel shells near the water's
edge, while the women sat on shore, mending what looked
like fishing nets. Our men did nothing, for it is a feast day,
and while religious feeling runs stronger in some of the men
than in others, all were grateful for a day of respite from
their labors. Tomorrow we will resume work on the dock,
and perhaps learn more about our new neighbors.

Your loving brother,
Sancio

CHAPTER 5

THOUGH IT WAS A POOR SUBSTITUTE FOR the open sea, Sebastian enjoyed his new job as a river pilot. There was plenty to do. Ships came and went daily. Sebastian liked the feel of water beneath his feet, and without thinking about it he had begun to imitate the bowlegged gait of the sailors as he walked home each evening to have dinner with his mother.

What he liked best about the job, though, was that Ryerson trusted him in a way his father never had. Some of the ships he guided into port carried cargoes of considerable value, and if he led one onto a ledge, powerful men would lose money. Captains from Portugal and Castile, unfamiliar with the river's tricky currents, relied on him to guide them safely into and out of the harbor. Yet Ryerson left him alone. Sebastian was in charge of a boat with four oarsmen and a bow man, all paid by Ryerson.

Many bosses would have insisted on riding along the first few days, unnerving the new helmsman by constantly hovering over his shoulder and offering unsolicited advice. Ryerson did none of that. On the first day, he had introduced Sebastian to his crew, and turned him loose to escort a Portuguese trader down the channel.

The crew chafed a bit that first day. "He is but a boy," grumbled the lead oarsman, a swarthy man of some twenty-five years, half a foot taller and fifty pounds heavier than Sebastian.

"Hold your tongue, Burkett," Ryerson retorted. "I pay you to pull your oar, not to question who I put in charge. Young Cabot is your captain, and you will obey him."

Captain! Though it was only a pilot boat, Sebastian swelled with pride at his employer's words. And within a week he had earned the respect of his crew as well. The rowers were all large men, cut from rough cloth, selected for strength, not learning. They did not speak much among themselves when Sebastian was present, and they barely spoke to Sebastian at all. They knew who his father was, of course. But Sebastian was good at his job. He knew the river, and he knew how to handle the small boat on it, and when the oarsmen saw this there was no more grumbling.

Sebastian saw Ryerson at the end of each day, when he

handed over his fares, out of which the older man paid him. Ryerson owned several boats and employed many rowers and pilots. When the rowers were done with their day's work they took off, but Sebastian often had to wait around the docks to transact his business with his busy employer. Here he had a chance to mingle with men from the ships that had recently come into the harbor and to catch bits of news from around the ports of Europe. And it was on one such day, while waiting for Ryerson to settle up with another of his helmsmen, that Sebastian was approached by the mate of one of the ships he had that day guided up the river.

"You're Cabot's boy, aren't you?" the sailor said.

Sebastian didn't recognize the man. But then, Bristol was so full of sailing men that Sebastian could not possibly remember them all. His father was well-known along the waterfront, and some of his fame had rubbed off on his sons. It was not at all unusual for him to be recognized by people he considered total strangers. Sebastian could not remember ever having seen the man before today, when he had observed him on the foredeck of a returning merchant ship, barking orders to the crew as the tide carried them in.

The man's clothes were clean and starched, as befitted an officer of the deck. His cap was pulled down low over thick brown curls, and his face was tanned but still youthful. Sebastian drew himself to his full height and was pleased to discover that he was a couple of inches taller.

"I'm Sebastian Cabot," he said.

"Yes, well, I'm William Martin. Came in today on the *Rosalinda,* that small caravel yonder." He pointed out into the river, where the compact, two-masted ship lay tethered to a spar as the tide surged out around her.

"Yes, I guided you in."

"Aye, and a fine job you did, too, though I am from Bristol myself and probably could have managed it." Sebastian stiffened when he said this, and the man caught it. "Never mind, our captain is from Liverpool and a stubborn man, so it is just as well you were there to keep him off the shoals."

Sebastian nodded at the compliment, but said nothing. The man had approached Sebastian with a purpose, and Sebastian waited for him to get to it.

"We've been out for a month," the curly-haired sailor said. "Since before your father left. I presume he left on schedule."

"Twenty-eight days ago today," Sebastian replied. He looked down at the clove hitch that secured his boat to the dock post, made a show of tightening it. He was not eager to talk about his father. "They must be approaching the New Found Land he claims to have discovered, if they are not already there."

"It might interest you to know that at least one of his ships is nowhere near the New Found Land," Martin said.

Sebastian's head snapped up, and he looked directly into Martin's blue eyes. "What? You have news of him?"

"Of one of his ships," the sailor said. "It is said to be in Donegal Bay, in north Ireland, much damaged and unable to continue on across the ocean."

"Which ship?" Sebastian pressed. "And where did you hear this from?"

"From men we took aboard at Dublin, on our way home. They said that one of Cabot's ships had been driven back by a storm, and made Donegal Bay. I don't know much else."

"Surely not the *Pandora*," Sebastian said. "The *Matthew*?"

Martin shook his head and looked down at the dock. "I'm sorry. I do not know."

"But you have not seen any of her crew?"

Again, Martin shook his head. "I only heard it from those men who came on board at Dublin," he said. "Perhaps the news traveled overland."

"Will they be returning to Bristol?"

"Undoubtedly—either in their ship or another. Sailors are like rats, you know. We find a way to get where we must."

Sebastian kicked at the dock, deep in thought. "I should like to speak with these men," he said. "There was a storm, you said?"

"That is what I heard."

"And only the one ship made port at Donegal?"

"Again, I heard this from the mouths of men who were not there, but who repeated what *they* heard," Martin said. "They said there was only the one ship."

"Father would have got word to someone," Sebastian said. "It cannot be his ship, or Ludovico's. It must be one of the others."

"Perhaps only the one was driven back, and the others continued on their way west," Martin suggested. "Perhaps even now the fleet is nearing the coast of Asia."

Sebastian shook his head. "No. It has not been long enough. Last year he was thirty-five days out of sight of land, and the land he charted was no part of Asia. The world is bigger than that, despite what they claim in Castile."

Martin slapped Sebastian on the back, not hard, in a gesture of friendliness. "Well, that is what your father aims to find out, is it not?"

"My brothers are with him," Sebastian said.

"Your brother Lewis is cut from the same cloth as your father. He is a fine seaman, from what I hear. He is an oak."

"He is on the *Matthew,* with Captain Conway," Sebastian said. "And Sancio is on my father's ship." Sebastian looked out into the harbor as he said this, and could not quite keep the bitterness out of his voice.

"And there will be a joyful Cabot family reunion when they return," Martin said, giving Sebastian's shoulder a brief squeeze. "Here comes your boss. Chin up, young Cabot."

As Martin walked off, Sebastian frowned into the swirling brown water at his feet. His emotions were no less turbulent. Was the fleet in trouble? Had his father and brothers in fact come through the storm and continued on, or were they even now shipwrecked on some unknown shore—or worse, at the bottom of the ocean? Not knowing was the worst thing. Ships sometimes disappeared, their fates remaining a mystery for all time. Did Ludovico and Sancio and his father still live, or had they been swallowed by the storm? Sebastian prayed they were all right, yet at the same time he cursed his father for sentencing him to this uncertainty.

Richard Ryerson had heard the news, for little was

said on the Bristol waterfront that escaped his attention. Ryerson was in many ways the opposite of Sebastian's father. As far as Sebastian knew, the man had never been away from England in his life. Though he made his living on the waterfront and talked daily with men who had sailed over distant horizons, he expressed no desire to see those horizons himself. He was well-paid and respected by the merchants he served, and he treated his hired pilots and oarsmen fairly.

As they settled the day's accounts, they discussed the news, sketchy though it was. Sebastian knew his father's fleet had been cobbled together, for unlike Ferdinand and Isabella, Henry VII was a penurious ruler, who preferred to let Bristol's wealthy merchants finance the Crown's first forays into the Western Ocean. The flagship, the *Pandora,* had been newly built for this voyage; she was the largest and sturdiest of the five ships. The little caravel *Matthew* had proven her worth on the previous year's venture to the New Found Land and back. The other three ships were trading vessels their owners had deemed expendable. Though his father had inspected them all and pronounced them seaworthy, Sebastian knew they were far from the best Bristol had to offer.

"Nonetheless, they will want their ship back, if she

still floats," Ryerson said. "I should think they would dispatch someone to Ireland, to assess the damage and contract for repairs, if her crew cannot sail her home themselves."

"Has anyone said which ship it is?" Sebastian asked.

Ryerson shook his head. "Not the flagship, that's all we know. Words change shape when passed from mouth to mouth. Perhaps she is not damaged at all, but only lost her way in the storm. Perhaps we shall see her soon at the mouth of the river. We shall have to wait."

"I hate to wait," Sebastian said.

Ryerson laughed. "Impatience is the curse of the young, my boy. You, who have time stretched out in front of you like a seven-course meal, want to consume it all at once. As you grow older you will learn that things happen in their own due time, and that a man cannot speed up the world simply by wishing it."

Sebastian scowled. "My father told me much the same thing when he said I could not go with him. I would rather be lost in a storm than to have to wait in port, not knowing." Then an idea occurred to him. "Do you think it possible that I could be among the men dispatched to Ireland?"

"And what would I do, without my best river pilot?"

Sebastian knew Ryerson was flattering him simply to

cheer him up, but still he glowed inside. His father had never praised him like that, for anything.

"You got by without me before," he said, looking down at his shoes, not wanting Ryerson to see him blush.

"Sebastian, it is not even known what will be done, whether there will be a crew sent to Donegal to pick up your father's men. It may not even be necessary. When they return to Bristol, we will know the full story. There is no need for you to run off to Ireland simply because you have heard a piece of disquieting news. Besides, did you not promise to look after your mother until your father returns? Think of her. What would she do all alone?"

Sebastian thought his mother would do fine, for she was friendly with several women along their street, other wives of other sailors. And she had money from his father's contract with the king.

However, he debated with himself as he walked home whether or not to tell her the news he had heard. In the end he decided to tell her, because she would doubtless hear it eventually from somebody else, and because if he kept it to himself she would read in his face that he was concealing something from her. Secrets he could keep from his father, but his mother had a way of drawing them out of him. No, it was better to tell her right off, even though he did not want her to worry.

But Mattea was unruffled at the news. She had borne her husband's long absences ever since Sebastian could remember, never complaining, never staring wistfully out to sea, never failing to believe that he would come home. Even during that bad year when Sebastian's father was held prisoner in Arabia, when it was not known if he was alive or dead, his mother had carried on stoically, running her household as efficiently as any Venetian businessman.

"I suspect the sailors on that other ship had little stomach for the sea anyway," was all she said. "And the storm gave them the excuse they needed. A Caboto does not turn tail at the first sign of bad weather."

"He turned back two years ago," Sebastian reminded her.

"Yes, but only after days of westerly winds, and a near mutiny among his crew," his mother said. "This time he has a better ship. And you and I both know that if he is forced back, he will only be the more determined to try again."

For the next several days, Sebastian tried to find out more about the ship that had returned to Ireland. Each time he went to King's Road, he stared down the channel, out toward the open sea, hoping for a glimpse of the returning vessel, or a ship bearing men who had news of her. But nothing more was known.

There was plenty of talk, however, about other ventures—so much talk that from the flavor of it Sebastian could imagine the Western Ocean teeming with ships from all over Europe. He learned that Columbus had at last set off on another voyage to his so-called Indies, this time with eight ships divided between two fleets. Sebastian amused himself with thoughts of what would happen should his father meet up with Columbus on the other side of the ocean, for the two men did not like each other, and his father was more than a little jealous of the other's fame and glory. Such a meeting was highly unlikely, of course, for his father had sailed north and Columbus south, and his father was determined to find a western route to Asia while Columbus thought he was already there.

Sailors weren't allowed to talk about these things— they could be flogged, or even hanged, if they did. New trade routes and new lands were state secrets. But men talked anyway. The Spanish had established a huge colony on one of the islands Columbus had discovered, and were sending ships there regularly, at intervals of several months. The Portuguese were all over Africa, and challenging Spanish claims in the Western Ocean. Sailors from both countries swaggered around the docks like men from the real world visiting the provinces. What did they have to lose by bragging of their compatriots' discoveries? Nobody in England had done anything to match them.

But the truth was not always permitted to interfere with a good story. Though Sebastian listened to the Spaniards' tales of abundant gold and subservient Indians, he did not swallow them whole, and neither did anyone else on the waterfront. Columbus had certainly stumbled upon *something*. And the Spanish Crown had granted him a percentage of all profits, setting him up as a virtual king of his own island colony. Eight ships, plus the others already there, all at his disposal. Sebastian's father had barely scraped together a fleet, and had to come all the way to England to do it.

A week passed, then two. Sebastian grew irritated that there was no more news of his father's ship. A fishing boat came in from an extended run in northern waters. Her crew reported that they had waited out the same storm in Iceland, and had been forced to turn over half their catch before the Icelanders would allow them to clear port. They had heard nothing of John Cabot's fleet.

Commerce in Bristol continued as usual. Barges came across the channel loaded with timber and mutton and wool. Ships arrived from Venice and Portugal bearing fruit and olives and wine. Sebastian worked every day but Sunday, which he dreaded, because his mother had fiendishly arranged for Mr. Vigneron to come to the house after church. His Sundays were filled with religion and mathematics. He chafed at the routine of both home and waterfront. Someday, he told himself, as he stared out from King's Road toward the mouth of the Bristol Channel, he would build his own ship, and recruit his own crew, and sail off toward his own discoveries, with neither father nor priest nor professor nor boss to stop him.

On June 24, the anniversary of his father's landfall in the New Found Land, a small, lateen-rigged ship sailed into King's Road while Sebastian and his rowers waited at the dock. A short, bearded, dark-haired man disembarked and approached Sebastian. "You must take me up the river, for I have business in Bristol," the man said, scowling.

The man had not seen a barber in some time, and his clothes were caked with salt. There was a general mean-ness about him that Sebastian did not like; his face looked like it had not sported a smile in years.

"Passage is two pence," Sebastian said.

The man's scowl deepened. "Who're you working for, boy? Clarke? Bridgeman? Ryerson?"

"Ryerson," Sebastian said.

"Well, you tell Mr. Ryerson that I have urgent business with Mr. Edward Abercrombie, merchant and shipowner, and that he will make good my fare. He'd better, if he wishes to recover his ship from the Irish."

A jolt of recognition shot through Sebastian. Abercrombie was one of Bristol's wealthiest merchants, and part of the consortium that had funded his father's expedition.

"What ship?" Sebastian asked eagerly.

The man was already getting into the boat. Now he fixed Sebastian with his dark, malevolent eyes. "I am Matthew Holliday, lately master of the caravel *Eliza,* under Captain Charles Morgan, out of Bristol," he said. "We were nearly shipwrecked in Ireland, and the Irish, damn their eyes, are demanding compensation for their help in repairing her. Now, may we go? It has taken me much longer than I anticipated, and I am in no mood for more delays."

Sebastian didn't move. "You are one of my father's men," he said.

"Damn it, boy, we can talk on the way upriver. Cast off and let's go!"

"Do you not know who I am?"

"You are an impertinent boy who is trying my patience."

"I am Sebastian Cabot. The *Eliza* is one of my father's ships."

Now Holliday laughed, but there was no merriment in it. "Well, Sebastian, it seems I have not seen the last of your family after all! So you are the other son! A river pilot! Well, if you can take me up to Bristol with all due speed, it would please me greatly."

Sebastian cast off quickly and gave orders to his rowers, and the boat eased out into the channel. The tide was turning, and Sebastian maneuvered the boat into the current, which was slow at the mouth of the river but would pick up speed as the channel narrowed. Holliday sat near the stern and scowled at everything.

"We had heard you were forced back by a storm," Sebastian said.

Holliday's only response to this was a grunt. He didn't seem too happy to be home.

"Have you any news of my father?" Sebastian asked.

Holliday looked at Sebastian for several seconds without saying anything. His scowl deepened.

"Your father is dead," he said.

CHAPTER 6

GIOVANNI CABOTO RETURNED TO VENICE from Arabia in 1489 a changed man. Gaunt, half-starved by his Arab captors, given up for dead by most of the Venice business establishment, he was also very nearly broke. Robbed of most of his goods before he reached Mecca, he had been imprisoned there as a spy when he had attempted to recoup his losses in the open marketplace. Upon his escape, Giovanni and three of his compatriots had crossed miles of open desert, disguised as Arab nomads, to reach Alexandria. There they talked their way aboard a Venetian ship whose captain at first refused to believe they were who they said they were. They did not look anything like the prosperous traders who had set out the year before.

Venice had changed as well. Giovanni heard no more talk on the streets of bold, speculative ventures into the unknown. Instead, there were worried murmurings of the growing influence of the Moors in the west and the Turks in the east. Caboto's ill-starred expedition to Arabia had only underscored Europeans' fear of Islamic armies massing all around them.

Giovanni Caboto had a family to support, and a picture of the world in his mind, made more vivid by his travels. Far to the east, beyond the lands of the Turks and Arabs, was a rich land brimming with spices and teas and other goods much desired by Europeans. If he could find a way to get there directly, he would be rich beyond his dreams.

He also had friends, many of whom came to see him in the days and weeks following his return. Years later, Sebastian would remember the late-night gatherings of men around the table, where the wine and the talk flowed as freely as the murky water in the Venetian canals. These were men with whom his father had done business over the years, many of them well-traveled and well-connected, men who had made money by keeping their ears open and knowing what their rivals were up to. Sebastian and his brothers would often lie awake in the bedroom they shared, listening to the talk and wondering where it would lead. Their father regaled his listeners with tales of his adventures in Arabia; the other men, in turn, filled Giovanni in on events that had occurred in Europe during his absence. And always the talk was rife with speculation. Had the Portuguese really rounded Africa? Were there islands in the ocean beyond the Azores? What if the Western Ocean could be crossed safely with these new, speedy caravels? What would it mean for Venice, the jewel of the Mediterranean? The talk often went long into the night and seldom reached any resolution, but Sebastian and his brothers, as they lay in their beds waiting for sleep to come, sensed its direction, and knew their lives were soon to change.

"Our friend Columbus has been agitating all over the western kingdoms." This was reported one evening by a man named Lorenzo Pasqualigo, a large, well-traveled Venetian sailor whose booming voice reached every corner of the house. "He and his brother have gone up and down the coast, petitioning the royal courts for a fleet to sail out into the Western Ocean, to seek Asia through the back door."

"That has been tried before," Giovanni said.

"Yes, but this man Columbus, he is quite determined," Pasqualigo said. "He has been turned down twice by King John of Portugal, and once by Ferdinand and Isabella. He has even dispatched his brother Bartholomew to England to appeal to King Henry. Of course, he got nowhere with that miserly old bean counter. But he is a charmer, our old friend. He will keep at it until he gets his ships. And Queen Isabella, she seems to have an eye for him."

"How did you hear all this?"

"Oh, I have my sources, Giovanni. Times are changing, my friend. Venice is no longer the center of the world."

The two men were seated at the table in the main room of the house, a flagon of wine between them. Lorenzo, whose wife had died years earlier, was a frequent dinner guest. Older than Giovanni, he traveled frequently in western Europe as a representative of several Venetian businesses.

"Speak to me more of Columbus," Caboto demanded. From his bed in the darkened adjacent room, Sebastian could see his father lean forward, his elbows on the table. He saw his mother pass in front of the table and go out again. He could not see the other man at all. Sancio snored gently in his bed on the other side of the room, but Sebastian thought Ludovico was, like himself, still awake, listening.

"It is an obsession with him, this 'Enterprise of the Indies,'" Pasqualigo said. "He will talk of nothing else. He went to King John and told him, Look, your ships are sailing fifteen hundred leagues down the coast of Africa. The westward distance to the Isle of Cipangu off the Asian coast cannot be more than half that. Of course, the king has reaped great profits in Africa, in slaves and gold and ivory, but he was interested."

"Yet Dulmo and Estreito found nothing," Giovanni said.

"It was reported that they found nothing. But remember, it is a capital offense in Portugal to reveal new discoveries."

"Yet it is reported all over Venice that Bartholomeu Dias found the southern end of Africa. And that was but a year ago."

Lorenzo chuckled. "There are always men willing to risk their necks, if they are paid well enough," he said. "Even powerful nations cannot keep secrets forever."

Caboto shook his head. "I have been to the Azores," he said. "They are difficult to get to, because of the westerly winds. If I recall, they were discovered not from Lisbon, but from Madeira, and by accident, by a ship blown off course. To sail west from the Azores . . . well, it would be a difficult and frustrating venture, I should think."

"As Dulmo and Estreito discovered," Pasqualigo said.

"Then you don't doubt they found nothing?"

"We would have known—there are no long-lasting

secrets among seafarers. But that does not deter our friend. He proposes a more southerly route, west from the Canaries. He claims that a fair wind could carry him to the Indies in a matter of days, because the distance between Lisbon and Cipangu, from east to west, cannot be more than seventy degrees of the whole Earth's circumference."

At this, Giovanni Caboto burst into laughter. "Oh, my," he said. "Our friend Cristoforo may be an able mariner, I will give him that. But he knows nothing of geography."

"Well, King John didn't buy it either," Lorenzo said.

"Look," Caboto said. "I have just spent a year among the Arabs. And while they may be brutal in their customs, they are skilled in the art of mathematics. Why, we would not even know of Euclid, or Pythagoras, had not the Arabs kept their discoveries alive while all the bright boys of Europe were being snatched up by the Church. The Greeks knew how big the world was, hundreds of years ago. And the Arabs know it today. Columbus is a fool if he thinks the journey across the Western Ocean will be a short one."

"There is much debate about that," Pasqualigo conceded. "Columbus contended that Ptolemy's estimate of the Earth's circumference is too large, and that the eastward extent of Asia is greater than is shown on most maps. Then he added the supposed distance from the Asian coast to the Isle of Cipangu—which Marco never saw, mind you—and he came up with a sailing distance of only seven hundred fifty leagues west of the Canaries."

"Preposterous," Caboto scoffed.

"I'm just telling you what he's saying, Giovanni. And he can be very convincing. He is a true believer. I have heard him speak. Unpleasant mathematical facts do not bother him. He uses Toscanelli's figure for the Earth's circumference instead of Ptolemy's. He ascribes the greatest possible eastern extent to Marco's travels and the islands of which he wrote. His estimate of the length of a degree is smaller than anyone else's. Everything is manipulated to present his enterprise in the most favorable light—even God. 'Do not the scriptures say that the world is six parts land and one part water?' he says. 'How, then, can there be any great extent to the Western Ocean?' He speaks with the fervor of a preacher converting the nonbelievers."

"Yet King John turned him down."

"Yes, because the commission could see that his figures were wrong. As you say, he is no geographer. But he is a man with a mission."

Caboto got up and paced around the small room. "Have you ever heard of a man called Eratosthenes?" he asked after several seconds of silence.

"No."

"Neither had I," Caboto said. "But he is known to the Arabs."

"Who is he? He sounds like a Greek."

Caboto nodded. "A Greek mathematician who lived in Alexandria," he said. "He lived long ago, before we started counting years the way we do. Before Christ. Well before Ptolemy."

"What did he do?" Pasqualigo asked.

"He calculated the circumference of the Earth."

"You mean he guessed," Pasqualigo said.

"No, I mean he figured it out." Caboto returned to the table, but remained standing. "It was quite ingenious. See, Eratosthenes heard that at noon on the twenty-first of June, the sun was directly overhead in Syene, and an obelisk cast no shadow. In Alexandria, an obelisk always casts a shadow, even on the longest day of the year, when the sun is at its farthest north." Caboto drew an imaginary curve on the tabletop with his finger. "Eratosthenes fig-ured if he could measure the angle of the sun at noon, and if he knew the north-south distance between Alexandria and Syene, he could calculate what percentage of the whole curve that distance covered. So at noon on June twenty-first he measured the angle of an obelisk and found that the sun was seven degrees from overhead. He deduced that the distance from Syene to Alexandria covers seven of a circle's three hundred and sixty degrees. It works out to about one fiftieth of the whole circle. Therefore, the circumference of the Earth is fifty times the distance from Syene to Alexandria."

Pasqualigo was staring at him in wonder.

"I had a lot of time on my hands after I was captured," Caboto said, laughing gently at his friend's astonishment. "A lot of time to think. A lot of time to scratch calculations in the sand, and wipe them out again, and start over."

"And what *is* the distance from Syene to Alexandria?" Pasqualigo asked. "Do you know?"

Caboto smiled. "It was easier for the ancients to measure angles than distances," he said. "But my best guess would be around a hundred and fifty leagues. Which would give the world a circumference of seventy-five hundred leagues at the equator. Columbus proposes to sail but one tenth that distance, and at a southerly latitude. I guarantee you he will not find his Isle of Cipangu."

"But why does not Columbus do a calculation like the

one you have described, and discover this for himself?"

"Because it has never occurred to him," Caboto said. "Just as it never occurred to you, or to me, before I heard an old Arab tell of it. We are not taught to think that way. Columbus would prefer to think of him and his ships as sailing on the breath of the Holy Spirit, cupped in the palm of the Blessed Virgin, carried along to their destiny."

"You are growing cynical in your old age, my friend."

"Has not our Catholic Church turned its face away from the world?" Caboto said. "The Arabs adhere to a fierce faith whose mysticism and promises of miracles have not blinded them to physical reality."

"I hope you are wise enough to keep those opinions to yourself," Pasqualigo said. "It would not serve you well to let the elders of the city hear you talk like this."

Mattea entered the room, bringing more wine. "Don't get him going on the faults of the Catholic Church," she said to Lorenzo. "Giovanni would have you believe that the Church wishes to keep men in ignorance, even though it was in the Church that he learned his letters, and his sons learned theirs." She poured herself a glass of wine and took a seat at the table with the two men.

"So that we could read the Bible as though it were the sole source of truth in the world," Giovanni said.

"Without the Church, what reason would men have to treat one another with respect and decency?" his wife asked. "The Church is the glue that holds civilization together."

"And holds men in place," Giovanni Caboto muttered. But his tone had softened since his wife had come to the table.

"It is not holding Columbus in place," Lorenzo said. "He is determined to try his westward route, if he can but raise the money."

"Where is he now?" Caboto asked.

"In Cordova, at last report," Lorenzo said. "His road out of Portugal was paved with debt. But Isabella has set him up with a small salary, as some sort of royal adviser."

"Adviser of what?" Caboto said. "How to change the shape of the Earth?"

"It would be a mistake to underestimate him, Giovanni. Men as single-minded as he have a way of getting what they want."

"Bah! The man's an idiot. He has had stars in his eyes since boyhood. Were I to attempt to reach Asia by sailing west, I would do it farther north, where the distance is less. I would navigate the world as it is, not ask God to shrink it for me."

"Oh, stop it, Giovanni," Mattea said. "Belief in God does not make the man a fool. You would do well to invoke His help now and then."

"Columbus is not likely to get funding from Castile anytime soon, in any case," Lorenzo said. "Much as the queen may like him, she has her hands quite full with the Moors in Granada."

Sebastian lay awake for a long time, his mind churning with the things he had heard. How would these changes in the world, of which he knew so little, affect his family, his life?

What would his father do next?

Giovanni spent two months at home with his wife and sons, and put back some of the weight he had lost in Arabia. Toward the end of the year he traveled to Barcelona, and early in 1490 he took passage on board a Venetian ship that stopped in Cádiz, Lisbon, and Bristol, in southwestern England. These trips were not paid for by his employers. To finance them, Caboto sold his interest in the saltworks and raised the rent on his income property in Venice. The tenants grumbled, but they had little choice but to pay. Housing in Venice was much sought after. The Cabotos were fortunate to live in a house that had been owned by Mattea's family. Otherwise the recession would have hit them harder than it did.

Caboto was welcomed everywhere he went. Information was like gold to the mariners of western Europe. Few of them had traveled in Arabia, and their eyes sparkled when Caboto told them of the marketplaces filled with spices and other goods from the East. In Lisbon he met a man named Vasco da Gama, who wanted to follow Bartholomeu Dias's course around the tip of Africa and continue on to the islands where pepper was grown. A reliable supply of pepper could make a man's fortune, da Gama said.

In exchange for geographical details, Caboto told da Gama of the spice markets in Mecca. Da Gama said that the journey around Africa was long and perilous, with high winds and swift currents swirling about treacherous shoals and headlands. Dias had discovered the route by accident, he said—he had been blown offshore by a storm, and failing to resight the coast upon turning east, had gone north until coming upon an unfamiliar shoreline that trended to the northeast. Only after his panicked crew had forced him to turn back did he realize that he had rounded the long-rumored but never-seen tip of Africa.

And did he take a sighting? Caboto asked. Surely he must have. Any competent mariner would have.

Reluctantly, and after Caboto had confided some wholesale pepper prices, da Gama told him that the end of Africa was as far below the equator as Lisbon was above it. To get there required a ship to pass through eighty degrees of latitude! And that was just to reach what was probably the halfway point on a journey to the Spice Islands. Caboto could see why Columbus, with his faulty math and fanciful geography, was convinced that the easiest way to the riches of Asia lay to the west, across the ocean.

Caboto knew that a circle connecting the Earth's poles had to have the same circumference as the equator; the nature of a sphere dictated that this must be so. For both circles had as the center the center of the Earth itself, and thus had to have the same radius. Therefore, a degree of longitude at the equator was equal to a degree of latitude along any north-south meridian. Moreover, the parallels of latitude, north and south of the equator, were not "great circles," but circles of progressively smaller size, which meant that the length of a degree shrank the farther from the equator one sailed.

The more he thought about the problem, the more convinced Caboto became that Columbus was wrong in the particulars but right in principle. Africa presented a fearsome physical obstacle, and the Turks and Arabs a no less daunting human one. Even if the western route proved longer than the journey around Africa, it might turn out to be more practical.

In Bristol, Caboto used his Venice connections to introduce himself to that city's wealthy merchant community, but he also spent time on the docks, admiring the high-sided oceangoing ships and talking with the sailors.

Caboto heard many stories. He heard of the myth of St. Brendan, an Irish monk who had supposedly sailed in a leather boat to a land far to the west a thousand years ago. He heard tales of Norse sailors who had settled on a treeless land beyond Iceland, where the winters were nine months long and people lived underground in houses of sod and stone, and where wooded beams were hewn from timber brought back at great risk from lands still farther west. And he heard of the vast schools of fish discovered in broad, shallow banks off the shores of an island known to the Bristol fleet as the "Isle of Brasil," but not set down on any chart. Though some of the stories were probably exaggerations, Caboto began to suspect that they contained a central truth: There was land out there, unknown to the rest of Europe, in the cold north reaches of the Western Ocean, and the Bristol sailors knew how to find it.

But he came away from Bristol with nothing more than that—tantalizing bits of information that only hinted at his future. Unlike Columbus, Caboto had no royal patron willing to back a scheme based mostly on speculation. He needed a job. And in Valencia, on the Mediterranean coast of Aragon in what was now the united kingdom of Spain, he found one.

"I am to be commissioner of their new port," he announced to his family upon his return to Venice. "I have convinced them that it is in their interest to construct a deepwater harbor for oceangoing ships, and they have hired me to oversee its design and construction."

"We will be leaving Venice, then?" his wife asked, as their three sons stared silently at him around the table.

"Yes," Giovanni Caboto said. "Before the end of summer."

Mattea took the news with characteristic calm. She knew her husband. Almost immediately, she began making plans. "We shall have to put the house up for sale, and the rental property," she said. "There is some money in the bank. . . ."

It did not seem to trouble her that she was being asked to leave the home she had inherited from her parents, possibly never to return. She had known since the day she married Giovanni Caboto that this day might come. He was not a Venetian by birth, after all, and his roots had never grown deep. His window was the horizon, his home the deck of a rolling ship. But Sebastian and his brothers were stunned. They had been Venetians all their young lives; now their father intended to uproot them and place them among strangers who spoke a different language. Ludovico asked the question that was on all their minds. "Venice is the finest port in all of Europe," he said. "Everyone from everywhere comes through here. We are in the middle of everything. Why do you want to move us out to Aragon and start over?"

"Venice is far from the Western Ocean," his father said. "And although we think of ourselves at the center of the world, the truth is that we tend to look east, toward the ancient civilizations and the old ways of the past. The future lies in the West. And I intend to look to the future."

CHAPTER 7

Dear Sebastian,

There is much to tell you, and scant time to write. The dock is nearly completed, the mast hewn and shaped, and Father says we should be able to bring the ship in on the high tide of the full moon. Once the mast is stepped, we will be able to sail away from this place.

Work on the dock has kept everybody busy from first light until dusk. The natives have been an unexpected source of help. They have brought us food, mostly fish, but also squashes and delicate ferns that, when lightly boiled and salted, are delicious. Several native men have spent days working alongside our crew, moving rocks to help fill the pilings. I have watched their women at the water's edge when the tide is out, gathering shellfish. I have even gone out fishing with them, at Father's encouragement, in their frail-looking but strong little boats.

You would think that I, who have crossed an ocean and survived the most terrible storm I ever hope to see, would not have been frightened on a simple fishing trip not far enough even to lose sight of land. But the native boats terrified me. They are so low to the water that they disappear between the waves. And yet the natives handle them expertly.

They fish with nets, weighted on one side with fist-size stones. The nets are made of fibrous plant material; I have seen their women sit on the shore for hours, weaving them together. Two or more boats work in tandem, spreading the nets between them and hauling them up together. The slippery, silvery fish wriggle all over the inside of the boat in their struggle to escape. Most of them are about a hand's breadth in length, though a few are larger.

On shore, the fish are gutted and laid out to dry, either on flat ledges or on racks made of wood. There is always a great gathering of seabirds, wheeling and screaming and darting in and out to grab pieces of flesh. Some of the native boys amuse themselves by throwing stones at the birds, and I have seen them bring down a few. The feathers are plucked and kept, and sometimes the claws are taken, but the bodies of the birds are thrown into the sea, for they do not make good eating. The drying fish are seldom left unguarded. Some of the fish is not dried, but eaten raw, on the spot, which I find a bit disgusting. Some of it is cooked in stews, along with roots and herbs.

I am afraid I am not much help to the natives in their fishing expeditions. They are like cats in their sense of balance. They haul aboard quantities of fish that weigh the boats even lower in the water, and then, with the boats full, they bring their catch safely back to shore. It is a miraculous thing to see. I am in the way more than anything else, constantly fearful that the small boat is going to capsize. The natives show no such fear. But these are their boats, and this is their land. They have been doing this forever.

But what land is this? And who are these people? Where did they come from? Like the savages Columbus paraded through Valencia, they seem ignorant of civilization as we know it. They have never suspected the existence of Europe and its cities, nor of the lands and peoples of the Bible. They appear to have no books at all. When Father Cartwright attempts to speak to them about Jesus entering Jerusalem, when he holds up the cross and recites Mass, their faces are blank.

They live most of the year in a village several leagues from here, in a valley behind the low hills that line the sea's edge. In the summer they come to the ocean to fish and harvest shellfish. They travel from place to place along the shore, making temporary settlements wherever the fishing is good. They have set up half a dozen temporary houses, fashioned with poles and sewn-together hides, a short ways down the shore on a flat, grassy area at the top of a cliff, overlooking the bay. These can be put up or taken down in a matter of minutes. A group of perhaps twenty natives, including women and children, has taken up residence there. Others come and go. There is always activity, whether it be fishing, or net mending, or shellfish gathering, or play among the children.

The Pandora remains an object of curiosity to them. Since that first day, Father has limited the number of natives invited onto the ship at any one time, and he has made certain that they are carefully watched while on board. I am not sure they even understand the concept of theft. I have seen nothing that would pass for money among them. They seem uncorrupted by the idea that one must attach a monetary value to everything.

Trade, though, they understand, and there has been a brisk exchange of goods. Father presented the leader with a sweater of thick Hebrides wool, which he has taken to wearing out on the ocean while fishing since discovering that it retains warmth even when wet. The natives are adept at sewing bits of mica and brightly colored shells into clothing. They make all manner of decorative shirts and sashes and headdresses, and though these things are purely ornamental, some of our men are much taken with them. I myself am wearing a necklace of bleached shell and bone. It was given to me by one of the boys I went fishing with, after I survived that first frightening expedition.

Father wants me to find out more about this land—how big it is, what lies beyond it. I am still just learning their language, though, and it is hard to talk about anything that is not right in front of us and can thus be pointed out. It is easy, for example, to hold up a fish and say what it is in both our languages. Sun, moon, sea, ship, man, woman—I have learned their words for these. But other things for which we use words are more difficult. Even names present a problem. Each of the natives has several of them. Their names are not given them at birth, as ours are; rather, they are called by some feature of their character or physical attribute. A person with a scar on his forehead may be called Lightning Brow, for example, though he was called something else before the injury that caused the scar. The boy who gave me the necklace is called Red Hawk by his fellow fishermen (for his keen eyesight), but the women at their encampment call him Bending Reed, because he is tall and thin and sways when he walks, like one who spends much of his time on the water. It is all very confusing.

I am going fishing again tomorrow—me in one native

boat, Peter Firstbrook in another. Every time one of us goes out, some of the natives help carry stones and timbers for the dock. Father seems happy with this exchange of labor, for the natives are strong and eager to help. What a mystery they are! As we must be to them.

There is more to tell you, but it is the end of the day and I am exhausted.

Your loving brother,
Sancio

18 July 1498

Dear Sebastian,

The dock is finished! It is an impressive structure, made entirely of the materials we have found here, as solid and sturdy as the docks of Bristol. At low tide I can stand on the mud beside it and not come close to reaching the top. There will be plenty of room for the Pandora.

Father has declared a day of rest for tomorrow, and plans to bring the ship in the day after that. The dock will remain here long after we are gone, for it would take a strong storm indeed to wash it away.

We have just about given up hope of the other ships in

the fleet finding us here. It has been weeks. I do not want to spend too much time thinking about this. Since the storm, I still have not heard Father speak of Ludovico.

There are fewer natives here now, no more than a dozen. The boy they call Red Hawk left yesterday in a group of three native boats, headed east along the shore. The fish are moving, and the fishermen must move with them. I was sorry to see him go, for we have become friends. He, more than anyone else, has helped me with their strange language. And he even made a fair pass at pronouncing my name. Red Hawk said that he would return this way, and indicated the moon, three-quarters full in the afternoon sky. He made a circle with his arms and held up two fingers, and although I could not follow all of his words I took this to mean that he would be back in two months. We will be long gone by then.

As we stood on the deck of the Pandora *this evening, when the work was finished, I asked Father which way we would sail. "West," he said. "We have lost a month here, and there is still far to go."*

"Will we not go in search of Ludovico, then?" I asked him.

He met my question with silence. It was the first time I have asked him such a thing directly. Red clouds had formed over the trees on the western side of the bay, and the sun had set behind them.

I tried again. "He may be shipwrecked, somewhere behind us," I said.

Father stared out into the ocean, still saying nothing. He is a hard man sometimes, as you well know. Yet he brought us safely through the storm, and he has maintained discipline, and seen to the construction of a dock from which to repair the ship. Not many men share his determination about things. Ludovico does. Father, I think, is counting on this hardness to see our brother through.

At length he spoke. "Does your friend Red Hawk tell you anything," he asked, "about land to the west?"

I had been anticipating this question, but I did not know how to answer it. "They talk about this land as though it is a single thing," I finally said. "They do not think of themselves as living on the way to anywhere."

"But we have seen them move from place to place, and they are capable of traveling long distances," he said.

"Yes, but they think of it differently than we do. They do not draw maps, nor divide the land with imaginary lines."

"But an island has its own boundaries," Father argued, "even a large island, like England. Can you not ask them if there are other islands to the west?"

I bowed my head. "I do not think," I said, "that they know they are on an island."

We fell silent for a moment, me looking in toward the darkening land, Father staring off at the glow in the western sky, his mind on Asia. "It may be," he said, "that the world is quite different than we have suspected."

"How do you mean?" I asked him.

"We know only that which we have read about, or heard about," he said. "Until the Portuguese sailed down the coast of Africa, it used to be said that people could not live in equatorial regions, because of the heat. Yet they found those regions full of dark-skinned savages who had never heard of Europe. It may be that there are many people, in places we have never been, untouched by our civilization down through the ages of Man. The men Columbus brought to Valencia were surely not Asians, nor are these people here. They may have lived for untold generations in ignorance of us. And we of them."

"There is much we could learn from them," I said, "about living on the land."

"Yes, I have seen their skill at hunting and fishing," Father said. "And yet . . ." I waited for him to continue. When he did, it was with a different thought. "Ever since we encountered them, I have asked myself, How did they get here? Where did they come from? But perhaps these are the wrong questions, Sancio. It is meaningless to ask a Venetian where he came from, or an Englishman, for there have been men in those places since the beginning of time. If that is true with these people, if they have always been here . . . well, why have they not built cities, and roads, and great ships, as we have done in Europe? Is it not in the nature of man to build, to explore, to bend the world to his will? Why have they not done these things?"

I didn't have an answer, nor did he expect one. But we will sail away from here in a few days, once the ship is fixed, and the water casks filled, and the larders topped off with dried meat and fish and squashes that the natives have given us. In the morning Father will tell the men that we will continue to the west in search of Asia, even though the summer grows old. Perhaps he will find his answers over the western horizon.

Your loving brother,

Sancio

24 July 1498

Dear Sebastian,

It is done! The new mast stands amidships and the Pandora is ready to sail. Today the men finished attaching the spars and rigging, and on tomorrow's high tide we will tow the ship back out into the bay, raise sails, and leave this place, after more than a month.

What an adventure, just to tow the ship to the side of the dock! I was reminded of the maneuvering of ships on the approach to Bristol. The bay is wider than the river, it is true, but the currents are unpredictable. Twice the Pandora was nearly swept down onto a ledge. In Bristol the currents have been studied and charted, and besides, there is a harborful of boats ready to assist. We had only the longboat. The natives put two of their boats in the water and circled around, watching. God only knows what they thought. We probably should have enlisted their help. They almost got to see our proud flagship pile up on the rocks. A month's work, nearly rendered useless by a moment's carelessness!

I don't know what we would have done, Sebastian, had we lost the ship while trying to guide her in to be repaired. We would have been stranded here, to live among the natives, until King Henry sent out another ship to look for us. Or until one of the other ships in our fleet came upon us. But I am now convinced that isn't going to happen. A month is time enough to sail back to England, and I pray that is what the other ships have done. As I write this, it is my deepest hope that you and Mother and Ludovico are sitting down to dinner together. There was some talk among the men that we, too, should return, but Father silenced that immediately.

Perhaps he should have been thinking less about Asia and more about the task at hand. He chose a calm evening and a slack tide, but things began to go wrong quickly. The men had trouble getting the anchor up as fast as Father would have liked—it had been set for a month and must have lodged against something hard on the bottom. By the time they had the anchor clear a breeze had picked up. It would have been nothing to a ship at sea, but in the confines of the bay it was troublesome, because the wind's direction was at right angles to the course to the dock. The rowers in the longboat struggled against it, and the great bulk of the ship began to drift on them. Soon the oarsmen were struggling just to keep the ship in line with the dock. By this time the tide had begun to ebb, and Father, who had planned to have the ship secured before this happened, contemplated raising some sail to try to stand off. He could have aborted the whole thing right then—sailed off and dropped the anchor and made the attempt another day—but here was where his vision of Asia and his impatience to pursue it nearly wrecked our ship. It was Eliot Morison who saved us, by leaping into the water with the end of a line and swimming it to shore. He walked it around to the dock, and through the combined

efforts of several strong men on the dock and the men in the
longboat, we were able to pull the ship to safety. Father was
white-faced afterward, and didn't say much to any of us.
He knew how close he'd come to dooming the entire
expedition.

The stepping of the mast, the next morning, went much
more smoothly. Here was where the building of the high
dock paid off, for when the tide went out and the ship
grounded, the men could work from above. Father placed a
shiny Venetian coin underneath the mast as it went in, for
luck. The hull was covered with barnacles and weeds and
other sea life. We spent most of two low tides scraping it
clean. A ship needs to be moving, Father said, or else it
becomes little more than a floating house for every parasitic
form of life in the water below. Truly he is anxious to get
going.

This evening, Father gathered Stephen Conant and a
few of the other men around him, and attempted to chart
where we have been and the likely course ahead of us.
He took the chart from last year's voyage—the same one
he laid out in front of us in our house the week before we
left—and spread a new piece of paper on top of it. He
traced the known shorelines first, including the jagged
peninsulas of the New Found Land past which he sailed
last summer. Then, dropping down to the south and west,

he attempted, with the men's help, to sketch in this new land, which he labeled "New England" at the insistence of the priest. Near this bay he outlined the coast with a great deal of accuracy, for we have climbed the nearby hills and seen it. As to the extent of the land, we have only the vague, imperfectly understood reports of the natives.

It will be good to feel the moving deck beneath my feet again, the sails filled with wind, the ship restored and heading for new horizons. Despite the disappearance of the other ships and the delay in our journey, I can see the fire in Father's eyes as we prepare to press on. We shall leave a cross and banners at the top of our dock so that other ships from Europe will know that we have passed this way. But for now, it is on to the west. Asia awaits.

Your loving brother,
Sancio

CHAPTER 8

His mother, Sebastian reflected, set a fine table, even when his father was not present. She had been to the marketplace that morning and picked out a rack of lamb, two plucked chickens, fresh cabbages, carrots, celery, and leeks, and she had prepared a brawn pudding and a trayful of tarts for dessert. Sailors and businessmen and family friends expressed their appreciation with satisfied grunts, loud burps, and a few verbal compliments. For the first time since his father's departure, the dining room filled with the sounds of men enjoying themselves.

More than a dozen people had gathered in the Cabot home on this Sunday afternoon in early August. Richard Ryerson had brought his wife, but aside from Sebastian's mother, she was the only woman there. The dinner had been Mattea's idea—a way to bring together those Bristol men involved, in one way or another, with John Cabot's voyage. Talk was flying all along the waterfront. Ships were disappearing over the horizon, and every sailor in Europe wanted to be part of the adventure.

But where was John Cabot? That was the question most on the minds of the men who had assembled in his house to sift through the various reports.

"It has been more than three months," said a man named John Day, seated to the left of Sebastian's mother. Sebastian knew Day by reputation—he was an educated man who dealt in the commodity of information. Skilled in writing, he found employment with Bristol's wealthy merchant class by making himself their mouthpiece, composing letters to the king and to their business partners and drawing up legal contracts. He was much interested in the commercial possibilities of new discoveries in the West, and had accordingly ingratiated himself with Sebastian's father. Day talked with a great many people, but Sebastian's impression was that he took in more information than he gave out.

"Three months is not a long time," said Richard Ryerson, "when you consider that the destination lies halfway around the world."

"Indeed, it took Marco two dozen years to return

from Asia." This was spoken by Lorenzo Pasqualigo, his father's old friend from Venice, who now made his living as a mapmaker. Several of the men around the table laughed.

"But Marco lived among the Chinese for most of those years," Day said. "And he traveled on foot, not in a swift caravel."

"He was given up for dead," said Lorenzo. "When he returned to Venice, most of his countrymen did not recognize him."

"Perhaps Cabot will return with a boatful of Chinamen," someone else said, to more laughter.

"If he returns at all," mumbled Matthew Holliday, the sailor Sebastian had ferried upriver upon his return from Ireland. "Perhaps he is even now resting on the bottom of the ocean."

Sebastian stiffened at this; his eyes flicked to his mother. But her face was impassive.

"I have sailed to many ports with Giovanni Caboto," Lorenzo said. "We have braved ocean passages together, to the Madeiras, the Azores, up and down the coast of Europe. Never have I met a more capable mariner, a better judge of wind and weather. He is out there somewhere."

"Then why have we heard nothing?" John Day asked.

"Perhaps," Ryerson put in, "he has found the route to Asia after all, and is even now trading with representatives of the Great Khan."

"Would he not have sent a ship back, upon finding the passage, to report the discovery?"

"Perhaps not," said the portly merchant Edward Abercrombie, one of the investors in the voyage. "Cabot knows that the waterfront is full of spies. The Spanish and the Portuguese would pay good money to learn what he has discovered."

At this, John Day looked down at his plate, and sawed at a piece of meat.

"They are all over the Western Ocean with their own ships," Lorenzo said. "Columbus has planted quite a colony on his island of Hispaniola. There is regular traffic between Spain and his supposed Indies. And he has gone there again, with two separate fleets."

"But that is far to the south," Abercrombie said. "Columbus knows nothing of what Cabot may have discovered in the north."

"What makes you think he has discovered anything at all?" Holliday said. "We know there is land in the north. There is violent weather there too. Not many ships could have survived that storm."

Sebastian could remain silent no longer. "Yours did!"

Holliday turned his bearded face toward him. "Because we had the sense to run from it, boy. Even so, we were barely spared. Your father is so obsessed with finding his route to Asia that he will allow nothing short of death to stop him."

"At least he is no coward," Sebastian said.

"Sebastian!" his mother snapped. "These are our guests. I invited them here for this very discussion. You will be polite to them!"

Sebastian sat back in his seat and glowered, but said no more. He had disliked Holliday from their first meeting. The man was a pessimist, his glass always half-empty. Such a man could easily stir up discontent on board ship, dooming an expedition before it began. His father, in Sebastian's opinion, was well rid of him.

Lorenzo Pasqualigo smiled across the table at him. "Columbus was gone nearly three years last time out," he said. "Surely there is no need to worry after only three months."

"But Ferdinand and Isabella have many ships," John Day said, "and knew of Columbus's activities from ships that sailed out and returned during that time. Columbus was not sent out alone into the unknown."

"I hear he has made quite a mess of things," Abercrombie said, taking a large bite out of a chicken leg.

"Yes, well, he is a headstrong man," Day admitted. "Queen Isabella has made him rich and powerful. But she wants to increase her wealth and power in return. If he has not found the golden cities of Cathay, what choice does he have but to extract gold from the natives of those places he *has* found?"

"Money," Sebastian muttered. "That's what it's all about, isn't it?"

"As it always has been, and forever shall be," Lorenzo said good-naturedly. "Do you think your father left Venice and came to Bristol for any reason other than to bring wealth to himself and his family? Do you think our miserly king in London would have spent one shilling on his journeys if he did not see potential profit for the Crown? Columbus may make a lot of pious noise about bringing his heathens into the Catholic Church, but you will note that his contract with Ferdinand and Isabella makes him viceroy and governor-general over all lands he discovers, and secures to him one tenth of all profits obtained. He has taken care of himself, first and foremost. Your father would kill for such a deal."

"King Henry is not one to throw money at foreign

sailors," Abercrombie said. "He would rather use the money of men who have earned it in business. He is no fool, our king. And while we shall profit if Cabot finds his way to the Great Khan, our king will send his tax collectors to our doors with their hands out."

"Yes, it is we who are assuming most of the risk," said Thomas Foley, another of the merchants at the table.

Mattea glared at the man. "It is Giovanni Caboto who is taking the most risk," she said. "While you men sit and eat and contemplate your assets, he is out there on the open sea, battling storms and charting new coastlines." Her dark eyes swung to the face of Matthew Holliday, who looked at his plate, unable to meet them. "Let us not forget that."

"A thousand pardons, madam," Foley said. "I phrased that awkwardly. And we are all praying for your husband's safe return."

Sebastian glanced over at Holliday, who shoveled a forkful of vegetables into his mouth and did not look up.

"Yes, and we are most grateful for your hospitality," Abercrombie said. "How easily we forget what it must be like for you, to wait month after month, not knowing his fate."

"Oh, I know he will return," Mattea said, shooting

one last glare in Holliday's direction before turning to smile at Abercrombie. "Giovanni has always been able to find a way home. Were I the worrying kind, I would have married a man of finance, rather than a seafarer."

Abercrombie clasped his hands across his belly and laughed, and soon many of the men around the table were laughing with him. Sebastian was not among them. He noticed that Matthew Holliday wasn't laughing either.

Sebastian turned to Edward Livingston, another of the sailors from the ship that had been beaten back to Ireland. "Was it very bad?" he asked. "The storm?"

Livingston, a small man who looked older than his thirty years, forced a smile. He had a kind face, weather-roughened, with pinpoint-blue eyes and deep crow's-feet that became more prominent when he smiled. "Storms in that part of the Western Ocean are always bad," he said. "It is a matter of degree. But I would say this was among the worst I've ever seen."

"The worst," Matthew Holliday put in uninvited. "It would have been madness to continue."

"And Captain Morgan?" Sebastian persisted, ignoring Holliday's comment and directing his attention solely to Livingston. "He concurred in this, and ordered the ship back to Europe? Or did the men aboard force him into it?"

"He made the decision," Livingston said. "We were out of sight of the other ships, and taking green water over the bow. When he decided to turn back, the men rejoiced."

"But your crew was mostly prisoners and conscripts, was it not?" Sebastian said. "There were few real sailors on that ship."

"Sebastian!" Mattea snapped.

"Why is Captain Morgan not here with us?" Sebastian asked his mother, ignoring Holliday, who looked ready for a fight.

"I sent word to his family," Mattea said. "He has gone to sea again already."

"To Bergen, for a load of potash and pitch and straight pine," said Abercrombie. "He departed last week, with my brig *Eliza*. I wish he could be here to speak with us, but business is business."

"Another venture into northern waters," Sebastian said. "It seems the storm did not discourage him too much."

"A sailor knows there will be storms," Livingston said. "It is part of the unwritten contract one agrees to when one goes to sea. The Western Ocean is filled with the watery graves of Bristol men."

"The prudent ones know when to turn back," Holliday muttered.

Sebastian turned on him angrily. "Why are you so certain that my father and my brothers are dead? You come as a guest to my mother's house, eat the food she has prepared, and then poison the air with your talk of storms and drowning and the loss of an entire fleet! Yet you have no proof that this has happened, none!"

The look on Holliday's face lay somewhere between annoyance and amusement. Sebastian was of only average size for his age, but had he not been in his mother's dining room, surrounded by some of Bristol's most important men, he would have challenged the sailor to a fight right there. Sebastian knew that some of his father's crew still did not like being commanded by a foreigner, even after last year's successful trip to and swift return from the New Found Land. Yet it was Bristol men who had turned back, who had looked into the face of the storm and flinched. His father—Sebastian clung to this as a certainty—had stared it down and willed his way through it. Ludovico, too, for there was nothing in the world that frightened him.

And his father, foreigner or no, Sebastian thought,

would have thrown Holliday out of this house on his ear had he been here.

But Mattea Cabot found the right words for the moment. "You are right, Sebastian," she said gently. "Mr. Holliday has no proof that anything has befallen the fleet save for a storm that he feels lucky to have escaped. All he has is an opinion. I think his opinion is wrong, as do most of these men." Her eyes swept the table. "But we are here to have an honest discussion, and no one should be forced to hold back an opinion simply because it is an unpopular one."

"You are a courageous woman, Mattea," said Annabelle Ryerson, clutching her husband's hand. "I am happy that Richard has chosen to live his life on the river, within sight of the friendly hills of home."

"Every woman must learn to accept her husband for the man he is," Mattea replied, with a smile that contained the barest hint of sadness. "Giovanni has dreamt of ships and voyages since he was a little boy in Genoa. I could not change that even if I wished to."

After most of the guests had left, Sebastian helped his mother clear and wash the dishes. The sailors departed quickly, their bellies full, in search of a tavern open on a

Sunday evening. Some of the merchants lingered a while longer, huddling in a corner of the living room in quiet discussion. Sebastian managed to slip away long enough to catch Lorenzo Pasqualigo, the Venetian mapmaker, on his way out the door.

"I should like to know more about the lands Columbus has discovered," Sebastian said.

"As would we all," Lorenzo replied. "As the Spanish would like to know what your father has found. It is a game, my boy, full of guesswork and speculation."

"But you do have some information," Sebastian persisted.

"I have my sources," Lorenzo said.

"Has he really found the coast of Asia, as he claims?"

The older man's face twisted into an expression of amusement. "Well, that is part of the game," he said. "Certainly it is to his advantage that others think he has reached the Asian mainland—especially his king and queen. They are the ones paying him, after all."

"But do *you* think so?"

Lorenzo studied Sebastian before replying. "Tell you what, lad. When you are done on the river tomorrow, come by my office on Baldwin Street. I will show you what I know."

The tide was low the following evening, so Sebastian got off work early and made a beeline to the mapmaker's office. To his surprise, John Day, who had been at his house the previous evening, was there also. A large sheet of ruled map paper lay spread out on the office's central table between the two men.

"Ah, come in, my boy, come in," Lorenzo greeted him, setting down his pen and meeting Sebastian by the door. He clasped his hand in a firm handshake, and with his left hand led Sebastian by the elbow to the map table. "I was just discussing the size and shape of the Western Ocean with Mr. Day here. Like you, he is most interested."

"Hello, Sebastian," John Day said. He was a tall man, well-dressed and well-groomed, with lean, artistic hands more accustomed to holding a pen than a rope. Sebastian noticed that Lorenzo's hands were thick-fingered and rough, in contrast to the delicate lines he drew with them.

Sebastian nodded politely in reply. His eyes roamed the small office. The table, made of oak, took up half the space; a desk in one corner was piled high with correspondence. There were books, and shelves with small, built-in cubbies from which rolled-up maps protruded. A wooden cabinet half the height of a man stood against the far wall. A clay pot atop this cabinet held a variety of pens, rulers, and paintbrushes, some of which also lay strewn about the big table. Hanging from nails on the walls were a variety of straightedges, protractors, and measuring sticks, as well as an astrolabe and draftsman's compass. Amid the papers on the desk lay a globe much like those his father had fashioned. There were also sketches of ships, tide charts, and one or two works of decorative art having nothing to do with navigation or mapmaking. The cluttered office reflected Lorenzo's mind, for he was a man much interested in the world, and indeed, he had seen a lot of it with his own eyes.

He had his sleeves rolled up, and a lock of his thick gray hair had fallen down over his forehead. His rumpled look contrasted sharply with that of John Day, who stood with his arms folded, every button on his expensive shirt fastened. Sebastian imagined that if the man had an office, everything would be in its assigned place.

"You wanted to know where Columbus has been, and where he is now, in relation to your father," Lorenzo said.

"Something like that," Sebastian said.

"I will show you our best guess." He ran a hand through his hair, sweeping it back, then turned his attention to the map laid out on the table. Sebastian recognized the coast of Europe, drawn in outline only, and the familiar shapes of

Britain and Ireland. Maps in Venice and Valencia had invariably placed the Mediterranean at the center and worked outward from there, but the mapmakers of Bristol habitually placed the British Isles at the center. Lorenzo had placed the Strait of Gibraltar halfway between the top and bottom along the map's eastern edge, as a native of a Mediterranean state would. It was a sensible arrangement, as it allowed him to draw in the curve of Africa down to the Canaries and the Cape Verdes and still have room at the top for Scotland, the Hebrides, the edge of Scandinavia, the Faeroes, and Iceland.

The well-known European coastlines had been drawn quickly, copied from other maps, and showed little detail. Lorenzo had spent more time and attention on the lands, reported and rumored, out in the Western Ocean. The Azores were there, a hand's breadth due west of Lisbon. "That is as far west as I have been," Lorenzo said, indicating the small Azorean island of Santa María. "Everything beyond is based on what I have learned from your father, or from men who have been west with the Spanish fleet, or upon second- and third-hand information from those who have spoken with them."

"Columbus drew detailed maps," Day said.

"Indeed, and some who have seen them risked their

lives to copy them, or draw them from memory," Lorenzo said. "As I told you, boy, a man can find out much if he keeps his eyes and ears open."

Sebastian was looking at the map. "So this is my father's landfall?" he asked, pointing to a ragged strip of land in the map's upper right corner.

"No. This." Lorenzo traced a finger south, to a group of islands lying off a peninsula that stuck out from the map's eastern edge. The largest of the islands featured a much-indented coastline on its southern side that ran east to west. "Your father followed this shoreline after he had already turned back toward England," he said. "He reported that it was a rocky shore, with areas of woods and open grass, and that there were many long bays, and islands and bold headlands. A dangerous bit of navigation. But his original landfall was farther to the west."

"Here," Sebastian said, pointing to the peninsula. "The Asian mainland?"

"We don't know that for sure," John Day said.

"Your father made a great show of having discovered the way to Asia for king and country," Lorenzo said. "But privately, he had his doubts."

"I know," Sebastian agreed. "That's why he was so eager to try again." He bit his lower lip and stared at the map. Below his father's New Found Land there was a large gap where Lorenzo had drawn in nothing. Farther to the south, however, directly across from the curve of Africa, Lorenzo had drawn an extensive chain of islands. Some were large, some were small, and they were laid out along a nearly east-to-west line. The westernmost island was easily the largest, thin and elongated, its far end nearly touching the map's edge.

Lorenzo let Sebastian have a long look. "This is based on what we know at present," he said finally. "There will be more information as more of the men who shipped out with Columbus come home." His face twisted into a smile. "Ships leak more than water, you know."

"These are Columbus's islands, then?"

"The Indies, as he insists on calling them," Lorenzo said. "And, according to his agreement with Ferdinand and Isabella, he is now supreme ruler of them all."

"Except for Cuba," John Day put in.

Sebastian looked at Lorenzo for an explanation.

"Cuba," Lorenzo said. "Here." He ran a stubby finger along the outline of the long island near the map's edge. "Columbus maintains that it is not an island at all, but rather the outermost peninsula of the Asian mainland. He claims that a man could walk there from Europe, if he had the time. As Marco walked to Cathay."

"But you have drawn it as an island," Sebastian protested. "How do you know?"

Lorenzo smiled again. "I had to judge for myself which of my sources were the most reliable. Look here." Lorenzo pointed to the second-largest of the islands, just to the east of the long one. "This is the island he has named Hispaniola, where he wrecked the *Santa María,* and where he left his men to die after that first trip. They have built a city of sorts there, called Isabela, after their queen. It is Columbus's base of operations. In spite of their initial disaster, which I suspect they brought upon themselves through ignorance or cruelty to the natives or both, they have succeeded in planting a Spanish colony there, of which Columbus, as per his contract, is lord and master. Resupply ships now arrive there regularly from Spain. I gather there has been some trouble with the natives, but as they have neither guns nor metal, Columbus's men have been able to subjugate them. And he has convinced—or coerced, more likely—several of the natives to be his guides in his search for the Great Khan."

"That doesn't answer my question," Sebastian said.

"Patience, my boy," Lorenzo admonished him, though the mapmaker was still smiling. "Why is it that youth wants to know everything at once? Columbus left his lieutenant, Alonso de Hojeda, in charge at Isabela, and set out to find the Asian mainland." Lorenzo traced a finger along the shape of Cuba. "You must understand that the man has bet his reputation that this is the way to the riches of the Orient. He scouted the south coast of this land for many leagues, but he encountered no Asians, only half-naked savages like the ones in Hispaniola. Still, the coast trended south and west for as far as the Admiral could see. According to the men I've talked to, however, they made slow progress. After many days of trying to work to windward, and several groundings and near wrecks on the shoals, he turned back. *He turned back!* But he forced his crew, under penalty of fines, flogging, or torture, to sign a document stating that the land was a peninsula, and part of the Asian continent. Now, I happen to know that some of the men knew differently. The natives *told* them it was an island. But imagine your-self on a leaking ship, thousands of leagues from home, and your only way home at the command of a captain who insists that his every assertion is right, and who brooks no disagreement. They signed; they had no choice but to sign. And Columbus went back to Ferdinand and Isabella and told them he had reached the Asian mainland."

Sebastian took a moment to digest this tale before replying. "My father says Columbus could not possibly have sailed far enough in the time he claims to have reached the Orient. And yet my father was not entirely truthful in his reports to King Henry either. He saw no Asians."

"Columbus wants to get there first," said John Day. "He wants the credit for opening up the Western Ocean. But ambitious men like Hojeda—and, I daresay, like your father—are nipping at his heels. Columbus is a proud man. Vain, but proud. He wants to be the one to march into the court of the Great Khan, and to return to Europe and say, 'See? I told you so.'"

"It seems," Sebastian said, "that in this business, much depends on who is the better liar."

Lorenzo laughed. "My boy, you are learning fast," he said. "No one is rich enough and sailor enough at the same time to finance and carry out his own expeditions. For that, one must depend on the wealth of kings. And kings, invariably, want to know what's in it for them."

"So if Columbus doesn't come back with spices or gold . . ."

"Ferdinand and Isabella will drop him like an anchor," Lorenzo finished for him. "Unless he can string them along with promises that the riches of the Orient are just around the next headland."

Sebastian ran his hand over the blank spot on the map. "What of this area?" he asked. "It looks like empty ocean."

"That is because no one from this side of the ocean has ever charted it," John Day said.

Lorenzo's fingers traveled across the map from Portugal to the Azores. "Remember, it has only been within this century that we have known of these islands," he said. "And men have tried sailing west from them, but none of them found land. I have been to the Azores. The westerly winds are relentless—they would beat back any ship. No, the only way is to go south, as Columbus did, or far to the north, like your father, and the Vikings before him."

"Your father's idea was to find the northeast corner of the Asian mainland and follow the coast as it fell away to the south and west," John Day said. "A workable theory, if that is indeed the lay of the land. We shall have to wait for his return to find out if he has succeeded."

Sebastian recalled his lessons. "The farther north one goes," he said, "the shorter the distance from east to west."

"True," said Lorenzo. "And the land tends to cluster nearer the pole. From Scotland it is less than a hundred leagues to the Faeroes, then nearly the same distance again to Iceland, and the same again to Greenland. But there is the question of climate. Storms from the north can be fearsome, as you heard the sailors say last night at your mother's table. And the sea around Greenland is reportedly full of ice."

"Our ships have not called there for many years," Day said. "It is a forbidding place."

"My father had no plans to sail by way of Greenland."

"No, but his letters from the king gave him authorization to explore the ocean to the north, east, and west," Day said. "Not to the south. King Henry has no desire to provoke a confrontation with Ferdinand and Isabella. Theirs is a much richer country, with many more ships. England would get the worst of a conflict with them."

"But you said . . ."

"He must first go west," Day said. "If he is correct in his picture of the world, he will find the coast of Asia at a point far north of the lands of the Great Khan. By following the coast, he will reach temperate latitudes, but well to the west of Columbus and his fleet. Should he sail south too soon, and encounter Spanish ships, I am afraid it would not go well for him. The Spanish can be brutal in protecting their interests."

"My father and Columbus have known each other

since they were children," Sebastian protested. "They aren't friends exactly, but I can't believe Columbus wishes him harm."

"Men change," Lorenzo said. "Power, especially, changes them."

"And Columbus is not the only one out there," John Day added. "They have a veritable navy in those islands, well-financed and well-armed. They mean business."

"As the Moors discovered," Lorenzo said. "And the Jews."

"I know," Sebastian said. "We lived in Valencia, during the worst of it."

"They would treat a fleet of Englishmen with no less dispatch," Day said. "Let us hope your father steers clear of them."

CHAPTER 9

VALENCIA, ON THE MEDITERRANEAN shore of the Iberian Peninsula, was nothing like Venice. But Sebastian's mother never complained about leaving her home and extended family. He and his brothers struggled to adapt to a new land, with a new language and new customs. And his father, though well-paid and respected by the council of businessmen who ran the city's affairs, found himself frustrated by continual delays and indecision as he set about designing Valencia's new port.

The family moved into a spacious house on a sandy bluff overlooking the beach. It was more room than they had enjoyed in Venice or would have in Bristol, but then, Valencia was neither a commercial capital nor a thriving port. They had a steady flow of money again, and the small community of Genoese and Venetians that could be found in cities all along the Mediterranean helped ease the transition.

Sebastian learned to write and speak Spanish, and Sancio picked up the language even more quickly. There were wide, sandy beaches along the warm sea from which to go swimming, and groves of citrus and almond trees just outside the city where an ambitious boy could find a day's work and come away with some money in his pocket. The weather was warm and pleasant and the pace of life, after Venice, seemed languid. Sometimes ships came to call; they anchored far off the beach and their crews rowed ashore in longboats. But most travelers and most commerce came overland, from Barcelona, Seville, and Madrid.

The potential port would require the construction of breakwaters and the creation of a deepwater area where ships could tie up to docks and off-load cargo. The city planners had dreamed of such a thing for generations. It had, until now, remained a dream. But the unification of Aragon and Castile meant that there was more money to go around, and the men who ran the city's affairs hoped to lobby Ferdinand and Isabella for some of it. Giovanni Caboto had been to many ports; he had seen how they were constructed and how they operated; and he had dealt with people in positions of power. If he was unused to being an administrator, he was at least well-suited for the job.

Caboto had his own agenda, of course. A port at Valencia would be an excellent spot from which to fit out and launch an expedition to the west. In many ways, it was better than Lisbon, the Portuguese capital, or the Spanish port of Cádiz, both of which lay outside the Mediterranean. If a westward voyage was successful in reaching Asia and returning to Valencia, the prized goods could then be easily transported to Venice and throughout Europe, avoiding the Islamic lands altogether. Giovanni Caboto's fortune and reputation would be made. And Ferdinand and Isabella would be sitting atop the richest trade route in the history of the world.

But Ferdinand and Isabella had many other things on their minds. There was the ongoing military struggle to drive the Moors off the peninsula and back to Africa. There was the question of what to do with those Jews who refused to convert to the kingdom's official Catholic faith. There was the conquest of the Canary Islands, won by Ferdinand and Isabella in exchange for their agreement to leave the African slave trade to the Portuguese. And there was Giovanni Caboto's old friend Christopher Columbus, who had been living in Spain for several years.

Always a keen observer of people and events, Caboto

kept his eyes and ears open and learned what he could. He paid particular attention to any news of his old friend and rival. Columbus, it was said, had made an impression upon Queen Isabella, for they were kindred spirits, each imbued with a sense of divine mission. Caboto, his associates told him, would have more luck trying to win over the scheming and hardheaded King Ferdinand, whose family had ruled Valencia before the marriage.

Giovanni traveled frequently to consult with the king's advisers or to meet with the king himself, leaving Mattea to care for the house and their three sons in her accustomed, capable fashion. When Giovanni was home, there were often meetings at the house lasting far into the night. Visitors from other parts of Europe called occasionally, and a few old friends from Venice made their way to the house as well, among them Lorenzo Pasqualigo, who would follow the family to Bristol.

Ludovico, Sebastian, and Sancio dutifully attended church each week with their mother, and the family observed all the requisite fast days. Giovanni, when he was home, sometimes attended services with his family, which pleased his wife and surprised his sons. It was important, he told them in the privacy of their kitchen, that he be seen as a good Catholic. He was a foreigner in a place where the hot winds of religious intolerance blew across the face of the land, and if attending a few church services helped him fit in with the local business community and won him favor with the Crown, he was willing.

From time to time soldiers came through town, and there were rallies in the plaza, at which local boys were sometimes recruited to go off and take part in the siege of Granada in the south. The armies of united Spain had numbers on their side and a determined king behind them. Every so often news would reach Valencia that another Moorish town had fallen, and then there would be a bonfire in the plaza and a night of celebration.

Sometimes Sebastian and his brothers would stand on the fringes of the crowd as an officer on horseback whipped it into a frenzy, exhorting families to send their sons into battle for the glory of king and queen. Boys only a few years older than Sebastian would come forward, begging for the chance to join the holy war that would drive the infidel from Spain. The soldiers took boys as young as eleven. The tall, serious-faced Ludovico, who looked older than his thirteen years, would have been a prime candidate had he been born in Valencia. But his mother sat him down one evening, after Sebastian had given a breathless account of soldiers in glittering uniforms and plumed helmets, and said, "You are a Venetian. You have no stake in this. We may live in this country, but they will not have my sons to fight their wars." She looked at Sebastian and Sancio as well when she said this, young though they were, to emphasize the point.

Soldiers recruiting young men for the battle in the south were not the only strangers to pass through town. Itinerant traders dealing in gemstones, fabric, and printed books, which were still rare, came and set up shop in the plaza. Sometimes groups of travelers, many of them Jews, carrying what possessions they could, came through Valencia looking for passage on a ship that would take them to Marseilles or Genoa or some other destination away from Spain. Sebastian and his brothers often saw whole families on the move, leading mules with packages piled high upon their backs, often stopping in the marketplace to trade precious gems for currency to buy their way aboard a boat in Barcelona, Alicante, or, if a ship happened to be in, from Valencia itself. Many of these families were anxious to leave, which puzzled Sebastian, for his parents had sold quite a bit of their property in order to get here. The West was the future, his father had said. Yet these Jewish families were willing to part with their gemstones for a fraction of their worth if it meant they could get aboard a ship bound for other parts of Europe.

The Jews in Venice had been set apart but not perse-
cuted. Many of them had tried to fit in to the city's
day-to-day life and commerce by adopting Christian customs and dress and speaking the language of the street, and
they often held positions of some influence. The doctor
who treated an infection on Sebastian's foot when he was
six years old was a Jew, as was the real estate broker who
sold the family's rental property prior to the move.

Things were different in Valencia. Sebastian could feel
the fear. He had heard the stories of the occasional Jew
being set upon and beaten by peasants in the countryside,
but that sort of ignorant violence happened all over
Europe, and could be dismissed as a rough sort of mob
sport. But Spain's Jews lived in fear of a more organized,
more powerful form of persecution, its instrument not
a temporary mob, but the Catholic Church itself.

In a small building off the plaza, a group of friars
had set up an office whose function was a mystery to
Sebastian. These friars were not men of Valencia, but had
been sent there by officials of the Church, and with the
blessing of the king and queen, to convert nonbelievers to
the official faith and to inquire into matters of heresy.
Sebastian had little idea what went on inside the building,
whose doors were always closed, but he knew that people

who were arrested by the king's police were often taken there, and that a wide area in front of the building's stone steps was avoided by many of the townspeople.

One day Sebastian and Sancio were returning from a walk on the beach when they saw a crowd of people headed toward a flat, open area outside the city walls. Ludovico, who had spent the morning picking fruit, fell in beside his brothers. "What's going on?" Sebastian asked.

"I don't know," Ludovico replied. They followed the mass of people out onto the plain. It was a sunny day, one in a recent string of such days that often blessed this part of the Mediterranean shore, and the sea sparkled below the bluff until it disappeared in a layer of haze on the horizon. Behind the town, the olive-green mountains rose into a clear blue sky. The crowd stopped and formed a wide circle around an area where a large scaffold had been placed and a pole, into which had been hammered two large iron rings, set into the ground. Sebastian and his brothers jostled for position, trying to see, but they were hemmed in by people all around them, shoulder pressed to shoulder, necks craned for a view of the scaffold. As they watched, three friars clad in simple brown robes led a man and woman, bound at the wrists and around their torsos with chains, out into the area in front of the scaffold. The crowd drew back a little as one of the friars ascended the scaffold and passed a length of chain through the loops on the pole.

Sebastian gasped. "I know them!" he said. "I have seen them at service!"

"They may have walked in the house of the Lord," said a grim-faced man next to them, as tall as Ludovico but gray around the temples, "but they are the Lord's enemies, and they deserve what's coming to them."

"What are they doing?" Sancio said, at Ludovico's elbow. Sebastian, on tiptoes, could see the friars and several other men piling sticks of wood at the base of the scaffold, but Sancio was several inches shorter, and his view was blocked by the people in front of him. A low murmur of anticipation swept through the crowd.

"They're going to burn them," Ludovico said, his voice even.

"What?" Sancio cried. "Why?"

"Because they spring from the seed of the men who killed Jesus," the man next to them said, his chin jutting upward as he watched the friars lead the couple onto the scaffold.

"But I have seen them in church," Sebastian said. "I have watched them kneel and take the sacrament. They are as Christian as you or I."

"New Christians," the man said, his voice full of contempt. "That is part of their evil way. They accept baptism in order to gain the favor of righteous men, so that they can do business and own property and live like Christians. Meanwhile they practice their devilish rituals in secret."

Now the crowd stirred and pushed forward. The man and woman were chained to the stake, their backs to each other. The woman was dark-haired and still young; her eyes looked wildly around at the mob of people who had come to watch her die. The man, dark-haired also, with a close-cropped black beard, was naked to the waist. Red lash marks crisscrossed his torso. Both man and woman were barefoot, their clothes ragged, their hair matted against their foreheads. The crowd roared as one of the friars came forward with a lit torch and touched it to the woodpile at the base of the scaffold. Sebastian felt the heat immediately. He looked at Sancio and saw that his younger brother was crying. The flames shot up and licked at the base of the scaffold. Sebastian saw the woman look skyward and call out, but her words were lost in the crackling of the flames and the cheering of the crowd. Now people pushed backward as the heat surged outward. The air filled with cheers and shouted curses and the screams of children. Sancio ducked between the legs of people around his brothers and him and was gone.

"Sancio!" Sebastian cried.

"Come on," Ludovico said. "We cannot take part in this."

Sebastian followed Ludovico as his older brother pushed and elbowed through the crowd. Bodies pressed all around them. The stench of burning flesh reached Sebastian's nostrils. He fought back the reflex to vomit. "Sancio!" he called again. But his brother had disappeared.

They found him at the edge of the bluff overlooking the beach, sobbing. The crowd, deflated after the frenzy of the spectacle, dispersed, some people heading back toward the city, others to the orchards and fields. The friars and their assistants remained to tend to the dying fire and the charred remains of the couple. Sebastian sat down next to his younger brother and put an arm around his shoulders.

"That was horrible!" Sancio cried, his body shaking. "How could they just stand there and watch? How could a whole city stand by and do nothing?"

"It wasn't the whole city," Ludovico said, kneeling at Sancio's other side. "That crowd was mostly peasants and day laborers. Good people stay away from such things."

"But why?" Sancio wailed. "Why did they burn those poor people?"

"They must have committed some crime," Sebastian said. "They must have done something more than say a forbidden prayer. People cannot be put to death for such small things." He looked at Ludovico questioningly. "Can they?"

Ludovico stood and squinted at the smoldering remains of the scaffold in the distance and the people lingering around it. "It is a strange country," he said.

"I hate it here," Sancio said, sniffling and wiping at his face with the back of his hand. "I wish we were back in Venice."

Sebastian helped his younger brother to his feet. The three of them walked back to their house in silence.

It happened to be a week that Giovanni was home, and he had heard about the execution at his office. It was the sole topic of conversation that evening around the dinner table. Sancio, though he had been comforted by his mother, was still upset. Ludovico, as was his way, betrayed little emotion. Sebastian, the image of the man and woman crying out their last words to the sky as the flames rose around them still fresh in his mind, wanted to know what his father thought about it.

"There is no violence like religious violence," Giovanni Caboto said.

Mattea's dark eyes flashed. When the boys had arrived at the house that afternoon and told her what they had witnessed, she had knelt with them before the small statuette of the Virgin that stood in the living room. She had prayed for forgiveness for the friars who had carried out the burning, and made Sebastian and his brothers join in her prayer, though Sebastian had said his "Amen" softly and without much conviction and Sancio had not said his at all, for it was hard to forgive such cruelty. And she had prayed also for the souls of the man and woman who had been burned, for they had been baptized as Christians and earned forgiveness for their sins.

"It's wrong to blame the Church for the excesses of a few," she said to her husband.

"Is that what you think?" Giovanni Caboto asked his wife. "Do you really believe that what took place today was the act of a few friars, taking the law into their own hands? Well, you're wrong. Those men answer directly to the inquisitor general, a man named Torquemada, who answers directly to the king and queen. The burning of Jews is official policy."

"But there are many Jews here," Mattea protested. "Surely they do not intend to burn them all."

"Ah, but that is the frightening thing," Giovanni said. "For while it is no crime to be a Jew, it is a crime for a Catholic to commit heresy against the Church. And Spain is full of Jews who have accepted baptism and sworn allegiance to the Church. For them, the utterance of a single Jewish prayer can mean a death sentence."

"Why do they not openly remain Jews, then?" Sebastian asked.

"For the same reason that you are learning to speak Spanish," his father said. "The king's own doctor is a Jew, as is Luis de Santángel, the royal purser. In matters of money and medicine, learned Jews have made themselves indispensable. But ordinary Jews are always under suspicion. They are seen as loyal to their own kind first, the Crown second. Some say they are secret allies of the Moors."

"And how do you know all this?" his wife said, her voice calm but challenging.

"I must make it my business to know things, if we are to get our port built," Giovanni said, a small smile alighting on his lips. "The war in the south will be won very soon, I think. The Moors cannot hold out much more than a year or two, maybe less. Then, there will be money for public projects, like our port. I intend to have the plans ready, and in the hands of the king's advisers, on the day the war ends."

Events moved even faster than Caboto predicted. The burning witnessed by his sons took place in June of 1491, and was followed in the next few days by two others (which Sebastian and his brothers stayed away from), before the friars moved on to the next town and the next group of heretics. Reports continued to filter back to Valencia from the campaign in the south. One Moslem town after another fell before the Catholic armies of Ferdinand and Isabella. As the Christmas season approached, Giovanni Caboto and his crew rushed to complete their surveying and drafting work. In the second week of the new year, the news came.

"Granada has capitulated! Long live the king and queen!" Bells rang out from the cathedrals near the plaza; people poured from their houses to celebrate in the streets and to welcome the returning soldiers. Throughout the night, people gathered around bonfires to pass skins of wine and sing triumphant hymns and patriotic songs. During the next few days, the plaza buzzed with word-of-mouth accounts of the final siege and the glorious procession, behind the cross and the royal colors, into the last Moslem stronghold on the peninsula. By God, they would have to go back to Africa now! The armies of Christendom might even pursue the infidels across the desert, might indeed chase them all the way back to Arabia! All hail Ferdinand and Isabella, saviors of Spain!

Giovanni Caboto, former Venetian merchant and cur-

rent port commissioner of Valencia, watched it all unfold
with the eyes of one who had seen world-scale changes
before, and knew that within such change lay opportunity.
He was forty-one; his sons would be grown men soon.
With his aides, he completed the plans for the harbor,
and then sent a messenger to the royal court, which was
then in Santa Fe near Granada, overseeing the transfer of
the city from the defeated Moors. Caboto requested an
audience with the king at his earliest convenience.

Three weeks passed before the messenger, one Aurelio
Rodriguez, returned. He was a small man of both Venetian
and Spanish heritage—his mother was from Valencia and
his father was a Venetian sailor who had come to Spain
many years before. Rodriguez had proven valuable to Caboto
because he could speak both languages, and because he understood both the hardheaded business sense of the Venetians
and the proud, emotion-driven nature of the Spaniards.
Caboto had relied on Rodriguez to help him win the confidence of the Valencians, and he hoped the man would
represent his interests to the king as capably.

But Rodriguez returned without a commitment. "The
king is a busy man these days," he told Caboto in his office,
where plans for the developed port lay across a wide table
and the Mediterranean stretched uninterrupted outside

the small courtyard. In his mind, Caboto could gaze at the water and see the vision on the paper, a harborful of ships from over the horizon, bearing goods from distant ports. But it would take money to make the vision real.

"This is the time to approach him, when he is flush with victory," Caboto said. "He has the gold of the Moors in his pocket. And I know he wants a port here."

"I was told that in the spring, perhaps, when the court returns to Barcelona, the king might hear your proposal."

"Were you able to speak with anyone who might have his ear?" Caboto asked.

"I spoke with the royal purser, Luis de Santángel," Rodriguez said. "He informed me that ours is not the only request before the king, that indeed the court has been beset with proposals from all over Spain as to how best to distribute the wealth of Granada."

"Santángel has much influence at court," Caboto said.

"Indeed. That is why I spoke with him. But others are speaking with him too. Your friend from Genoa, for one."

"Columbus? You have seen him?"

Rodriguez nodded. "I am told he was in the royal procession that marched into Granada the day after the Moors surrendered."

"He is like a pesky insect that will not go away,"

Caboto said. "Like a mosquito, buzzing round and round, making a nuisance of himself until he either draws blood or someone swats him."

"More like a bee, I should think," Rodriguez said. "There are those at court who wish to keep him around, on the chance that he will pollinate the right flower."

"He is still telling everyone that the Western Ocean is only seven hundred leagues wide?"

"Oh yes, and anything else they want to hear, anything that will further his own personal ambition," Rodriguez said. "He talks of undiscovered islands along the way that Spain could add to her empire. He calls up visions of caravels returning from the Orient groaning with gold and pepper and silk. This westward voyage to the Indies is his personal Crusade. He rode into Granada with Ferdinand's cavalry, but he cares nothing for the fate of the Moors or the glory of Greater Spain. All he wants is money for his enterprise. And there are those at court— Santángel among them—who deem it an acceptable gamble to give it to him."

"And the queen likes him, of course."

Rodriguez nodded. "And the queen likes him. But she still has not given her consent. And Santángel is the king's man, not hers."

"He is also a Jew," Caboto observed. "Which, given present circumstances, ought to limit his influence at court."

"Perhaps," Rodriguez said. "But the king and queen defer to him in matters of money. He is useful to them. You can be sure that those influential Jews who are close to the king and queen will be treated differently than the great mass of Jewry in the cities."

Caboto rubbed his chin and looked out the window. "What does Santángel say about our port?" he asked the messenger.

"That there is an excellent chance it will be funded," Rodriguez said. "Queen Isabella is a romantic, like your friend Columbus, but the king is a pragmatist. My guess is that once things settle down at Granada, they will go ahead with it."

In April 1492, Giovanni Caboto was summoned to Córdoba to present his plans for the port to the king and his commissioners. They were impressed with his thoroughness, and Caboto was told to return to Valencia and await delivery of a contract. In that same month, the queen issued a royal decree mandating that all of Spain's Jews convert to Catholicism or leave the country within four months—exempting, of course, those Jews within the royal court. And in May, the queen gave her blessing to

Christopher Columbus's plan to sail across the Western Ocean in pursuit of a new route to the Indies. Luis de Santángel pledged to put up half the money himself.

"Well, he is going to try it," Giovanni Caboto told his family at dinner on the day he heard the news. "They are giving him three ships, and one tenth the value of all the goods he brings back." Sebastian watched his father ladle a spoonful of soup into his mouth and scowl down into the bowl. "One tenth of nothing is still nothing," he said.

Caboto wanted to travel to Palos to see Columbus before his departure. But business demanded that he remain in Valencia. Besides, the roads were choked with Jewish families, their worldly possessions packed atop mules, heading for the port cities to board ships for other parts of Europe. It was a pitiful exodus. Those Jews who did not travel in large groups were often set upon by bandits in the countryside and robbed, and many an unscrupulous Spaniard made money by purchasing gems and valuables at a fraction of their worth from desperate families who needed the money to book passage aboard a ship. The ports themselves swarmed with Jewish families anxious to leave the country before Isabella's deadline. So busy was the sea traffic that Columbus was twice forced to delay his departure, for the business of expelling the Jews took precedence over a speculative venture to the west. Caboto imagined his single-minded friend pacing the dock in frustration, undisturbed by the deportation of much of his adopted country's intellectual and commercial wealth, eager to get on with his destiny. Finally, in mid-August, word reached Valencia that Columbus's three-boat fleet had sailed, bound first for the Canary Islands, and then westward into the uncharted ocean.

For the remainder of the year, Caboto stayed busy negotiating the contract for the new port to be built at Valencia. He heard nothing more of Columbus. He traveled twice to Barcelona to meet with the king's advisers, and each time he heard the promise that a contract was imminent. Christmas came and went, and the calendar turned to 1493. Finally, in February, he was summoned once more to Barcelona, where he was received personally by King Ferdinand and given a contract to begin construction in the spring. Valencia was finally going to get its port, and Giovanni Caboto was to be its master.

CHAPTER 10

Dear Sebastian,

We have found land again, and Father is not happy about it.

On the second day out, we came upon two low, rocky islands, topped with grasses and trees and surrounded by flocks of seabirds but apparently uninhabited by humans. We looked for a place to land, but finding none, and judging the islands too small to support game animals or a source of fresh water, Father ordered the helmsman to stand off. "We are well-stocked anyway," he remarked, and it was true. Our water casks are full, and our native friends had bestowed upon us gifts of dried fish, cakes, vegetables, and fresh meat. We spent the last night ashore boiling most of the meat and salting it down, in preparation for a long ocean passage.

We had no sooner spotted the islands when William Hennessey cried out from the crow's nest. Several of us sprang into the rigging, but there was no need, for it soon became obvious that we were near land, and not just two scraggly islands, either. Here was a coast much like the one we had so recently left. Low, rounded hills rose up near the shore. They were greened with trees, though the tops of a few of them showed bare rock and glints of silver in the sunlight. The hills rose from a mostly flat shoreline that was broken up by bays and inlets and innumerable small islands. Father ordered the lead heaved and found varying depths, in places ten fathoms or less, and nowhere more than forty. As we drew closer to the land we saw another solitary hill off to starboard that appeared to be on an island by itself, though it was hard at a distance to separate one island from another, there were so many of them.

"What is this place?" Father said aloud to no one as he puzzled over the vista before the ship. "I should not have liked to come upon a broken shore such as this at night."

The day was clear and the wind gentle, just strong enough to move the boat with the lateen sail rigged and the square sails trimmed in on the starboard side. We were heading north into a large bay. The bay was filled with rocky, tree-topped islands, a few of them sizable enough for homesteads or even settlements, but others just drops of land, like batter in a pan, some too small even to support trees. We passed close to one of these ledges, where perhaps two dozen seals had hauled themselves out of the cold water to bask in the sun. There were quite a number and variety of birds, including one with a fat, colorful beak and black-and-white feathers, and another that circled high in the sky before dropping like a stone into the water and emerging with a fish. Clearly this coastline, wherever it was, teemed with life. But it looked like a treacherous place to navigate with a ship such as the Pandora. For if there were crowns of rock that barely broke the surface of the ocean, there must be others, unseen, lurking just below.

And then, suddenly, there they were—three native craft, each with three men, bobbing out toward us over the waves. The boats were slightly rounder and deeper, but the people in them looked just like the natives among whom we had stayed for the previous month and a half. When they drew near, I shouted out a greeting in the language of Red Hawk's people, and I could see that the words were recognized by the natives in the nearest boat. "Not Asians at all," Father said, by my side, "but more savages."

He ordered several of the men into the rigging to shorten sail so that we would not outpace the small native boats. For an awkward few minutes our crew and their boatmen stared at one another across the small stretch of water that separated us. "Try saying something else to them," Father urged me. "Ask them where they live, where they came from."

"Ask them where their women are," suggested Eliot Morison, bringing laughter from most of the men.

I tried to talk to them, using what words I'd picked up from Red Hawk and his people. But although the language sounded similar, I was unable to understand most of what they said.

After much faltering and pointing and pantomime, it was agreed that we would allow them to guide the Pandora into safe harbor for the night. The afternoon was drawing on, there was a fresh onshore breeze, and Father did not want to be caught out in the dark among the ledges and small islands.

But he was disturbed. He had not expected to find another shore so soon. As he stared out over the ship's rail at the islands and headlands all around him, I could see his mind turning. If this was not the farthest fringe of Asia, what was it?

We followed the native boats toward the reddening sun as it sank behind the hills. They led us into a small, well-protected harbor, guarded from the ocean swells by a small island at its mouth. The natives beached their craft in the grass of the inner harbor and disappeared into the trees. As it was getting dark, Father ordered everyone to remain on the ship for the night.

He gathered several of his men around him, and said that a party must set out in the morning to climb the highest of the hills, to ascertain the lay and size of the land. The men were restless, and Father sensed this—he was restless himself. He ordered watches posted according to the regular schedule. All of us had expected to be at sea for longer than two days, and the continuation of sea watches served to remind us that we would soon put to sea again.

Where are we, Sebastian? That question is on everyone's lips tonight as the stars appear: the Scorpion and the Archer low in the south above the ocean, Polaris shining steadily over the rocky hills. Just as before, the bulk of the land lies north of us. Is it possible that this land and the land of Red Hawk's people are connected, and that we have done nothing but cross the mouth of a large bay, like the Bay of Biscay? Remember when we came to England? Halfway between Cape Finisterre in Spain and Brittany in France, one can see no land, yet the land is all of a piece, though different tongues are spoken on each peninsula. If that is the case with this land, if it is all connected, it is a large land indeed, larger than anyone suspected.

The lamp in Father's cabin remains lit, though it is past midnight. I imagine that he is poring over his charts, trying to figure out where this land fits in with what is known of the world. Just now he went on deck with the astrolabe to take a fix on the Pole Star. He has no more idea than any of the rest of us where we are. We can only hope to find out more when the sun returns in the morning.

Your loving brother,
Sancio

2 August 1498

Dear Sebastian,

We are on our way again, after a severe disagreement among the crew. Many of the men wanted to set course for Bristol, to report what we have discovered, but Father and a few loyal crewmen argued that we have as yet discovered nothing, and that this expedition would be a waste if we quit now. But a faction of the men, led by Adam Keane, held that this land would be best explored by a fleet of vessels that could return next summer. Father replied that the men had signed on for a year, and that this expedition had been prepared to spend a year at sea. Father is the captain, and his will prevailed, but not without considerable grumbling from Keane and other like-minded sailors.

When we went ashore this morning, a group of natives was there to greet us. Father brought out some of the

Venetian jewelry, and their leader presented Father with a necklace of shells. He noticed the shells hanging from my neck, and fingered them, and said something I didn't understand. Again, we tried to communicate with them in their own language, with little success. Like the other natives, they dress mostly in clothes made from animal skins, and they are fond of smearing their faces with some sort of reddish material, a kind of grease.

Again, Father tried some words in Arabic, which brought from them only blank stares. Their tongue sounds nothing like Arabic, nor any language I have ever heard in Europe. I tried some of the phrases I had learned from Red Hawk and his people, and both groups were pleased to discover some signposts of familiarity, though we could not yet understand one another.

Father directed Stephen Conant to lead a party of a half-dozen men to the top of the largest hill, which the natives called something like "Megunticook." Their language, like the language of Red Hawk's people, is full of sounds like that—a lot of "g" and "k" sounds formed back in the throat, unlike European languages, which use the tongue and teeth and lips. They are primitive in everything else; it is no surprise that their language is primitive as well.

It is an impressive hill, and I wanted to see the view, but Father ordered me to accompany him to the natives' village.

It was not far from the harbor, a walk of perhaps an hour. Father selected a dozen people, including me, my friends Peter and William, Adam Keane, and Father Cartwright to accompany him, and he left Eliot Morison in charge of the Pandora. We followed the natives up a small stream through stands of leafy trees and along the base of a high, rocky cliff that bore the stains of spring runoff. The land was green and lush; moss covered the trees and rich green undergrowth carpeted the forest floor. The native men led us along a path until the woods abruptly ended and we found ourselves on the edge of a freshwater lake. The natives stopped to drink, cupping the water with their hands, and after watching them, most of us did the same.

It was a beautiful spot. The lake was long and narrow; we could not see all of it, for it disappeared around a point behind two small islands. The cliff we had been following extended all along one side of the lake, leaving a small, flat area by the water's side. The rest of the lake was surrounded by low, rolling hills covered with trees. We stood at the spot where the lake flowed into the stream that carried its water down to the harbor. The slope had been gentle all along the path, and had the stream not been flowing beside us we would not have been conscious of walking uphill at all. The lake looked like what it was—a flooded valley between verdant hillsides. Undoubtedly the lake was filled with fish, the forests with game. There was abundant timber for building generations of houses, and a ready supply of fresh water. A safe harbor was just a short walk away. Were this place in England or Spain, I thought, men would have built a city here. But then the trees would have been cut down and the lake fouled and the rock cliff quarried for cathedrals and banks and prisons. Perhaps it was better in the hands of these natives.

I took off my shoes and rolled up my trousers and waded out a short distance. The water was sweet and clear, and as the day was warm, I thought about swimming.
But one of the native men pointed to a cluster of buildings along the side of the lake, where a flat peninsula below the cliff extended out into the water. I could see several structures there, and the smoke from a small fire.

The village consisted of perhaps ten buildings of varying size surrounding a central area where there was a stone fireplace. They had cleared some land for crops, and there were several boats—smaller versions of the boats they used on the ocean, along the shore, and out on the lake. There was a house of sorts on one of the islands as well, and it looked like people had cleared the land there, too.

The houses were long, low, and curved. Their frames were made of bent tree limbs embedded in the ground, their walls fashioned from branches and skins. I wondered why they had no timbers, until I spotted a native woman digging in the ground with an implement made from a curved shell bound to the end of a stick with a strap of animal hide. Then I understood. These people had no adzes or metal tools with which to shape trees into the planks and timbers needed to build strong houses, or strong ships, for that matter. They could not sail to England even if they knew of England's existence, because they could not build a ship capable of taking them there.

But like the natives we had met previously, they shared food and drink with us and invited us into their homes. Each house had its own hearth and central cooking area, with a vent in the ceiling and areas for the storage of food, tools, and clothing. They do not use much in the way of furniture beyond simple stools, preferring to sit and recline upon skins on the dirt floor; their bedding, likewise, is made up of piles of skins and furs. I found myself wondering how they pass the winter, and what winter is like in this place.

I could tell that several of our men were disturbed at the sight of the villagers' houses and our brief glimpse of their day-to-day lives. Women and children flitted in and out of every home and all around the village. No doubt the scene served as a painful contrast to the emptiness and uncertainty of their own lives. A few of our crew stared openly at the native women, and I am sure this did not escape the attention of the native men.

We did not stay long, however, for Father wanted to get back to the ship and meet up with Conant and his party. They arrived back at the harbor shortly after we did, and their news was not encouraging.

"The land extends for as far as a man can see to the north, east, and west," Conant reported. "To the north the land rolls away in a series of higher and higher hills. There are many lakes, and a few rivers. Offshore, the sea is speckled with islands, like the coasts of Ireland and Scotland."

"What about the direction of the coast?" Father wanted to know. "Does it continue in a straight line, or does it curve around on itself?"

"I would say it continues to the southwest," Conant said. "Though it is no straight line. Many fingers of land reach out into the sea. But the coast appears to trend in the same direction." Conant lowered his voice. "We are not on an island, Captain. Or if we are, it is a very large one— as large as Britain itself, perhaps larger."

"A new land, unknown to Europe," said Adam Keane. Turning to the priest, he said, "We must claim it for the king."

"There is another possibility, Captain," Eliot Morison put in. "It is possible that we have reached the Asian mainland after all."

Father shook his head. "I cannot believe we have come so far west. And if we are in Asia, would these people not have some knowledge of the riches of the Orient? Would they not have silk, and other Asian goods—much as Roman coins can still be found in England? No, I agree with Mr. Keane. This is a land previously unknown to us. We are the first Europeans to see these shores."

"Then we must return to England, and tell the world what we have found," Keane said.

Father did not reply for long seconds. "Were we to do that," he said finally, "the Spanish would claim this coast as theirs. We are west of the Pope's line, and the Pope gave none of the western seas to England. No, we will weigh anchor tomorrow, and follow the coast southward, and see where it leads."

The argument went on long into the night. Many of the men were not convinced, and held that this land must be a far-flung part of Asia into which the culture of the Great Khan had not penetrated. Others said that we should return to England, regroup the fleet, and return to this latitude with more ships, this time avoiding the stormy northern route. Still others said that we should turn northward along the coast and map it as we go, while looking for the other ships in the fleet. Only a few agreed with Father's plan to follow the coast southward, though this seemed to me the most sensible course. If the trend of the coast continues, we will be getting farther west the farther south we sail, and if there is a passage to Asia, it surely lies in the direction we are headed.

Nonetheless, it is a divided and disgruntled crew that now stands off this coast, whether it be part of Asia or not. I think the sight of the native women has reminded some of the men of the loneliness of sea travel. There were two fights today, over stupid things like a piece of a biscuit and the proper handling of a line. Father had to clap one of the men in irons until he cooled off. He does not like to impose discipline, but he is the captain, and no ship can long afford that kind of disorder. He himself spends long hours on the deck, pacing and staring out at the sea.

Who can fault him for not being able to sleep? He is a man on the doorstep of destiny. When we return to England, Sebastian—and I cannot say when that will be— we will bring with us the certainty that a great mass of land, reachable by ship from the shores of Europe, does indeed lie in the Western Ocean. It is Father's discovery, and he will become famous for it. I daresay the world as we know it will never be the same.

Your loving brother,
Sancio

4 September 1498

Dear Sebastian,

Oh, my brother, we are in trouble. The Pandora *sits stuck in the mud near the shore of a wide bay surrounded by marshlands. We have been here for several days, and now Adam Keane and a few of the other men have aroused the anger of the natives. No one knows what is going to happen, and everybody is on edge.*

They have been so long without women it has made them crazy. Still, there is no excuse for what they did. Two of our men are dead—Richard Cunningham and Michael Ballard— though Keane, who started all the trouble, escaped without a scratch. Father had to order the use of the muskets to frighten the natives away. At least two of them were struck by musket balls before Father ordered the men to stop firing.

He is not naive enough to think that they won't attack again. They can shoot their arrows with deadly accuracy, and the woods around the ship are full of eyes. I am sorry to have neglected this journal for the past month. It has been a month of danger and uncertainty. We have followed the coast far to the south, then north again, then south once more, and Father has spent much time with his charts, attempting to place each new landmark. It seems certain now that we are on the shores of a hitherto unknown continent. A great body of land lies between Europe and Asia in the Western Ocean. It is populated by people who have never heard of us. Father now says that Columbus must have made landfall on some islands lying offshore of this new continent, but that he is too stupid and stubborn to know what he has discovered.

Father has kept a careful record of the distance we have traveled and the lay of the coast. Though we can only guess at our westward distance across the ocean, we can figure out how far west we have come since then, and Father says it is nowhere near far enough to have reached any part of Asia. We have sailed as far south as the latitude of Lisbon, where Marco located the Great Khan's kingdom, and we have seen no hint of Asian riches. There is no other conclusion but that we have reached an entirely new land, and that if there is a western route to Asia, it must lie far to the north or south of here.

We have navigated into several bays, which unfailingly narrow into river channels lined with dangerous shoals. We were lucky to extricate ourselves the first few times this happened. This time we were not so lucky. We have tried to pull her off with the longboat. The tides are not so large here as they are farther north, and as we grounded at nearly high water, we cannot simply wait for the tide to float her off. We cannot move. We have off-loaded many of our supplies in an effort to lighten the ship and float her free, but we remain stuck, surrounded by hostile natives.

All the watches are now armed, but there is a great deal of nervousness, especially at night. Just last night I was wakened by shots. One of the men on deck thought he had seen something move in the trees and fired, and two of the men on watch with him discharged their weapons as well. In the morning there was nothing. Father has warned everyone that we have a limited supply of gunpowder and that the muskets should be used only as a last resort, but everyone is afraid. It is a bad situation we have gotten ourselves into.

I'll try to write more when I can. Father wants to make peace with the natives, for the freeing of the ship will be an easier undertaking if we are not under constant threat of attack. He wants to go to their village and speak with their leaders, and as I am the most adept at translating native languages, I am to accompany him. The priest stepped in and told Father that since this is not Asia but an entirely new land, it was his duty to claim it for England and to baptize the natives into Christianity, by force if necessary. Father told him rather abruptly to be silent.

It will not be easy to convince these people that the kidnapping and rape of three of their women was all a misunderstanding. Such a thing would not go unpunished in England. Here, there is little Father can do except clap the men involved in irons or have them shot. However, there is no chance of replacing any of the crew on this side of the ocean. We have already lost three men since leaving Bristol.

Oh, Sebastian, the shores of Europe would be a welcome sight right now! I pray that you and Mother and Ludovico are well, and I know that we are in your prayers. Still, Father has been through trying times before. If anyone can get us out of this latest mess, he can. But for the first time since the tide swept our fleet out into the Bristol Channel, I find myself wishing that I had been the one left behind. How delightful it would be to sit at our table and share a meal again, to sleep once more under a roof, to walk out in the morning into streets full of civilized people going about their business.

The natives of this new continent meant us no harm until we wronged them. In Europe these matters would be settled by the courts of civilized men. How does one settle such things with people so strange to us, whose language we can barely understand? If we do not make matters right, I fear that the mark we will leave in this place will be one of shame and distrust, and that future meetings between men from Europe and this new world will be filled with bloodshed on both sides. I pray that does not happen, but I find myself awaiting the morning with a knot of dread in my stomach.

Be well.

Your loving brother,
Sancio

CHAPTER 11

IS SONS HEARD THE NEWS BEFORE
Giovanni Caboto did. They spent much time out
in the streets of Valencia, among other youths,
and when someone arrived in town they usually knew it
first. Thus did Sancio Caboto overhear a conversation in
the marketplace in Castilian Spanish and, understanding
its import, rush to tell his brothers.

Their father was bent over a detailed drawing of the
port when Ludovico, Sebastian, and Sancio burst through
the door of his office. It was mid-March; construction
was to begin in May, and Giovanni was going over the
plans with Alfonso Cuneo, who owned the quarry from
which the stone for the breakwater was to come. Caboto
looked up when his sons entered the office; the first
expression to cross his face was irritation at being interrupted in his work.

"What are you boys doing here?" he said. "Can't you see I'm busy?"

"I know, Father, but we have heard important news," Ludovico said.

"So important that it could not wait for the dinner table?"

Sebastian couldn't contain himself, and shifted nervously from foot to foot. "Columbus is back," he blurted. "And Father, he has been to the Indies!"

Giovanni Caboto straightened to face his sons: Ludovico, tall, nearly a man, calmly meeting his father's eyes with his own; Sebastian, nervous and fidgety and unsure of himself; and young Sancio, who, though still a boy, bore an expression of sly intelligence, as though he knew more than he let on. Cuneo, a short, rotund man of about forty, folded his hands over his stomach and said nothing.

"Where did you hear this?" Caboto said.

"A man came into the plaza this morning," Sancio said. "A seller of musical instruments. I heard him talking about it with some of the other merchants."

"What did he say, exactly?"

"He said Columbus had returned, and landed in Lisbon," Sancio said. "And that he claimed to have come from the Indies, and not from Guinea or any other

Portuguese possession, and that he had some Indians with him to prove it."

"But he has been gone only a few months."

"I am just telling you what I heard in the plaza," Sancio said.

Caboto exchanged a look with Cuneo before turning back to his sons. "And this man, he has seen Columbus?"

"My impression was that he had only heard about his return, from people he has talked to in his travels," Ludovico said.

Sancio nodded. "He has talked to people from Lisbon, though he did not come from Lisbon himself. Columbus is there, he said, with two of his ships. King John had him brought to the court, to question him."

"I would like to speak with Cristoforo," Caboto said.

"If he has reached the Indies," Cuneo said, "it will change everything."

"We cannot be sure of information passed from one mouth to another," Caboto said. "Men have made claims before that have turned out to be false."

"It is the talk of the plaza," Ludovico said.

Giovanni Caboto grabbed his coat from the peg on the wall and flung it over his shoulders. "Alfonso, we will continue this later," he said. "I need to go see this man myself."

"I'll come with you," the quarry owner said, going for his coat.

The plaza buzzed with the news. But to Giovanni Caboto's frustration, there was little more specific information than what his sons had told him. Columbus had arrived in Lisbon, with two of his three ships, and reported the discovery of several large islands off the Asian mainland. The third ship had apparently been wrecked on a reef, and Columbus had left forty of his men behind in a fortress they had built on one of the islands. He had dispatched a letter to Ferdinand and Isabella, and would soon travel to Barcelona, where the royal court was currently in residence, to present the news of his discovery to the sovereigns in person.

And that was all. For the next several days nothing more was heard about Columbus, though each evening Caboto pressed his sons to tell him anything they might have overheard in the plaza. Rumors swirled—that Columbus had landed on a wild island populated by people with tails; that the third ship had not wrecked at all but was on its way back to Spain via the tip of Africa, on a course that would take it clear around the world; that Columbus had landed in Asia and presented a letter from Ferdinand and Isabella to the Great Khan himself. Caboto dismissed such talk, but the excitement behind the rumors made him nervous. What had his old friend found? And what would he tell the king and queen?

More information arrived with subsequent travelers. Shortly before Easter, 1493, Caboto learned that Columbus had sailed from Lisbon and arrived in Palos. The newly anointed "Admiral of the Ocean Sea," summoned to Barcelona by the king and queen, had set off overland from Seville with an entourage that included several of his officers, priests, servants and scribes, and the "Indians" he had taken captive on his voyage. New arrivals in Valencia gave breathless reports of the procession. At each town, Columbus stopped and gave a speech, and allowed the residents to gawk at his Indians and the exotic items he had brought back from the voyage.

The route from Seville to Barcelona reached the coast at Valencia, and every day the Valencians looked out at the mountains to the west, wondering when the admiral would appear. No one awaited his arrival more eagerly than Giovanni Caboto, for he wanted to hear from Columbus's lips the details of his transoceanic voyage, and to see for himself the people he had brought back and the charts he had made. It was difficult for Giovanni to keep his mind on plans for the harbor with reports of Columbus reaching his ears daily.

At last the day arrived. On a sunny, mid-April morning, the procession snaked down out of the hills on the road to Valencia. Even from a distance it was evident that Columbus had spared nothing to create an image of triumph. He was accompanied by more than a dozen men, half of them on horseback, the others walking alongside. Two horsemen out front carried long pennants that waved in the breeze; the sun glinted off polished shields and brass helmets, and those on foot followed in an orderly formation. Businesses closed, and the activity of the plaza markets came to a halt to welcome the parade; every resident of Valencia was outdoors to witness the spectacle of the admiral's arrival.

Sancio, Sebastian, and Ludovico stood with their mother and father near the edge of the plaza as the parade entered the city between the lines of cheering people. A small wooden stage had been set up near the center of the square. The flag bearers dismounted and took up positions at either side of the stage, displaying the royal colors and the banner of Pope Alexander, who was especially revered in this part of the world because he was a Spaniard, and had the ear of Ferdinand and Isabella. Next came several men carrying wooden crates filled with plants and shrubs, which they set on the ground in front of the stage.

Across two of the crates, a long board was laid out, and covered with a purple cloth, and on it two more men began placing ornaments made of fish bone and trinkets of hammered gold. Columbus himself, dressed in a flowing red cloak and a smart, three-cornered hat studded with jewels, sat tall upon his horse and looked out into the crowd, soaking up the welcome.

"Count on Cristoforo to milk the moment," Giovanni Caboto muttered to his family.

A priest, also on horseback, rode beside Columbus and carried a small golden cross. Two men on foot carried small wicker cages, which held birds with bright plumage of red, yellow, and green—beautiful, large-beaked birds that drew appreciative comments from those close enough to the stage to see them. Behind Columbus, two men led a group of six bewildered, dark-skinned men, naked save for tiny loincloths, onto the stage. They stood silent and stoop-shouldered, exchanging looks with one another, their dark eyes every now and then darting quickly into the crowd. Despite the flags and the finery, it was these strange people who drew most of the crowd's attention, and there was much whispering and pointing. "Father, why do they wear no clothing?" Sancio asked. But Giovanni shushed him with his hand, for Columbus was about to speak.

With a nod and a small wave to the people who had gathered round, Columbus dismounted, shook the hands of several people near him, and stepped onto the stage between the flag bearers. He was taller than most of the men around him, a fact that the low wooden stage emphasized. He took off his hat and waved it at the crowd, and a cheer went up.

Columbus asked the priest to lead a prayer of thanksgiving to the blessed Virgin for carrying his crew across the Western Ocean and safely back again. Then he began to speak of his voyage.

"For thirtytwo days we sailed westward from the Canaries," he said, "and on the night of the thirtysecond day I saw a light in the distance ahead. The next morning we came upon a low, sandy island covered with dense forest and surrounded by reefs. It proved to be just one of many islands in that sea, of varying sizes. We charted these islands for several months before returning to Europe by way of the Azores. I am certain that the islands we explored are in the Indies, and that the Isle of Cipangu and the lands of the Great Khan lie not far beyond them. Good people of Valencia, the way to the West lies open!"

Another cheer rose from the crowd. Giovanni Caboto pushed forward toward the stage as Columbus continued speaking. Ludovico could see over the heads of the people in front of him, but Sancio and Sebastian could not, and they began to inch forward behind their father. "Stay with your mother," he told the boys. "I want to talk to him."

Columbus went on, describing his first encounters with the Indians, praising them for their peaceful nature, and allowing the crowd to ogle the six captive men behind him on the platform. He called attention to the smattering of gold trinkets laid out on the makeshift bench, and promised that on his next voyage—which had already been approved by the king and queen and for which preparations were even now under way in Palos and Seville—he would locate the Asian kingdoms from which this gold surely originated. Sebastian stood on tiptoes beside his mother, trying to see, but Sancio could not remain in place. Picking a moment when his mother was looking the other way, he darted between the legs of a tall man in front of him and wormed his way toward the front of the crowd. He heard his mother call after him, but she was too late. Using his small size to his advantage, Sancio squeezed forward until he was close enough to see the whites of the admiral's eyes. He looked at the assortment of odd plants, necklaces, and carvings that had been laid out at Columbus's feet, at the brightly colored birds in their cages, and at the near-naked men, who certainly did not look like Europeans but did not look like Africans, either, nor like any people he had ever seen. Venice had been full of people from far-off places, and Valencia had its share of foreigners, but these people did not resemble any of them.

"And so, by undertaking a sea voyage to the west, which no one had ever before tried, I have shown that the land described by Marco Polo and long talked about by men of Europe can indeed be reached from the shores of the Western Ocean, and in a reasonable number of days," Columbus proclaimed. "No more will we need to risk expensive caravans to the banditry of Arabs and Turks or the harsh terrain of mountain and desert. Nor must we make the long and perilous journey round the tip of Africa. West! West, across the ocean! By the grace of God the Father, the sea has yielded up her secret. I shall report to my king and queen that I have found the way to Asia, and that the throne of Spain, in its wisdom for sending me on this noble voyage, shall prosper from it, in the name of Christ our Lord!"

Another cheer rang out from the crowd. Sancio felt a rough hand on his shoulder. "I thought I told you to stay with your mother," Giovanni growled.

Sancio flinched. "I . . . I couldn't see," he protested.

"And everybody wants to see what the great admiral has brought back from the Indies," his father said. "You are a willful and overly curious boy."

"Yes, Father," Sancio said meekly.

"That curiosity of yours will get you in trouble if you aren't careful."

"Yes, Father, I know, but—"

"Never mind. You're here." The elder Caboto nodded toward the stage, where Columbus was accepting congratulations from several of the sellers whose spots on the plaza had been usurped for the welcoming ceremony. "He's quite full of himself, isn't he?"

Sancio said nothing, relieved that the anger had gone out of his father's voice. One of the priests in Columbus's entourage approached the admiral, and introduced him to a man Sancio recognized as a priest at the church he and his family attended. The two men shook hands warmly.

"Come on," Giovanni said, taking hold of his youngest son's arm. "Let's go see if we can have a word with him."

They moved forward with the flow of the crowd, and as they did so, Sancio caught his father looking over the plants displayed at the front of the stage, then squatting to rub a broad, stiff leaf between his fingers. Then Caboto moved toward the spot where Columbus and the local priest were conversing, and maneuvered himself into Columbus's line of sight.

"Cristoforo," he said.

Columbus turned his head, and Sancio saw a brief look of confusion in his dark eyes. It lasted only a moment, and then his self-satisfied smile returned. "Giovanni!" he exclaimed. "Giovanni Caboto, my old Genoese friend! What a surprise to see you here! How *are* you?"

The two men embraced, and then held each other by the shoulders for a long moment. "I am well," Caboto said. "But look at you! The conquering hero returning."

"It is a long way from the docks of Genoa," Columbus conceded, looking down at his regal attire with a show of modesty. "How long has it been since I last saw you? Five years? Six? In Lisbon, as I recall."

Caboto nodded. "You were working on a chart of the Azores, and I had just come from there."

Columbus laughed. "As I have come from there recently myself," he said. "They were not inclined to believe me when I informed them that we had arrived from the Indies."

"My congratulations on seeing it through," Caboto said. "You have always refused to believe that anything is impossible."

Columbus laughed again. "Yes, stubbornness has served me well," he said. "But what brings you to Valencia?"

"I am port commissioner here," Caboto said. "We are in the process of constructing a harbor, though the actual building is still months away. But that is nothing, compared with what you have done!"

"I always knew the Western Ocean could be navigated," Columbus said. "Now I have shown that it can be done."

"Were there many storms?" Sancio asked at his father's elbow.

Columbus looked at the boy, and then back at Caboto.

"My son, Sancio," Caboto said, giving him a pat on the head that was a little bit rougher than necessary. "He has never quite learned when to keep his mouth shut."

Columbus laughed. "Do you remember," he said, "pestering the men who came in off the ships in Genoa? Do not be too hard on the boy, Giovanni. We were boys once."

"What of the weather, then?" Caboto asked. "You found fair winds from the Canaries, to take you across the ocean?"

"Indeed." He looked down at Sancio. "The only storm we encountered was on the way home. I had not intended to call at the Azores, but the winds had other ideas."

"I should like very much to sit down somewhere with

you and hear about your adventure, perhaps over a glass of ale."

Columbus glanced around at his people, who had started to put away the various displays. "I should like that as well, but we must make all due time to Barcelona, for their majesties have summoned me."

"Surely you have time for a drink with an old friend."

Columbus shook his head. "I regret that I do not," he said. "The king and queen are awaiting my report, and these people are eager to get moving." He glanced around at the men in his party as they packed up the plants, neck-laces, and other items. "I will be fitting out a return trip, with many more vessels," he said. "I could use an experi-enced captain."

"I have a job here," Caboto said.

"Very well." Sancio couldn't help but notice how quickly Columbus dropped the offer. It was evident that the admiral didn't really want a rival of his father's stature.

Caboto's attention turned to the plants that were being loaded into boxes. Many of the people in the crowd had begun to drift away now that the spectacle was over and the procession was preparing to continue on toward Barcelona.

Caboto bent to examine the same plant he had looked at before. "What is this?" he asked Columbus.

"I believe it is a variety of the aloe plant," Columbus said, "which, as you know, is traded in the Far East for its healing properties."

Caboto shook his head. "I have seen aloes in the markets of Alexandria and Arabia," he said. "This does not look like them, nor does it have the same smell when it comes away on your fingers."

Columbus shrugged. "I am not a botanist," he said. "But it has the same general shape as an aloe plant. I believe they are related. We will find true aloes, I am sure, when we uncover more of the Asian coast."

"Were you able to trade for pepper, or other spices, or silks?"

"No, but they cannot be far. We have found the leading edge of the continent. When we return, we will find the way to the great cities and the islands where the spices are grown. And gold!" The admiral nodded at the boxes into which his men had returned the golden trinkets. "There is plenty more gold where that came from."

But Caboto was now looking at the near-naked men, who stood at the back of the stage, flanked by their Spanish captors. He walked up to them, met their eyes, and then said something in a language Sancio did not understand. Apparently the dark-skinned men did not understand it either, for they stared blankly back at Sancio's father. Caboto tried again. Sancio realized that his father was speaking in Arabic. One of the men uttered something in a language that sounded like nothing Sancio, who had heard many languages, had ever heard before. His father attempted other words, accompanied by movements of his hands miming the movement of a ship. Three of the dark-skinned men spoke briefly among themselves, but Sancio could understand none of it.

His father tried more words in other languages, with the same result. Sancio glanced over at Columbus and caught an expression of impatience on his face, which was quickly replaced by a thin smile the moment the admiral realized that Sancio was looking at him. Caboto was now holding up different numbers of fingers and saying the name for each number in various languages. The strange men responded with their own strange words, and Caboto shook his head in frustration. Finally he gave up.

"If those are Indians," he said to Columbus, "then I'm an Englishman."

Columbus's smile disappeared. "It is time we were on our way," he said. "It has been good to see you, Giovanni."

"My sons would love to hear more about your adven-tures," Caboto said. "And my wife sets a fine table. Can you not take time to be our guest at the midday meal?"

Columbus shook his head. "I am afraid not, old friend. As eager as your sons may be to hear about our trip to the Indies, the king and queen are more eager still. And I must answer to them first, since they are the ones who sent me there."

"You have charts of the lands you discovered?" Caboto asked.

"Of course we made charts," Columbus said—more haughtily than was necessary, Sancio thought. "But you must know that they are for the eyes of the king and queen, and not for public display. King John asked me to show them to him, and I refused. The king and queen shall see them first, for it is to them I owe my allegiance."

"Father! There you are!" Sebastian rushed forward through the dissipating crowd. "Did you talk to him? Did you ask him where—" He stopped when he saw Columbus, who flashed a quick glance in his direction and just as quickly returned to the business of packing up. Mattea and Ludovico stood a short distance away, watching.

"My family," Caboto said. "The tall one there is

Ludovico, and this is Sebastian. And my wife, Mattea."

Columbus said something to one of his men, and then stepped down off the stage. He lifted Mattea's hand to his lips and kissed it gently. "It is my pleasure to finally meet you, madam," he said, and Mattea dipped her head in acknowledgment. "You have three fine sons."

"Sailors all," Caboto said, "and Venetians at heart, though Genoa runs in their blood."

"As it does in mine, though I am a Spaniard now." Columbus turned back to Caboto's wife. "It is his Genoese blood that makes him look to distant horizons," he said. "But you are his home, no matter where his house is."

"Godspeed on your journey to Barcelona," Mattea said. "And on your next passage across the ocean."

Columbus nodded his thanks. "You are a lucky man, Giovanni," he said.

Caboto placed a hand on his wife's shoulder. "Yes, I know. But you have been blessed by fortune as well, Cristoforo. Of all of us who talked of sailing into the Western Ocean, you are the first to actually do it and come back. All over Europe men will be speaking your name."

"I could not have done it without God's help."

"And the king's and queen's," Caboto said.

"It was God who provided the wind."

"We must have that drink sometime."

"Come to Palos," Columbus said. "Though if things go well I shall be there only a few months—just long enough to get the fleet ready. The adventure is just beginning."

Columbus's horse was brought forward, and with a final wave to the people who remained around the plaza, he mounted and the procession moved out toward the road that led north along the coast toward Barcelona. Giovanni Caboto stood with his wife and three sons and watched them depart, the horsemen out front with Columbus in their midst, followed by the porters, the priests, and the dark-skinned captives. Some of the shops had already opened their doors, and a few merchants began setting up tables in the square. Slowly, but before the procession was out of sight, the town of Valencia returned to business as usual.

"He is an impressive man," Mattea said. "He will make a fine presentation at the royal court."

"Yes, I'm sure he will," Giovanni said. "They will give him his ships, and his titles, and his money. He has made a name for himself, that is certain. But he has not been to Asia."

"Jealousy does not become you, Giovanni," Mattea said.

"I'm not jealous. But I know a fraud when I see one. Why would he not sit and discuss the details of his venture with me? Why is he in such a hurry to see the king and queen and secure their blessing? He is afraid that someone will find him out. He could not have sailed all the way to the Indies and back in the time he says he did."

"But what about the plants, and the people?" Sebastian asked.

"Those are no Asians," Caboto said. He looked hard at his middle son. "In Arabia I saw people from the Far East. I spoke with them; I traded goods with them. Those naked men did not understand a word of Arabic. Nor did they recognize any of the simple words of the Indian languages I heard in Arabia. Their skin has never touched silk. They have never drunk coffee. They wouldn't know a spice if they saw one. And his plants don't look like anything I saw in Arabia either. His aloes aren't aloes. As far as I could see, he did not bring back one thing that proves he reached the shore of Asia, or came anywhere near it. Thirty-three days, even in a fast caravel with a fair wind, is nowhere near enough time to sail halfway around the world."

"He has been somewhere, though," Ludovico said. "Those strange men did not fall out of the sky."

"Everybody knows there is land out in the Western

Ocean," Caboto said. "My old friend has simply come upon some islands we have not seen before. And since he told the king and queen that he was seeking a new route to Asia, he must convince himself, and them, that he has found it."

"Are you so certain he has not?" Sebastian said. "You could be wrong, you know."

"I'm not wrong!" Caboto snapped, so harshly that Sebastian shrank back against his mother. "I know more geography in my left foot than Cristoforo Colombo knows in his whole body! Not even the great admiral can shrink the Earth to suit his purposes. He found some islands out there, and now he's boasting that he was right all along. The man's a self-serving, pompous blowhard."

"But a very convincing one," his wife said quietly. "Come, let's go home and eat. It's been quite a morning."

It was a grim meal, no one saying much of anything, as Giovanni stewed in the injustice of his old friend's success, and the likely reception he would receive from Ferdinand and Isabella. Afterward he went out, to his office and to the offices of city officials, and he returned home that evening in an even fouler mood, because everyone in Valencia was talking about Columbus and his glorious accomplishment. His wife and sons knew enough to leave him alone.

The days that followed were dark ones in the Caboto household. Giovanni reflected that his wife was right: It didn't matter that Columbus's claims of reaching Asia were preposterous—if he could make people believe them. And Ferdinand and Isabella, locked in fierce competition with Portugal to open up the Western Ocean and secure the riches on its far shores, were eager to believe.

The news that came out of Barcelona in the ensuing weeks was all bad. An appeal was quickly made to the Pope to grant exclusive rights to discoveries in the Western Ocean to Spain, with Columbus becoming the lands' governor-general. Columbus was granted royal approval to assemble a fleet of seventeen ships and twelve hundred men for a second voyage to his so-called Indies. As if this were not bad enough, several men who had been contracted to work on the port at Valencia announced that they would instead seek to accompany Columbus. The enthusiasm for the port shifted to this new westward adventure.

Finally, in late May, the hammer dropped. Word came by royal messenger that all funding for the port at Valencia had been canceled. Once again, Giovanni Caboto was out of a job.

CHAPTER 12

IN MAY OF 1499 TWO CARAVELS APPEARED at the mouth of the Bristol Channel and bore down on King's Road. At first Sebastian, who spotted the tall ships as he waited for the afternoon's passengers to complete their business before the return trip upriver, took them for two of his father's ships, and a lump rose in his throat as he contemplated their reunion. With what news would the old man be returning? What would he have to say to the son he had left behind? Would Sancio and Ludovico present him with gifts from the courts of Asia, underlining that they had been along on the adventure and he had not? For an hour or more Sebastian steeled himself. He did not relax until he saw the Portuguese flags flying from the tops of the ships' mainmasts.

Not his father, then. Sebastian was surprised to discover

that his reaction was mixed. For months now, he had been watching the horizon for signs of the returning fleet. He knew that many of his father's backers were worried. And yet he had come to like his position on the waterfront and the responsibility of holding down a job. The ship captains knew him by name and spoke to him. His boss treated him well, and had even given him a raise at the beginning of the new year. He was an accepted member of the loose brotherhood of river pilots, who watched out for one another and shared stories at the end of the day. Sebastian liked hearing news from the ports of Europe as it arrived on the lips of sailors. He liked mingling with the great cross section of people—Viennese, Norwegians, Basques, Irishmen, Jews—who came through Bristol on the fishing and trading ships. He liked being in the middle of things, and he liked it even more that his position had nothing to do with his being the son of John Cabot.

When his father and brothers returned, likely flush with success, they would be celebrities, and Sebastian would become the third brother, the one who had stayed behind. Was that why he had felt as he did when he saw the caravels? Did he secretly wish his father would *not* return? If so, it was a terrible thought, one he would have to cleanse from his soul the next time he attended confession. For surely it was a sin, wishing ill fortune on one's own family.

The Portuguese caravels hove to off the entrance to the river, and the captain of one of them was rowed in to the dock. Sebastian watched as the captain spoke with the two boys who tied up his longboat. He knew by now to wait. One of the boys pointed in his direction, and the captain started down the dock toward him.

He was a bearded, olive-skinned man of medium height but regal bearing. Sebastian thought there might be some Basque blood in him. In heavily accented English, he introduced himself as Miguel Corte-Real, and asked the rate for passage to Bristol. Sebastian quoted him a price double that which he charged his regular passengers, for the captain was a foreigner, and he knew that Portuguese captains were paid almost as much as their Spanish counterparts. Besides, how else was the man to get to Bristol? All the other river pilots did the same thing, with the tacit approval of their bosses. Corte-Real handed over the inflated fare without quibbling.

Though he refrained from asking the captain directly, Sebastian burned to know what the two Portuguese caravels were doing here. They had not come to trade, for then they would have wanted to bring the ships all the way up the river instead of lying at King's Road while the captain went on his errand. The man could travel upriver on tonight's flood tide and return on the ebb in the morning, and the ships could be on their way within hours. It made sense if the ships were pressed for time. And the caravels, invented by the Portuguese and now copied by everybody else, were the fastest sailing ships in the world. Sebastian's father had returned from the New Found Land in only fifteen days in the Bristol-built caravel *Matthew*.

The Portuguese captain took the seat nearest the stern. Sebastian made small talk, hoping Corte-Real would reveal something he could share that night over ales with his fellow pilots. "The tide is not so strong near the quarter of the moon," he said as the rowers eased the boat out into the channel. "It is a good time to bring ships such as yours into the harbor."

"Your harbor is famed for its tides," Corte-Real said. "I have been told it can be treacherous."

"Not if you place your ship in the hands of a competent pilot," Sebastian said.

The Portuguese captain chuckled. "Spoken with the confidence of youth," he said. "Still, I shall be content to see it for the first time from a boat such as this. One that can maneuver quickly—in the hands of a competent pilot, that is."

Sebastian allowed himself a smile. "The currents can be tricky," he said. "It has taken me most of a year to learn them."

"Then it is good that I am your passenger," Corte-Real said.

Silence passed between them until Sebastian pulled the boat alongside the dock at Hung Road to pick up three additional passengers, regulars who gave him the usual fare. Sebastian hoped that the Portuguese captain did not observe the transactions too closely.

"You have not been to Bristol before?" Sebastian asked when they were once again out on the river.

"No," Corte-Real said. "But I have met men from Bristol in every port along the shore of the Western Ocean, from Lisbon to Thule. Their reputation for bravery is well-earned."

The mention of Thule, or Iceland, stirred something in Sebastian's chest. Only fishermen and explorers went there, and the twin caravels were not set up for fishing. His father had called at Iceland on his first attempt to cross the Western Ocean, when gales had beaten him back. It was a mysterious place, at the edge of the known world. What was this man, with his two ships, up to? And what was his business in Bristol?

"We are coming up on Avon Gorge," Sebastian told him. "It's the fastest part of the river, and the reason why Bristol has so seldom been invaded."

The gorge was indeed impressive, with high, steep sides from which a defending army could shower down arrows and rocks upon any enemy ship. The river narrowed as it passed between the granite banks, and as a consequence the strong tidal current ran even more rapidly. Sebastian concentrated on his helm and the work of the rowers as the boat glided smoothly through. As usual, he felt the surge of excitement. He took pride in his ability to handle the boat, anticipating the eddies and whorls along the sides of the passage, and compensating for them with his rudder. He had become a good river pilot in the past year. Someday soon his father would be back, and would see him in action. And then, how could he refuse to take him on the next great voyage, perhaps as pilot of one of the vessels in the fleet? His father would see that he had been wrong to leave behind such a sea-worthy son.

"You steer well, lad," Corte-Real said as they came out of the gorge, and Sebastian thanked him with a nod. He *did* steer well. But he still longed for a chance to prove it on the open sea.

"Which side of Bristol are you bound to?" Sebastian asked, though from the man's dress and rank he knew already.

Corte-Real reached into his cloak and pulled out a small piece of paper, which he unfolded. "I am to see a man named Edward Abercrombie," he said. "At an address on Redcliffe Street. I hope that you can direct me."

"I know where it is," Sebastian said. But there was suddenly a hollow feeling in the pit of his stomach. Abercrombie was one of the men who had put up the money for his father. Why was he receiving a Portuguese captain with two caravels? Was he hedging his bets, financing another search for Asia in case his father failed to return? What was going on? Sebastian wanted desperately to ask more questions. Where were the caravels bound? What were Portuguese ships doing in waters so far north of Portugal? And why had their captain come to call on one of Bristol's richest merchants? But to ask would have been impolite, and might have aroused the captain's suspicion. Better to wait for word to get around the waterfront, as it would soon enough.

Sebastian steered the boat through the Frome-Avon confluence and toward the crowded docks at St. Nicholas Bank. The grand houses of Redcliffe Street, looking down over the harbor, came into view. Sebastian pointed out Abercrombie's house, and showed Corte-Real the bridge he needed to cross in order to get there.

"I am fortunate to have drawn such a knowledgeable and helpful pilot," the Portuguese captain said as the rowers pulled the last few strokes toward the dock. "You seem to know the river, and the city, as if you have always lived here."

"What makes you think that I haven't?" Sebastian said.

"Because," Corte-Real said in Spanish, "although you have a Bristol man's contrary nature, your English is accented. You speak it like a Spaniard."

Sebastian shook his head. "My family spent time in Valencia," he said, staying with English, which he spoke better than the captain. "But by birth and upbringing I am a Venetian."

"Ah, Venice!" A broad smile crossed the captain's lips. He switched back to English. "That explains why you are so at home on the water, having grown up in that drowned city. What is your name, my young friend?"

"Caboto," Sebastian said.

The smile disappeared from Corte-Real's face. "I see. And in Bristol, do they call you Cabot?"

"They do," Sebastian said.

"Then you are related to the Cabot who sails out into the Western Ocean?"

"He is my father," Sebastian said.

"I see," Corte-Real said again. Sebastian waited for him to say something else, but the man just gazed off at the houses atop the bluff on Redcliffe Street and said nothing. To Sebastian, he seemed deep in thought. What did this man's visit to Bristol have to do with his father? Did he know something Sebastian didn't, something he was unwilling to reveal, except to Abercrombie and his partners? Sebastian knew that rich and powerful men throughout the kingdoms of Europe were very much interested in this business of overseas exploration, that fortunes could be made or lost depending on who got where first, and that as a result information was closely guarded. But he also knew that the same information was traded at a price, and that the money in Bristol resided in the houses at which the Portuguese captain was now staring.

Sebastian spotted Richard Ryerson farther down along the waterfront, saw his boss watch the boat come in and then turn back to the man with whom he was speaking. He was right on time. It was a continual source of pride to Sebastian that his boss could count on him. He had worked hard to earn that trust.

The rowers shipped their oars as the young bow man tied up, and the passengers disembarked. Corte-Real handed Sebastian a small Portuguese coin, a shiny gold piece bearing the image of the late King John. "For your excellent service," he said, and stepped out onto the dock. "I thank you for the passage, Master Cabot," he added, with a small dip of the head. "Perhaps we shall see each other tomorrow, upon my return to my ship. Or perhaps we shall meet again somewhere out on the high seas."

He's flattering me, Sebastian thought as the elegantly clad captain walked off, but why? He would not be visiting Abercrombie unless he wanted something.

A year had passed since his father's departure. In these uncertain, fast-moving times, with ships departing regularly from the coasts of Europe for destinations previously considered unreachable, a year was an eternity. Sebastian hungered for news. No one in Bristol had heard anything from the fleet since that first ship had been beaten back to Ireland. What, if anything, did this Portuguese captain know? It was not beyond the realm of possibility that his father, returning from Asia, had missed England and made landfall in Portugal, or worse, Spain. Might he be imprisoned in one of those countries, his discoveries beaten out of him? Corte-Real had closed up like a clam upon the revelation of his name. What did he know, and to what use did he intend to put that knowledge? And where, on either side of the ocean, were his father and brothers?

Sebastian arrived home that evening to find his mother in conversation with John Day, the man of letters, on the front steps. Even before he drew close enough to hear their words, Sebastian could tell that Day had come with ill tidings. Mattea stood on the second of three stone steps, talking with her hands as well as her mouth, in that expressive way familiar to Venetians and Genoese but not the English. Day, smartly attired in finely tailored clothes as was his custom, stood at the bottom of the steps, on the street, arms folded across his midsection as though ready to defend himself against a blow. He looked like he wanted to be somewhere else.

When they saw Sebastian approach, they broke off the conversation, and his mother waved to him. "Hello, Sebastian," Day said, greeting him with a handshake, though his smile and the warmth in his voice seemed forced. "You're looking well. Life on the river appears to agree with you."

Sebastian looked back and forth between Day and his mother. Mattea had a smile for him, but there were clouds behind it. Sebastian realized now that she had been angry when he'd arrived.

"What is your business here?" Sebastian asked Day. "Is there news of my father or my brothers?"

"I'm afraid not," Day said. He sneaked a glance at Mattea. "Many of us are looking for his ships. He is overdue."

"Two ships came in to King's Road today," Sebastian said. "Two caravels, from Portugal. I thought they might have been from Father's fleet, until I saw the flags. I brought one of the captains up to the city just now."

Day cocked his head to the side. "A gentleman named Corte-Real, by any chance?"

"Yes! How did you know?"

"Miguel Corte-Real? Or Gaspar?"

"Miguel," Sebastian said. "Why? Who is he? He had a note in his pocket, with Mr. Abercrombie's address on it. Seemed in a hurry to see him." Sebastian took a step back and looked into Day's face. "Why is Mr. Abercrombie receiving a captain of Portugal? What is his business in Bristol?"

Mattea stiffened. "You didn't tell me anything about this," she said to Day.

"I did not know until just now that they had arrived," Day said. He turned back to Sebastian. "The new Portuguese king has become much interested in our northern discoveries, including your father's," Day said. "It is a touchy situation. All King John cared about was finding a way around Africa, but Manuel worries about the Spanish developments in the West. He has men in London, speaking with King Henry."

"And where does that leave my father?" Sebastian asked, bitterly.

"In competition with the Spanish, or in alliance with the Portuguese," Day said. "Depending on how far west he has sailed. We need to know. He has been gone longer than we had expected."

"He will be back," Mattea said. "Did he not tell you that the way to Asia would be longer than you think? Men of money have so little faith."

"And so now you are sending the Portuguese after him?" Sebastian said, beginning to understand his mother's anger. "What if he succeeds in finding the passage to Asia? What then? Does this Corte-Real swoop in and take the credit, while you and Mr. Abercrombie and the rest get rich from my father's work? Is that what's going on?"

Day looked briefly at his shoes, then up at Sebastian's face. "The Corte-Reals are commissioned by King Manuel," he said, "to explore the northern reaches of the Western Ocean and determine where the land lies. There are two brothers, Miguel and Gaspar. I suspect that Gaspar is in command of the other ship. When Mr. Abercrombie heard of this, he became concerned, because he is invested heavily in your father's voyage."

"So if he backs the Portuguese, too, he wins no matter who gets there first," Sebastian said.

"It's just business, Sebastian," Day said.

"I think you had better leave," Mattea said.

"Sebastian, Mattea, no one will be happier than I upon John Cabot's safe return," Day said. "Mr. Abercrombie will be happy, all his partners will be happy, King Henry will be happy. But ocean voyaging is dangerous business, and lately competitive as well. Men of business, as well as nations, have to look after their own interests."

"As do families," Mattea said coldly.

Day nodded in acknowledgment. "I respect that, ma'am," he said. "And I will speak with Mr. Abercrombie on your behalf. I wish you good day." He turned to Sebastian. "And when your father returns, I shall be among the first to congratulate him."

Mattea glowered at Day's well-dressed back as he walked down the street. Sebastian waited until he was out of sight before he spoke. "What was his business here?" he asked.

"Come, let's go in and eat," Mattea said to her son.

"Mother, what is it?"

But he could get nothing further out of her until she had sat him down at the table and set upon it two bowls of steaming stew, a loaf of bread, and a carafe of wine. Pouring herself a glass, she waited until her son had begun to eat, and then said, "Your father's pension will be paid until September. If nothing is heard from him by then, the payments will stop. That is what Mr. Day came here to tell me."

"The bastards," Sebastian said through a mouthful of bread.

"You heard what he said. It is only business."

"My father and brothers—only business! They are writing them off, like lost cattle!"

"You have to have faith, Sebastian," his mother said. "I have every confidence in your father. He is out there somewhere. And soon he will be back. I know it."

After dinner, Sebastian washed his face and hands and changed his clothes. "Where are you going?" his mother asked him.

"Where the sailors go," he said.

"Sebastian, be careful. Those places can be rough. You know I don't like you going there."

Sebastian heaved an exaggerated sigh. "Mother, I'm sixteen years old," he said. "I can take care of myself. Besides, men like John Day tell you only what they want you to know. To find out what's really going on, you have to talk to the men who've been out there, sailing from port to port, some of them because it's the only way to stay out of jail. Yes, they're a rough lot, but maybe one of them has news of Father and Ludovico and Sancio."

He saw his mother's face soften, and for a moment he thought she would cry. Then he realized what he had said. In the past year, the names of his brothers had gradually died from his and his mother's lips. Was it because they were fading, as individuals, from memory? Or was it the fear that speaking their names would bring them ill luck? Whatever the reason, as the months had piled up, Sancio and Ludovico had became "my brothers" or simply part of "Father's fleet." It had been a year now, and despite her outward show of confidence, the strain of waiting, Sebastian knew, had to be wearing his mother down. She lowered her eyes and busied herself with something on the table.

He went over to her and embraced her. "Don't worry, Mother, I won't stay out late," he said. "I can handle myself around those men. I see them every day on the river."

Mattea squeezed his elbows and smiled up at him. He

was several inches taller than she, not nearly so imposing a figure as Ludovico, but at least as tall as his father. "Yes, but on the river they are not usually drunk," she said.

Sebastian laughed with her. "I will be careful," he said. "I promise." He kissed her lightly on the top of her head.

The Bristol waterfront, peopled during the day by sailors and workingmen, boasted several establishments that slaked their thirsts at night. Sebastian's father had been regaled in all of them last summer during a memorable, debauched week of drunken parties following his return from the New Found Land and his trip to see the king. Mattea had not let Sebastian and Sancio stay out past nightfall, but Sebastian saw his father carried from tavern to tavern through the street one afternoon by a dozen drunken sailors, and he heard his father and Ludovico reel in on more than one night in the hours before dawn, singing songs of the sea.

His father had bought him his first mug of ale during that same week. Sebastian had sipped at it, unsure if he liked the taste, while men around him quaffed one mug after another in great, hearty gulps. He'd had two mugs and felt slightly sick afterward.

Tonight, he was looking for any Portuguese sailors who might tell him, with tongues loosened by alcohol, what the two caravels at King's Road were up to. Bristol, like all port cities, had a fair number of ethnic enclaves, and each group had its favorite watering spot. One tavern was run by Genoese. (It had been the site of the largest celebration of all for the Genoa-born John Cabot.) Sebastian decided that the best place to go was the Porto Santo, which was owned by two Portuguese brothers who had come to Bristol from Madeira.

Sebastian ordered a mug of ale and nursed it carefully as he looked around. A few groups were seated at tables, some other men were standing; there were about two dozen of them in all. Sebastian spotted Alonzo, one of his rowers, and approached him.

The big man raised his mug in greeting and smiled drunkenly. "Sebastian!" he cried. "Don't see you much around this neighborhood after working hours. Decide to cut loose for once?"

Sebastian patted Alonzo on the shoulder. "Did anybody but the captain come off of those two ships today, do you know?"

Alonzo shook his head. "Mebbe some of 'em came ashore in a later boat, but I haven't seen any of 'em around here."

"Thanks, Alonzo." Sebastian was already moving off, listening to the multilingual talk from around the tables.

He heard some men speaking Portuguese, said hello to them, but quickly determined that they were locals, relatives of the owner, who had undoubtedly not even heard of the arrival of the two caravels from their native country.

Instead, he fell in with a group of Spaniards arguing vociferously around a table over maritime politics in general and the Spanish-Portuguese competition in particular. Sebastian's Spanish was still good from the years in Valencia. The subject of the argument was Christopher Columbus. Sebastian did not tell the men at the table who he was, but when he mentioned that he had met Columbus in Valencia, they accepted him immediately.

They were sailors off a ship that had been in Bristol for a week, taking on a load of wool. One of the four men at the table—the one doing the most talking—had sailed on one of the ships on Columbus's second voyage. He had spent nearly three years in the new colony on the island of Hispaniola, while Columbus tried unsuccessfully to locate the passage to Asia. "You couldn't get me to go back there at any price," he declared. "Nothing but heat, and sickness, and naked savages."

Sebastian listened in fascination as the man described conditions in the new Spanish settlement. More than a thousand Europeans were over there now, including women and children, and nearly all of them wanted to return home. Columbus himself had taken ill at one point and had to be carried ashore, delirious with fever, and nursed back to health. Many men had died, but the deaths among the colonists were trivial compared with the toll to the natives. A system of tribute had been set up, the man said, under which each Indian had to supply a hawk's bill full of gold every two months. If they did not comply, they were punished brutally, their hands cut off or similar tortures inflicted. When, in revenge, the natives captured and killed several of the Spaniards, massacres were carried out in reprisal.

Sebastian was appalled. Was Columbus in charge of all this?

The man replied that Columbus was the governor-general of these new lands, by royal decree, and as such must be held responsible for whatever happened there. "But there isn't enough gold on that whole island to satisfy the tribute he has imposed, or even half of it," he said. "Columbus doesn't want to hear it. All he cares about is making Isabella happy, either by finding Asia or filling her coffers with gold. She took a chance on him, he says, and he'll die before he admits his enterprise is a failure."

Sebastian wanted to hear more. The man told him

about an overland expedition into the sweltering interior of the island, in search of a gold mine that existed only in Columbus's imagination. The campaign had been led by an ambitious, ruthless young man named Alonso de Hojeda, who had so terrorized the Indians that many of them killed themselves rather than face his inventive tortures. Many of the natives who managed to avoid being mur-dered died nonetheless of disease, for they had never before encountered the illnesses carried across the ocean by the Spanish pigs, sheep, and horses, and the rats that stowed away aboard every ship.

"Now there is a man to watch out for, that Hojeda," said another man at the table. "He was born angry."

The first man nodded. "And he will take what he wants, by any means he can," he said. "A pirate, that one. If he gets to Asia first, there will be a bloodbath at the court of the Great Khan."

"Who is he?" Sebastian asked.

"A truly frightening man, with a man's appetites and a boy's temper," the second man said. "The king and queen have sent him back over there, because it is too dangerous to keep him around the royal court."

"Their patience with the admiral is growing thin," the first man added.

"How so?" Sebastian asked.

The man rolled his eyes and took a huge swallow from his mug. He wiped his mouth with the back of his sleeve. "Look," he said, "Columbus got everybody excited when he came back to Spain claiming he had found the short way to Asia. But it's been six years now. Columbus keeps insisting that he'll find the Great Khan around the next point, or in the next bay, or beyond the next island. But he can't find any hard proof that he has, in fact, reached Asia, and it's driving him crazy. All he's found is a group of large islands, filled with savages who have an unfortunate tendency to die before they can be of any use, and not enough gold to cover the costs of outfitting the ships in the first place. There are those who have the ear of the king and queen who think these new Indies are nowhere near Asia."

Sebastian made an effort to keep his face impassive. "They have sent this Hojeda out to find Asia, then?"

The man laughed. "I don't think Hojeda cares about anything beyond his own nose. He is in it for the greater glory of Alonso de Hojeda, and he cares not a whit for the lives of anyone else—Columbus, you, me—or for a whole new continent full of heathens. Columbus wants to baptize them and make them subjects of the Crown. Hojeda wants to kill them and take their gold—what there is of it—and their land."

"Why do the king and queen employ him, then?" Sebastian asked.

"Because, at heart, Ferdinand and Isabella are as ruthless as he is. Columbus may have his grand vision of opening up the world for sea travel, but for Ferdinand and Isabella it has always been about power and money. Hojeda has been dispatched with his own fleet, and copies of Columbus's charts, to secure Spanish interests in all of the lands on the other side of the ocean, and may God help anyone who gets in his way."

Sebastian walked home through the damp, late-night fog that had settled over the city, his head spinning with all he had learned that day. He was amused that the pious and self-righteous Columbus seemed to be falling from favor. He was concerned that the Portuguese were making overtures to the merchants of Bristol. He was curious about the extent of the new discoveries—how much land was over there, anyway, and what sort of land was it?

But most of all, he was worried. And if *he* was worried, what must his mother be feeling, behind the calm, fearless face she showed him and the world? It had been a year. Where was his father?

CHAPTER 13

"**I**'VE GOT ONE WORD FOR YOU, GIOVANNI," said Lorenzo Pasqualigo. "Bristol."

"Bristol? You think I should move the family to England?"

"Why not?" The big Venetian sipped his wine and walked to the edge of Caboto's small stone patio. He looked out at the short waves breaking against the sand beach. "There isn't going to be a port. Your office is closed. What is there left for you in Valencia?"

"The king could change his mind again."

Lorenzo shook his head. "He isn't going to change his mind. He can't afford to send Columbus west with seventeen ships and still build your port. He can't do both." Lorenzo looked across the patio at his friend. "And as nice as this place is, Giovanni, you cannot afford to live here without a salary."

"I have some money still," Caboto said.

"Yes, but I know you, Giovanni. You are not a man of leisure. You are too young to retire to a beach house on the Mediterranean. You still thirst for adventure. And Bristol represents your best chance to prove Columbus wrong."

Caboto joined Pasqualigo by the low stone wall at the patio's edge. "I have been to Bristol," he said. "It is not nearly so pretty as this."

"But full of opportunity for a man like yourself. You would have no shortage of sailors or ships."

"Do you think King Henry would back me? He turned down Columbus twice."

"Henry will not want to sit on his hands while Spain and Portugal divide up the world between them," Lorenzo said.

"But he is a notorious miser," Caboto said.

"Perhaps. But there is money in England. And the Bristolians are an independent lot. They already venture far out into the Western Ocean, far beyond the Pope's imaginary line. They have known for years that there is land out there."

"I know—their fabled 'Isle of Brasil,'" Caboto said, a wry grin forming on his lips. "I have heard the stories."

"They are more than stories," Lorenzo said. "They have been there. And men from Europe have been across the

Western Ocean before, centuries ago, if the tales are true. You know this as well?"

Caboto nodded. "One can hear a lot if one listens," he said. "The Bristolians are great adventurers, daring seafarers. But they aren't explorers. They care about furs and fish, not a western route to Asia."

"That will change, now," Lorenzo predicted.

"Those stories you mentioned—you were referring to the old Norse sagas, were you not? What do you know of them?"

"Not much. In Venice, most people who have heard of them at all dismiss them as fairy tales."

"But the Bristolians believe them," Caboto said. "There is a land to the west of Iceland, called Greenland, though it is said to be a dismal place, where winters last nine months, and no trees grow. It was settled by outlaws from Iceland, centuries ago. Their descendants live there still."

"I have seen Greenland on some Bristol maps," Lorenzo said. "But no ship from Europe has called there in many years."

"Why would they? It is an appallingly poor place, by all accounts, with nothing of value to trade. Yet they have boats, and the ceilings of their houses are supported by beams—in a land with no wood."

"What are you saying, my old friend?"

"The wood had to come from somewhere. It did not come from Iceland, which itself is poor in wood, nor could it all have come from Norway, for the Norse no longer sail those seas. It had to come from some other land, to the west of Greenland. It is well-known that it is there. The Norse sailors visited it often, if the tales are true. And they encountered people there—not Europeans, certainly, and not Asians, but savages, much like the men Columbus brought back, though clad in skins and furs against a cold climate. They called them 'skraelings,' or 'wretched ones.'"

"Do you think there is some connection between this land west of Greenland and the land Columbus found?"

Caboto shook his head. "How could primitive people make such voyages? No, the only connection between the two lands is that neither of them is in Asia. Asia has a civilization equal to ours; it is not populated by savages with tools of stone and bone. If a western route to Asia is to be found, one must sail still farther west, find the tip of the Asian mainland, and follow it to the south."

Lorenzo clapped his hands. "Then you must go to London," he said, "and make a formal petition to King Henry. You must tell him that the back door to Asia lies in the ocean west of Bristol. And you must convince him that you alone know how to get there."

"Bristol," Caboto said, looking at the waves, mulling it over.

"I have connections there," Pasqualigo told him. "I could set you and Mattea and the boys up in a house, and introduce you to the people you need to meet. They will be much impressed with you, given the places you have been and the things you've seen. Not many Brits have been to Arabia! While everyone in Spain was falling all over Columbus and his displays, you could tell in a minute he hadn't been to Asia, because you have actually seen Asians, and Asian artifacts and medicines and such. I tell you, England is ready. Why should an island nation not rule the seas in an age of sailing ships?"

Caboto laughed gently. "Ah, Lorenzo, you have always been good at making speeches. Perhaps that is why so many men like you so much."

Pasqualigo joined his friend in laughter. "But what I say is true," he said.

The two of them looked silently out into the sea for several minutes. The Mediterranean Sea, Caboto thought, around which the civilization of his people had revolved for centuries. Phoenicia, Athens, Carthage, Rome, Alexandria, Constantinople, Venice—all the great ages of history had happened around this nearly landlocked sea. Of course, there were other civilizations around other shores, but a son of Genoa like himself could not help but regard the Mediterranean as the center of the world. The Mediterranean had been his home, and the home of countless generations of his ancestors. But its every port was known, its every island, shoal, and headland had been charted by men long since dead. There was no mystery in the Mediterranean. The challenge for his generation of seafarers and the generations to come lay in the immense, unbounded Western Ocean.

He would go to England, then, a place with one foot in Europe and the other dangling over the continent's bow into the waters of the unknown. Lorenzo was right—he was not a man to sit and contemplate the world. And Columbus, wrong though he might be about the way to Asia, had at least gone out over the horizon in pursuit of his idea. Could he, Giovanni Caboto, do any less?

"I shall not be unhappy to leave this place," he said to his friend. "Three years, and not a stone piling in place. Nothing but empty promises."

"You are not the first foreigner whom Spain has treated badly," Lorenzo said.

"Perhaps it will be better in Bristol," Caboto said.

Pasqualigo clapped him on the back. "At least they

have shipyards, already built," he said. "And docks, and warehouses—and wealthy merchants eager to acquire more wealth by building up their fleets. Trust me, Giovanni, it will be better."

The Cabotos packed up what belongings they wished to keep, sold or gave away the rest, and in October of 1494 embarked for Barcelona, where Giovanni had gone many times to consult with King Ferdinand or his advisers on the planning of the port. This time, there was no royal reception to welcome him. There was no one to welcome the family at all, save the captain of the trading ship they boarded, and Lorenzo Pasqualigo, recently returned from Venice, who would make the trip to Bristol with them and help them get settled. Sancio, Sebastian, and Ludovico stood at the rail as the Spanish coast faded into the haze and the ship drove south toward Gibraltar. They did not speak much among themselves, each of the brothers lost in his own thoughts about this latest uprooting of the family. They were the sons of a man who wandered the Earth for a living, and they were destined to wander as well.

Pasqualigo was as good as his word. A house, modest but comfortable, awaited the family in Bristol. He introduced Giovanni to the rich merchants of Redcliffe Street, who had made their fortunes in fishing fleets and lumber. They were keenly interested in this worldly Venetian who claimed he could find a better, faster route to Asia than the one Columbus was seeking. Like port cities all over Europe, Bristol had a small community of Genoese, and Pasqualigo made sure that Giovanni was accepted in that circle as well. He was introduced to shipbuilders and barge operators and river pilots and the managers of the docks.

Sancio, Sebastian, and Ludovico adapted quickly to their new home, for Bristol was an exciting place. Not as cosmopolitan as Venice, with its coffeehouses and book-shops and bazaars and tiled walkways and well-dressed women, Bristol nevertheless bustled with activity. Ships and barges came and went constantly, and the boys never tired of watching the traffic on the river. It was a rougher place than either the cultural crossroads of Venice or the sleepy, sun-splashed, beach community of Valencia. Trade here was in rougher goods—logs, wools, coal, and fish— befitting the Bristolians themselves, who were a rougher, less educated lot than either the Venetians or the Valencians. All three sons quickly picked up the language, which, like the people who spoke it, was coarser and less poetic than the languages spoken on the Italian and Iberian peninsulas. The consonants were harder, the vowels bitten off, words and sentences and even names chopped to their essentials. Bristolians routinely dropped the "o" at the end of the family name. "Ludovico" was too much of a mouthful for these hurried Englishmen; the oldest brother became "Lewis." And Giovanni Caboto, son of Genoa, longtime citizen of Venice, became known around the docks of Bristol by the name with which history would remember him: John Cabot.

From the day the family arrived, Cabot began preparing his case for launching an expedition to the west. The Redcliffe Street merchants were the key. He knew that he would need the king's backing, of course, but he also knew that Henry did not command the resources that Ferdinand and Isabella did. Like most misers, Henry had a jealous attitude toward other people's wealth. Cabot and the Redcliffe Street merchants used this to their mutual advantage. Columbus had reached the Indies, and returned with fantastic promises of a soon-to-be-realized fortune from Asian silks and spices and gold. King Henry now found himself in the position of a gambler who has bet too conservatively and missed the big score. The time was ripe. The merchants would win, for if they helped finance Cabot's quest for Asia they could expect to share in the profits of his success. Henry would win, because he would best the ambitious Spanish monarchs and tip the balance of power in Europe toward England. And John Cabot would win, because he would at last get the chance to test his theories in the Western Ocean with a ship and crew at his command, and to make his own name and fortune in the process.

For months, Cabot gathered all the information he could from the fishermen and sea captains who came into Bristol. He consulted old maps and books, and talked with astronomers, mapmakers, and monks who had kept alive the old stories of the seafaring saints of centuries ago. He assembled geographic knowledge and speculation from every source, and he constructed a globe, on which he illustrated the known surface of the Earth, paying partic- ular attention to the northern reaches of the Western Ocean and the chains of islands that brought one to the leading tip of Asia. In the early months of 1495, he sent a request to London for an audience with the king. Henry, who had heard of him already, quickly accepted. On the last day of March, Cabot, accompanied by Lorenzo Pasqualigo and several representatives of the Redcliffe Street consortium, including the scribe John Day, set off overland to London.

Cabot returned with signed letters patent from the

king—a contract giving him authorization to explore the Western Ocean under the flag of England. The shipyard owned by Richard Abercrombie was contracted to build one vessel—a caravel based on the Portuguese design—for Cabot's voyage. The consortium agreed to put up half the money; in return, Henry promised not to raise shipping taxes on the port of Bristol for the next three years. It was a deal designed to work out for everybody—the parsimonious king, the avaricious merchants, and the ambitious sea captain, who swept into his house upon his return, embraced his wife, and presented her with a dress he had bought for her in London with the advance on his pension.

"Giovanni, it's beautiful," she exclaimed, holding up the dark blue silk and running it through her hands.

"We are going to do it, Mattea," he said excitedly. "When I return from Asia, I will bring you a hundred such dresses. And you will wear them in our own house at the top of the bluff, where we can look down at our own fleet of ships! We're going to be rich!" He grabbed her by the shoulders and twirled her around, the silk dress in her hands catching the air and billowing out around them.

Later, he told his wife and sons all about the trip to London and the meeting with the king. Henry had been impressed with his presentation, becoming especially keen when Cabot told him of his travels in Arabia and his con-tact with traders from Asia, and the Arabs' knowledge of the true size of the Earth. Columbus could not have reached Asia, Cabot argued, because he had brought back no Asians, he had seen no evidence of the Asian goods that were sold in Arab markets, and he had not sailed far enough. Henry had examined the globe Cabot had fash-ioned, held it in his royal hands, turning it to follow the route Cabot intended to take across the ocean. On a globe it was easy to see that the northern route was shorter.

"The contract allows me to explore the Western Ocean to the north, east, and west," Cabot told his family that night at dinner. "That means everywhere the Norse went, I can go. Look here." He grabbed the globe, tucked it under his right arm, and began pointing to things on it with his left index finger. "You can go from here, up the Irish Sea, past Scotland, the Hebrides, the Faeroes, and there's Iceland, only a few days out of sight of land. These Bristolians make that trip all the time. Where do you think all these fish come from? Then here's Greenland, and we know there's land west of Greenland. I could sail that way, but there is no need to go that far north, because we know that Asia extends into temperate latitudes. The land west of Greenland runs to the south. Beyond it must be the shore of Asia."

"North, east, and west," said Ludovico, chewing a bite of lamb. "Why not south?"

"The king does not want to intrude in the squabbles of the Spanish and Portuguese," his father said. "He knows he would lose in any armed confrontation with either one of them. They have more ships, and better ships, because Henry has not seen fit to adequately finance a navy."

"Now you are speaking like your newfound friends on Redcliffe Street," Mattea said.

Cabot laughed. "The king doesn't want a diplomatic incident a thousand leagues out in the Western Ocean. So I am not to sail south from here. So what? That is not where Asia is. Let Columbus delude himself and everybody else that he has found the kingdoms of Cathay. It's a convenient distraction. When I return with real Asian goods, and proof of contact with the real civilization of the Orient, Columbus will be exposed for the fool he is."

"Why only one ship?" Sebastian wanted to know. "Columbus had three."

"And he wrecked one of them," Ludovico added.

"It's what the king and the consortium decided they could afford," their father said. "But she will be a good ship, brand new, built right here in Bristol. And I will oversee every minute of her construction."

The ship was built over the winter of 1495–1496. Stout oak logs were brought in by barge from the forest of Nye, across the Bristol Channel, and milled and shaped at the Bristol lumberyards. Construction was supervised by a little Portuguese man named Antonio Alvernaz, who had designed caravels for King John's fleets but had quarreled over money with Manuel, the new king, and taken up exile in Bristol. John Cabot, true to his word, visited the shipyard every day, often accompanied by one or another of the merchants who were backing him, or their representatives.

Cabot's first impulse was to name the ship *Mattea,* but his wife demurred, with the warning that naming a sailing ship after a living person could bring bad luck to both. They decided to call the ship *Matthew,* after Anthony Matthew, one of Egidius Caboto's friends in Venice who had helped the family move to Valencia shortly before his death. Besides, Cabot told himself with some satisfaction, *Matthew* was close enough to *Mattea* to reflect some honor upon his wife.

Construction went smoothly, if slowly. Bristol's tremendous tides provided a ready-made system for building and launching ships. Over the years, many "dry docks" had been created by digging out sections of earth abutting the harbor. At low tide, large wooden doors were put in place and sealed with clay. The excavated area, large enough to house an entire ship, was allowed to dry out for several days. Then the shipwrights took over. A single, massive piece of oak, shaped by skilled hands with adzes, was laid end to end in the bottom of the dry dock. From this backbone, the skeleton of the boat gradually arose. Most fascinating to Sancio and Sebastian was the steaming of the planks for the hull in the large oven above, so that they would bend over the frame and give the ship its curved shape. The tides ebbed and flowed and were held back by the sealed gate as the work went on. The genius of the system was that the *Matthew* would not need to be moved on launch day—the workers would simply tear down the gate at low water and let the ship float free on the tide.

Sancio and Sebastian observed the division of labor as various stages of the project were completed. There were crews who worked with adzes and axes and saws to shape each rough board before it was passed on to the discerning eyes of the shipwrights. Another group hammered strips of iron into nails, which were likewise inspected before being approved for use. Other men crawled along the outside and the inside of the hull fitting boards together and crimping the nails on both ends so that they would hold. Still others made measurements for the deck timbers and the dividing walls below, as well as the deckhouse and the holding pens for the animals that would start but not finish the voyage. Sebastian thought of the fleets he had seen, in Venice and on the Mediterranean, and for the first time in his life he felt awe at something larger than himself. If such effort, by such a conglomeration of people, was required to construct a single ship, it must take a great and committed civilization to build an entire fleet of them.

When the hull was completed, and the bottom of the boat covered with a first layer of pitch, the masts went up and the painstaking process of setting the rigging began. The *Matthew,* like most contemporary caravels, had three masts. The mainmast sat amidships and was stepped down through the deck onto the top of the keel. The forward mast, half the height of the mainmast, was placed so that it could carry a variable number of sails out front on the long, upward-jutting bowsprit. The third and shortest mast, set aft atop the high deckhouse so that it rose to the same height as the forward mast, would carry a lateen sail, adopted from Arab boats, which would allow the *Matthew* to sail closer to the wind than a traditional square-rigged vessel.

The *Matthew* was ready to sail in the spring of 1496. On launch day, the river water seeped over the brown flats and into the stall where the ship sat, and slowly rose about the hull, as the hull itself had risen over the months atop that first beam of oak laid for the keel. Sebastian watched as the finished ship, despite the great weight of rock laid in the bottom of the hull for ballast, came free from the mud and the wood frame around it and began to move in the way things move in fluid. As the tide filled in the dry dock where the ship had been built, men in rowboats attached lines to the *Matthew* and eased her out into the harbor.

John Cabot selected a crew of eighteen men. All but three were Bristolians, and all had been to sea before, some as far as Iceland. A few of them had been in trouble with the law, but that was hardly uncommon among sailors. They were experienced seamen who had crewed on fishing boats far out in the Western Ocean and survived storms to tell of them in Bristol's taverns. Cabot told them the *Matthew* would seek a northern route to the leading edge of Asia, and that he expected to find it at the latitude of Dursey Head in Ireland.

It was a triumphant day when the *Matthew* left Bristol, bound for the open sea. King Henry sent a delegation of a half-dozen members of his court to add an official presence to the departure. Sebastian hugged his father, wished him good luck, then stood with his mother and brothers by the side of the dock as the ship slid out into the channel.

Two months later, the *Matthew* returned, having found nothing. The crew, weary of beating into westerly winds, had threatened mutiny unless Cabot turned back. Cabot was discouraged but still determined. He argued with Abercrombie and his other backers for another chance, the following summer. "The way to Asia is there," he insisted one night when Abercrombie came to call. "All we need to do is find a way around the westerlies."

"Like Columbus did," Abercrombie finished for him.

Cabot pounded a fist on the table, rattling the plates and silverware. "It would take a year to get to Asia the way Columbus is going," he said. "He will be found out soon enough, I guarantee it. In any case, the Spanish would not take kindly to our sailing a southern route."

The three boys had been following the conversation with their eyes. But only Sancio had the temerity to speak up. "But what if you go north, Father?"

John Cabot smiled at his youngest son. "That is exactly what I plan to do," he said. "We will sail next June, close to the solstice, when there is near-constant daylight in the northern seas. If we sail first north and then south of true west, we will actually trace a shorter route than if we follow the parallel. Euclid proved this."

"It is risky, though," Abercrombie said. "Even in summer, you may run into ice and storms. The men may not stand for it."

"Well, I have an idea about that," Cabot said.

The idea, though he did not tell them of it that night, was that Ludovico, now eighteen and a good six inches taller than his father, would sail on the *Matthew* when the ship made its next attempt to cross the Western Ocean. Through his imposing presence and his unquestioned loyalty to his father, the young man would help maintain order aboard the ship.

Some refits were done over the winter, some repairs to sails and rigging, and more ballast was added. By early May of 1497, John Cabot and the *Matthew* were ready to try again.

With Ludovico at his side, and a crew of mostly new sailors (though there were a few holdovers from the first attempt), Cabot left Bristol on May 25, 1497. Nothing more was heard from him until August 6, when the *Matthew* appeared off King's Road, its crew shouting to anyone within earshot that they had found land—a considerable extent of land—on the other side of the ocean. Word spread upriver to Bristol even before the flood tide; by the time the ship made it into the harbor, a huge crowd had lined the docks to welcome the returning heroes who had sailed west to the coast of Asia. Sebastian was reminded of Columbus's triumphant march through Spain. John Cabot, already an important man on the Bristol waterfront, had become a celebrity.

And a national celebrity, at that. Word came from London that Henry VII wished to speak with the explorer in person. Less than a week after the *Matthew*'s return, Cabot made the overland trip from Bristol to London, accompanied by John Day, Lorenzo Pasqualigo, and three of Bristol's port commissioners. There, they hammered out a deal to equip Cabot with a fleet of five ships, to sail the following summer. Cabot's pension would be paid by the Crown, but the ships themselves would be supplied and financed by the port of Bristol, whose money came mostly from Redcliffe Street. The king agreed to put up the money for the construction of a new flagship. The *Matthew* and three other trading ships, all Bristol-built and Bristol-financed, would complete the fleet.

The city's printing presses lost no time in circulating the news. The Redcliffe Street merchants, who had conservatively backed the venture with enough money for a single ship, opened their homes to the Cabots and their bank accounts to the next voyage. Sebastian and Sancio found themselves invited to dinners at the huge houses they had previously admired only from down by the water. Their mother loved rubbing shoulders with the rich, and their father took delight in buying her expensive clothes that she could wear to such occasions. Ludovico usually sat with the men, nodding assent to his father's stories and occasionally, very occasionally, adding a word or two. Sancio always wanted to explore the mansions, to peer into every room, and he was frequently successful in enlisting Sebastian to accompany him. The boys had gotten in trouble more than once for slipping away during the after-dinner drinks and prowling around.

John Cabot apparently never expressed any doubt, to either the king or his Bristol backers, that the land he had found could be anything other than the edge of Asia. Even at home, alone with his family, he would not come out and admit what Sebastian knew he must suspect. "We must sail farther west" was the most he would say. But as the details of the voyage emerged over time at the dinner table and in conversations with Ludovico, Sebastian began to suspect his father of concealing the truth.

He and Sancio whispered about it at night when everyone else was asleep, and during the day they talked about it on a secluded bluff they sometimes walked to that overlooked the whole city. "He will be just like Columbus," Sebastian said on an autumn day that was so clear he had allowed Sancio to talk him into ditching lessons. They could see all the way to the channel, where two ships were working their way toward the mouth of the river. "He's going to be famous for something he didn't do."

"Maybe," Sancio said, tossing a pebble into the air and watching it disappear down the hillside in front of them. "And maybe he'll really find the way to Asia."

"He's walking around Bristol like a hero," Sebastian observed. "Everybody wants to congratulate him. We get invited to all those fancy dinners, and they all toast his success, and he loves it, every minute of it. But I wonder what he thinks, deep down. I wonder if he's lying to everybody about finding Asia, or if he really thinks he did it."

"What difference does it make?" Sancio said. "They're giving him a fleet."

"It makes a lot of difference," Sebastian insisted. "Do

you think it's right to lie to people, to lie to the *king*, even, just to get money?"

Sancio pondered this for a minute. "There's a difference," he said finally, "between lying and stretching the truth."

"Come on, Sancio! He brought back no more evidence that he reached Asia than Columbus did. Less—he didn't even bring back any people."

"He saw people," Sancio said.

"From a distance! And evidence of animal droppings. What's that mean, that there was a farm nearby? Ludovico said that the coast was rocky and the land was covered with trees and fields, but no cities. No towns, even. It sounds like a barren place."

"There are places in Europe that look forbidding from the sea."

"Yes, but do you remember how skeptical Father was about Columbus? How he questioned everything? He kept insisting that Columbus hadn't gone far enough, he'd just reached some island in the middle of the ocean and all that. Remember?"

Sancio nodded. "He still thinks that," he said.

"So how can he possibly think he's reached Asia, after sailing only thirty-five days in light winds? And back in only fifteen days, after following a coast that led back toward England? All his talk about Euclid and the Greeks and how they figured out the size of the Earth—it doesn't make sense that he'd just ignore all that the minute he spotted land."

"Sometimes you have to lie, Sebastian," his younger brother said.

"Why?"

"Isn't it obvious? Last year those rich Redcliffe Street men gave him money for one ship. This year, same thing: one ship—the same ship, even though they have ships running up and down Europe. One ship, and he had to beg and plead for the money. Now he's found the way to Asia—maybe—and look at the money pour in. When he sails next spring, he will command a fleet of five ships."

"I would like to go on one of those ships," Sebastian said. "Like Ludovico. I would like to see the Western Ocean for myself. See what's really out there."

"We will both get our chance, Sebastian," Sancio said, "if Father is successful."

The dry dock that had been used for the construction of the *Matthew* was enlarged for the *Pandora*. All fall and winter, a crew of Bristol's best shipwrights and carpenters, brought in and paid handsomely by the Redcliffe Street consortium, worked on the flagship, which was nearly twenty feet longer than the *Matthew*. It carried extra ballast below for better balance in storms, and its wide decks could house a larger array of animals to supply milk, eggs, and meat on the outward voyage. The hull was completed by January, the deck and deckhouse by March, and in early April the masts and rigging were in place and the *Pandora* floated free. Sebastian watched in amazement as his father directed the provisioning of the fleet. Cask after cask of dried and salted meat, fish, bread, flour, and beer went aboard each ship. John Cabot told his backers that the quest for Cathay could take a year, and that the fleet must be provisioned for a voyage of that length. When they questioned him, he pulled out a newly fashioned globe on which he had painted a considerable eastward thrust to Asia. The Asian coast, he said, was likely to prove long and treacherous before it reached the temperate latitudes where the great cities were. Sebastian grew restless with excitement as the departure date grew closer. Four weeks, three . . .

And then came the announcement that Ludovico would sail as first mate on the *Matthew*, instead of on his father's ship. They had discussed it, the two of them, before John Cabot told the family at the dinner table, for Ludovico's expression did not change. Sebastian felt his heart rise in his chest—would his father take him as well? He knew his way around a boat, and he was growing bigger and stronger, though he would never be a physical match for his older brother. But he could sail and he was learning how to navigate. He knew his knots and constellations, and he was unafraid of the ocean. He was ready.

Then his father turned to Sancio, and told him that his ear for languages could be of use aboard the *Pandora*. Would he like to come? Sebastian couldn't believe it. Sancio seemed surprised himself, and that night John and Mattea Cabot discussed long and loudly the dangers of an ocean voyage, and Mattea's fear, which she had never before expressed, of losing her family to the sea. "They are still boys, Giovanni," she said, "though they try to act like men." Late at night they reached an agreement: Sancio could go, but Sebastian must stay.

To his father he was cordial, for John Cabot demanded and received the respect of his sons, and a whipping was the price one paid for acting otherwise. But Sebastian could not hide his disappointment. He refused to speak to Sancio during the two and a half weeks before the fleet's departure. He did not meet his brother's eyes at the dinner table and avoided him during the day. If the rift between the brothers caused their father concern, he did not show it. He had made a command decision. He expected his sons to abide by it.

On the day the fleet sailed, Sebastian watched from the bluff he had so often shared with Sancio. Tears blurred his vision as the ships moved out on the tide. "Go find Asia then," he whispered fiercely. It should be me, he thought, over and over. It should be me.

He had shaken his father's hand, reluctantly, because his mother was there and he didn't want to hurt her, but when Sancio had held out his arms to him and said, "Don't be angry, brother," it had been too much.

"I hope you drown," Sebastian had said, too softly for anyone else to hear. But Sancio had heard it, and in the moment before he turned away, Sebastian had caught the look on his face. Then he'd fled from the dock, through the steep streets of Bristol, up here, where he could be alone. Where he could watch his father and his brothers sail off to their destinies without him.

CHAPTER 14

Dear Sebastian,

No doubt you have given us up for dead by now. It has been a year since we left Bristol, and I would dare to say it has been the strangest year for a boy from Venice since Marco left for China more than two centuries ago.

You will notice a gap of several months in these letters. That is because I have been separated from them, and from Father and the Pandora, *which is no more, and only the quick thinking of my friend Will Hennessey has preserved them for me—and for you, though God only knows when you will read them.*

Where to begin? How best can I tell you of the blood, the anger, the looting and burning of our ship, and my subsequent capture and the months I spent living among the natives of this new world? For that is what it is, Sebastian. There is nothing of Europe or Asia here. Father was right: Columbus was deluding himself, and the kingdoms of Europe

*have all been chasing after the same delusion. In searching
for a back way to Asia, we have stumbled upon an unknown
continent, and an undiscovered civilization. When we get
back to England, the truth will be known. Should we not
return, the fact of this great landmass blocking the way to
Asia must be discovered eventually. And then I fear for these
simple people, with their tools of shells and stone, no metals,
and no ships. They defended themselves against a handful of
drunken English convicts, but they will be no match for the
navies of England, Spain, Portugal, and France. Once the
royal courts get word of a virgin continent lightly populated
by primitive heathens, they will send cannons and guns and
soldiers and priests to secure it and make it their own.
Why do kings and queens want to possess everything they
see? And what of the people who already live here?
Certainly they can be savage, as we have seen, but what
people would not protect their own? It was not they who
started the trouble. It was our own men.*

*Most of the troublemakers are dead. I saw Adam Keane
take an arrow to the throat and fall from the deck of the
burning ship, spouting blood into the water. James
Worthington was clubbed to death by two native men as
he tried to flee into the forest. But others are dead too.
My good friend Peter Firstbrook was trapped forward
belowdecks in the fire. And Father Cartwright, who had*

hastened to his bunk when the fire broke out to retrieve his cross and Bible, stepped out onto the deck into the path of an arrow, which buried itself in his stomach. There was nothing anyone could do for him. He died as the ship burned around him, clutching his Bible and waiting to meet God.

Altogether, twelve of us survive. In addition to Father, William, and myself, there are Eliot Morison, Stephen Conant, Gardiner Morse, and six others, including David Garrett and the Irishman Patrick Daugherty, whom Father treats coldly because they were among the instigators of the trouble with the natives.

Until two days ago, I did not anticipate seeing any of them again. Indeed, I had begun to contemplate the possibility of living for years, and maybe the remainder of my life, among the natives here, cut off from family and home by an ocean, until such time as another ship from Europe might find me. I did not want to think about that. But I had seen the Pandora burn and men die, and from that awful day I had no news of Father or my shipmates for the next six months. You can forgive me, I hope, for thinking them all dead.

I will try to slow down and relate to you all that has happened, though I never thought to take up these letters again. The story will likely consume several. The natives do not have paper or pens; indeed, they do not write at all. I *attempted once to fashion writing implements from a bird feather, some of their dye, and a strip of tree bark, but I had to write the words in huge letters and they smeared. Running Fawn, the native girl who befriended me, watched, her head tilted to one side and her dark eyes wide with curiosity. Between her attention and the poor quality of my handmade writing tools, I became unnerved and then frustrated, and I gave up the attempt. Her mother later burned my scribblings. It is awkward to take up pen and paper again, but in our present circumstances it is also strangely comforting, like a lost part of myself returning.*

I am writing this hunched over in the bow of the longboat as we work our way along the low coast of this seemingly endless land. Father has rigged a sail amidships, and today the wind is fair, allowing us to make progress to the south. With twelve men aboard it is a bit crowded. There is little food and less water. Father was able to grab an astrolabe, some charts, and even several books from the burning ship, but the hourglass is lost, as well as all of our trading goods. William, bless his soul, saved this journal and my writing supplies, and held on to them throughout the winter, although he had little reason to believe he would ever see me again.

Father's plan—which, though he can see its necessity, must pain him deeply—is to follow the coast south in search of Columbus and his fleet. A European ship is our only hope of rescue. Our food will not last long and we cannot rely entirely on hunting and the help of friendly natives. We have three crossbows on board, but no more gunpowder. The longboat handles the sea reasonably well, and we can row when there is no wind, but several times squalls and rough weather have forced us to shore. Father says that any man who causes trouble with the natives will be left in their hands, and he has Eliot Morison to back him up, but his authority went up in smoke with our ship. We are reduced to a group of men struggling to survive. Father is our leader, but only so long as his leadership enhances our chances for survival. In the face of real danger, it will be every man for himself.

Father senses this, Sebastian. The loss of his ship and more than half his crew sits on him hard. He feels guilty over bringing me on this trip and exposing me to danger. For six months he had to live with the possibility that I was dead, or lost to him forever. And there is Ludovico, and the rest of the fleet, their fates unknown to us. Be glad that you are safe in England, and be glad for the small ray of hope your safety brings to our father, whose life's ambition lies in ruins.

It is the loss of his mission, more than anything else— more than the certain deaths of twenty-two members of his crew and the likely loss of other ships in the fleet—that hurts him most, I think. He will not be the man to pioneer a *westward route from Europe to Asia. Worse, he must now go seek out Columbus, humiliate himself before his boyhood friend and rival, and tell him the news of the new continent he has discovered. Perhaps history will remember him for this accidental discovery. But that is little solace to our father in the present, Sebastian. There will be no triumphant return to Europe for us, no parades along the Bristol waterfront, no claims of new lands and new riches for the king of England. If we are to return, it must be as passengers on a Spanish ship, for our own ships have surely returned to England or are at the bottom of the ocean.*

What is happening back in the Old World, Sebastian? I wish I knew. It is a strange feeling to be cut off from civilization like this, to have no word for a year and more of everyone you know and everyone you love! Have they sent out another ship to find us? Has Columbus returned to Spain, with more of his so-called Asian goods and people? What news from the rest of our ships? What are you and Mother thinking, as the days pass, and we do not return? Just one word of communication from home—from anywhere in Europe, all of which counts as home out here— would mean more to me than you can know. I remain—

Your loving brother,
Sancio

Dear Sebastian,

All right—I will try to start from the beginning. Father's goal was always to save the ship. I believe that if he had succeeded in floating the ship free, he would have then set course for England, in order to get back before winter and report our discovery. We might even now be sitting down to dinner in Bristol and mapping out new expeditions, instead of desperately trying to survive along a strange coast in an open boat. But a faction of the men, led by Keane, blamed Father for our predicament, and began disregarding his orders.

I don't know what they were thinking, or if they were thinking of anything at all beyond their own bellies and other parts of their bodies—you know full well what I am talking about, Sebastian, without me having to mention it. They had already stirred up trouble by capturing several of the native women. Father needed to get his ship free, and he absolutely depended on the goodwill of the natives. But his ship was stuck and the natives, who had been friendly until provoked, turned hostile.

Their village was built among the trees, back in the woods behind one of the marshy estuaries that fed into the bay. They kept their long, sleek boats—similar to the native boats we had seen farther north, but larger—on a patch of

grass around a bend in the river, out of the sight of anyone
approaching from seaward. The village had a permanent
look, even though it blended in among its surroundings in a
way that towns in Europe never do. The buildings were
made mostly of logs, roughly hewn and laid end to end, the
gaps stuffed with dirt and pine needles. Some smaller
structures had been constructed from bent wood, evergreen
boughs, and animal skins. One large building stood in the
village's central clearing.

Six of us went to the village that day, and all six of us are
still alive, proof enough for me that the natives' leaders did
not wish us any harm. What I think is that there were a few
hotheads on both sides. That's how matters got out of hand.

Most of the natives avoided us when we entered their
village. Women took hold of children and led them inside.
Young boys and girls peered at us from a distance. The group
that met us consisted entirely of adult men. They wore less
clothing than their northern cousins; many of the men were
naked to the waist, their bodies smeared with some kind of
grease. They smelled of the woods.

Father brought gifts—blankets, sweaters, what jewelry
we hadn't already given away, as well as some silverware
and a few metal tools he thought we could spare. The
natives took keen interest in the hammers and axes,
repeatedly hefting them to feel their weight and running

their fingers over the metal. I noticed a few small pieces of what looked like copper in the elaborate necklace worn by their leader, a stout man of about Father's age with shoulder-length black hair and a flattened nose. But metal tools were unknown to them. As I was to observe, they do all of their gardening work with handheld tools made from the thick shells they find in the bay. They attach them with thongs to the ends of sticks and thus create crude shovels, rakes, and hoes. But I'm getting ahead of the story.

Father brought me along in the hope that I could translate the native language adequately enough for him to communicate. But it was difficult to pick up. We had, after all, traveled a distance equal to that between Bristol and the Strait of Gibraltar since we'd encountered this coast; one might expect languages spoken that far apart to be different, just as they are in Europe. It was a tense meeting. Several of the native men carried bows and quivers of arrows on their shoulders. Stephen Conant had insisted on bringing his crossbow, and Father had agreed that it was a necessary, though regrettable, precaution. He laid the weapon on the ground when the meeting began, and the natives responded by laying down their bows and arrows.

I tried to find similarities in expressions between these people and those who had helped us repair the Pandora *at our first landfall. But it was hard. Their leader (whom they* call Wise Rock in their language, I would come to learn) accepted the gifts, and nodded when I attempted to tell him that they were a gesture of apology for the violent acts of our men. Father then tried to tell him who we were, that we had come from a land across the ocean. I was listening hard to Wise Rock's reply, trying to understand at least the general meaning of his words, when an explosion rang out from the direction of the water. There was only one possible source for a sound like that on this shore—the Pandora's small cannon.

We hurried to the shore—our party of six and about a dozen native men. The longboat was hauled out onto the grass beside the native boats. From the ship, out of sight, we could hear shouting. Then another cannon shot, and more whooping.

"What in hell?" Father thundered. "Get that boat launched!"

We sprang to the gunwales of the longboat and heaved her into the water. Even before we deployed the oars, two of the native boats, each paddled by two natives, were gliding out across the water. As they rounded the curve into the bay, a shout went up from the Pandora, mired along the far shore. We came around the bend into view of our ship at the same moment the natives spotted the wreckage of one of their craft, and saw two of their own people, one grievously wounded, floundering in the water.

It didn't take Father more than a second to deduce what had happened. Adam Keane was behind the cannon on the foredeck, with several men around him. Pieces of the native craft floated where the cannon blast had blown it apart. The wounded man cried in pain as the water reddened around him and his companion held his head above water. The two native boats got to them quickly. They lifted the wounded man into one of the boats, and I could see his arm hanging loosely from a ragged red wound at the shoulder.

Father stood in the longboat and waved his arms above his head at the men on the Pandora. "Cease fire!" he cried, cupping his hands to his mouth. "Get away from that cannon!" Keane and his men stopped shouting, but they remained where they were.

I have never seen Father so angry. I wondered if he would actually kill Keane, order him hanged as an example to the others. I have heard of ship captains carrying out such drastic discipline. I knew he had the authority. But I was terrified. Out here in this undiscovered country, there was no law to enforce a captain's will. He was at the mercy of his men.

We were halfway to the ship when the two boats overtook us, one on each side. I tried not to look at the wounded man. The natives all had bows and arrows. Stephen Conant reached for the crossbow. "For God's sake, put that down," Father snapped. "Keep rowing, and pray that we make it."

The natives did not attack, and they dared not approach the ship too closely. They hung back at a distance of several yards—though still within cannon or musket range—and allowed us to rejoin our men. Father ordered everybody on deck and demanded to know what had happened.

"They attacked us, Captain," Keane said. "They came out across there"—he pointed to a stretch of open water, seaward from the estuary that led to the village—"and started shooting arrows at us. They were getting closer and closer. So I fired."

"Why were they attacking you?"

Keane heaved his broad shoulders. "Who knows why those heathen savages do what they do?" he said.

I could see several of the men exchanging silent looks with one another. Father didn't miss it either. Something more was going on.

Father soon got the truth out of some of the other men. Keane and six others had gone ashore, supposedly looking for game but more likely looking for trouble. In Bristol (or in any other port in Europe) there would have been sailors' taverns and any number of people willing to fight. Here there were only the natives. Armed with crossbows (Father had forbidden the use of the muskets except in an emergency), they had gone out hunting deer, primed to shoot at anything that moved. One of the men—and none of them would say who—had heard rustling in the trees and let an arrow fly, hitting one of several native men who had been watching the ship from the woods. Keane and his group had left the dying man where he had fallen and fled back to the ship. When they saw the native boat approaching, they assumed its intentions were hostile and fired on it with the cannon.

Retaliation was sure to follow. We had the better weapons, but there were many more of them than us, and we were strangers in a land they knew well. Our ship was immobilized, stuck fast to the muddy bottom of the bay. I think Father knew how bad our situation was. He had come to trade, not to kill. He had sailed seeking the kingdoms of Asia, and had found instead a new, barely civilized land whose people had been friendly until we had made enemies of them at the moment we most needed their help.

For the next few days we confined ourselves to the ship. During the daylight hours we made several attempts to work the ship free, removing ballast and sending men along the shore and into the water with ropes, but all our heaving went for naught—the ship wouldn't budge. At night, Father posted guards, and everyone slept uneasily in makeshift bunks below or on the slightly listing deck. Morale was low; everyone was on edge. The nights were growing chilly, and the woods were full of eyes.

The attack came a week after the incident with the

cannon. I was to discover later that the area around the bay is populated by many more natives than we thought. A pattern of uneasy alliances, held together by trade, tribute, and arranged marriages, unites a series of native villages all within a couple days' walk of one another. Sometimes hostilities break out between them, but usually they leave one another alone. The arrival of our ship, however, and the murderous impulses of some of our men had convinced them that we represented a greater threat to them than they did to one another, and a council of elders had gathered to decide what to do about us. The throng that attacked us and burned our ship was made up of young warriors from several villages.

All this I was to learn later, when I lived with them. It had been quiet for a week. The moon was at the end of its cycle and the night was pitch dark. I was sleeping out on the foredeck, wrapped in a blanket, unable to abide Peter's snoring. (How I wish I could hear him snore now, God rest his soul!) There was no warning. The first indication I had that something was wrong was the sound of a splash in the water below me. I woke with a start. Flaming arrows were already flying through the air, landing on the deck. Back by the stern I could see one of our men struggling with two natives. The splash I had heard was the body of another of our men, posted as a guard, as he fell from the ship, his chest pierced by an arrow.

In seconds the ship was swarming with native warriors. Some had torches, which they applied to any surface that would burn. I struggled to my feet in time to see the priest go down. I heard a musket shot, and I saw Eliot Morison club one of the natives with the end of a musket that he did not have time to load. The fire leapt into the rigging. All around me was chaos. Arrows flew through the air. I kept my head down and made my way aft, looking for Father. Finally I spotted him, clutching a cutlass, an astrolabe, and the ship's papers, among a group of our men struggling to lower the longboat over the side facing open water. "Sancio!" he called to me. And that was the last thing I heard before a club came crashing down on my skull.

I awoke inside a dwelling in the natives' village. I was covered in deer-hide blankets and my head was wrapped in some sort of cloth that covered a poultice with the consistency of rotting leaves. A native woman came and changed the bandaging shortly after I returned to consciousness. I was to find out that I had suffered a nasty gash near the top of my forehead. They had cut back the hair and cleaned the wound, but I still have a prominent scar up near my hairline, and will probably have it for as long as I live.

I faded in and out during the first few days I lay there, still suffering from the blow to the head. The native woman and her young daughter looked after me, forcing me to drink water and eat some white mush that tasted surprisingly good. I didn't know enough of their language yet to ask after the Pandora and her crew. I did not even know how many days had gone by. But I was grateful that they had not killed me or left me to die. I could only guess it was because they had recognized me as the person who had tried to talk to them in their own tongue after the first incident. Maybe they recognized me as the son of our leader. Or maybe they just did not believe in killing without good reason. The mother and daughter, whose names were Moon Water and Running Fawn, treated me with kindness, and gradually my head began clearing.

From time to time other natives, both women and men, came into the small dwelling, but at night only the three of us slept there, Moon Water and Running Fawn on one side of the room and me on the other. I tried to talk to them, and tried even harder to listen to their conversations, for I wanted to know what they were saying about me and what my situation was. You can imagine what was going on inside my muddled head, Sebastian. Here I was in a home halfway around the world, being cared for by savages, with no idea of what had happened to Father or the rest of the men. In those first few days I might have given in to despair had they not been so kind to me.

When I was well enough to get up and walk about, I ventured down to the water and looked for the ship. It was gone. Only a few charred timbers remained above the surface of the water to show that it had ever been there. And then, Sebastian, I did despair. I cried. I sat on the bank and sobbed. All seemed lost at that moment. For all I knew, Father and the rest of the crew were dead. There was no sign of any of them. My whole world had been ripped away from me. In my sorrow, I wished the natives had left me to die on the burning deck. I did not see how I could go on living. I thought about simply vanishing into the woods, letting the crows discover my body after I became too weak to go on. It seemed better than the crushing loneliness I felt.

It was Running Fawn who convinced me to come back to the village. Without a word, she laid a hand on my shoulder as I sat there sobbing. I looked up, and in her dark eyes I saw the glint of understanding. I swallowed, and stopped my childish crying. Still bereft of hope, I stood and allowed her to lead me away.

For the next seven months I lived as one of them. My filthy clothes were replaced by the skins they wear, and I began to learn their language. Running Fawn and her mother lived alone because her father, White Oak, was killed in the attack on our ship. Six of the attackers died. I was surprised that Running Fawn and Moon Water bore

me no ill will for their loss, but they did not. They took me
in as a member of their household and taught me their
ways. Moon Water showed me how to sharpen an arrow
and hollow out a gourd. I helped Running Fawn harvest
pine nuts and acorns, and in the evenings we talked. The
girl was just a year younger than I, with long dark hair
that was usually braided but sometimes worn loose.
She had high cheekbones and bottomless dark eyes. Our
conversations eased the pain of her loss of her father and
my loss of mine. For I was sure I would never see Father
again. Though the natives told me much, they never told me
that Father was not dead. They never told me that some of
the men had gotten away on the longboat. Perhaps they did
not expect them to come back for me.

Winter came. And as the months passed, I gradually
gave up all hope of rescue. I devoted myself instead to
learning the language and the ways of the natives. The bay
was the source of much of their food, from fish that they
caught in nets to shellfish they gathered at low water. I
helped with the harvest of squashes and other vegetables,
many of which were strange to me. They were also skilled
at trapping animals and tracking them in the snow. I
traveled with a delegation to a nearby village for a
wedding; afterward, the young husband from our village
remained with his wife's people, as was their custom.

And I participated in the after-meal ritual of inhaling the smoke of dried leaves, burned in a long-handled pipe and passed around. At first this gave me raging headaches, but soon I learned to take in only a small amount of the sweet-tasting smoke, and to exhale it slowly. Eventually I found the sensation it produced quite pleasant.

You are probably wondering what happened to Father and his men during all this time. I did not find out until they returned for me. Father and the men who managed to make it off the Pandora *secreted the longboat in the tall reeds and salvaged what they could from the burning ship. Why Father did not immediately come after me was not clear. He had to suspect that I was still alive. How that thought must have tormented him. But his first duty was to his men. They passed the winter on a low, sandy island several leagues south of the mouth of the bay. The island was uninhabited and easily guarded. They built a shelter, and made forays in the longboat to the mainland for wood and to hunt. Even so, Eric Grindle died before the winter was out. He is buried on the island beneath a cairn of stones.*

No word of Father and his men reached me, though some of the natives must have known that they were still nearby. News travels between villages, and Father and the men weren't so far away that other natives would not have seen them and reported their presence. Yet my hosts told me nothing. I do not know the reason for this, but perhaps they are every bit as curious about our ways as we are about theirs. We are the ones who have sent great ships to their shore. They have not appeared in Europe, nor do they have the capability of traversing an ocean. We are the threat to them, with our gunpowder and steel. Why have they not developed these things? They are an intelligent people. The metal tools Father gave them were quickly put to use in the fields and forest. Imagine—for all of their lives and the lives of their ancestors they have been felling trees with stone axes! Things we take for granted seem miraculous to them.

Yet they are far from simple. Though they do not write, they have many stories, which are passed from the village elders to the younger people around winter fires. They have religion, and laws, and leaders. They don't seem to have anything resembling money, but perhaps that is a good thing. The village lives as a whole, and nobody goes hungry. I think of Bristol—the merchants in their huge houses and the beggars along the waterfront—and I wonder if their system isn't better.

I will write more later. But at present, the wind has come up and dark clouds loom over the land. Father has ordered the attention of all hands.

In haste—
Sancio

Dear Sebastian,

We have come to a crossroads. We have followed the coast as far as we can go, and now there is open water to the west. The long-sought route to Asia? There is much debate among our exhausted crew.

As we worked south, the land became flat and swampy, with long sand beaches meeting the ocean swell. Then a series of lush green islands, the thick trees coming right down to the shore. The water is clear and aqua blue and teeming with life, though not so rich as the stockfish-laden waters of the north. But it is warm. Hot, in fact, and sticky, relieved only by thunderstorms in the afternoons when the heavy air can hold no more water.

We have come, by Father's reckoning, nearly as far along this coast as the distance between Bristol and the New Found Land—and the last half of that distance without our ship. The makeshift sail on the longboat and the oars have brought us near the latitude Columbus sailed. And there is land to the south. Though we cannot see it, the clouds tell us it is there.

So—to head west into the unknown, or continue south in search of help? Most of the men favor the latter course, and I must say that I agree with them. Several of the men are ill. We cannot reach Asia in a longboat.

Even Father, for all his courage, must acknowledge this.

He could have left me behind. He could have sailed south immediately upon losing the ship, and reached this place six months ago. William whispered to me that there were those among the crew who demanded that he do exactly that. But Father never gave up hope that I was still alive, and that he would find me. And find me he did, one spring morning when Running Fawn and I had come down to the shore to gather the baby green ferns that grow there, and that the natives boil lightly and eat. We were wading in the marshland when Running Fawn straightened and cried out. Looking up, I saw the longboat approaching from the mouth of the bay. The sail was out to catch the following breeze. For a moment I did not recognize it. Then I saw the oars, and the ragged, bearded men. "Father!" I cried, waving my arms. "Over here!"

When they approached, Running Fawn looked like she wanted to bolt into the woods, but I gently held on to her wrist and told her it would be all right. I didn't like the way some of the men looked at her, though. I recalled too well how all our troubles with the natives had begun. Still, I wanted to introduce her to Father and to thank her for all she had done for me.

"You will go with them?" Running Fawn asked.

"Yes," I said. "They are my people, and I belong with them."

"It will make me sad to see you go."

"It will make me sad too, a little," I confessed, taking her hands in mine. The longboat was drawing closer. "That man there, standing at the back—he is my father."

"I recognize him," she said. "From the day you first came to our village." Her eyes darted toward the woods behind us. "Our warriors should not have burned your ship," she said. "Has your father come to take revenge?"

"I don't think so," I told her. "I believe his first concern will be to find a way to get us home."

The longboat drew near and landed. Father leapt out, and we embraced. Our first words were awkward. I wanted to know the fates of the shipmates I did not see, and he wanted to know how I had survived. I introduced him to Running Fawn and told him of the kindnesses of her people. He told me of Peter's death, their winter encampment, and his plan to sail south in search of a Spanish ship.

I took Running Fawn's hands in mine. "It is not good that you are going without saying good-bye to Wise Rock and the others," she said. "My mother will be sorry you have gone."

"We have brought enough trouble to your people," I said awkwardly.

"Will you return, Sancio?"

"I don't think so," I said.

She placed her lips gently against my eyelids, first one,

then the other. "I hope you find your home," she said. "At least you are with your father." Then she turned, and before I could reply, she disappeared into the woods.

I still see her face when I close my eyes, stretched out in my spot at the bottom of the boat, rolling in the waves. I wish her a long, happy life, and I hope it's many years before her bay is rediscovered by Englishmen.

And now I must put these letters away for safekeeping. For we are headed south into open water, toward the low clouds on the horizon. I can only pray that fate will be kind to us.

Your loving brother,
Sancio

CHAPTER 15

Whatever John Day had brought with him, it wasn't good news. Sebastian could see it on his mother's face when he opened the door. She had made tea; the empty cups and teapot were still on the table. It was a late afternoon in September 1499. A chill fog had descended on Bristol and Day was putting on his coat in preparation for leaving when Sebastian arrived.

"Sebastian," the man of letters greeted him. "How's the job?"

"The same," Sebastian said, looking warily back and forth between Day and his mother. He didn't know why, but the sight of Day always produced a knot of dread in his stomach. "Up and down the river, out to King's Road and back. And still no sign of the fleet."

Day said nothing. No word of hope, no encouragement,

not even a platitude to assuage his anxiety. Sebastian noted how well-dressed he was. Then he remembered. It was September—the deadline the merchants' consortium had set for his father's return. He guessed what Day had come to tell his mother. A glorified messenger, that's all he was, rubbing shoulders with the rich, carrying their wishes to the royal court, delivering life-altering decisions to the families of workingmen like John Cabot. Moving always under the protection of powerful and influential men, and living well in the process. What would a man like Day do in the face of a real adventure, such as a storm on the ocean, with all his protections stripped away? That was where a man's true character revealed itself. What would he, Sebastian, do?

"If there is anything you need, Mattea . . . ," Day said to Sebastian's mother.

"Send out another ship," she said. "Find my husband, and my sons."

Again, Day said nothing. Sebastian knew that Day could not make such a decision; at best, he could relate his mother's wishes to the men who paid his salary, the same men who had financed John Cabot's fleet. For them, every passing day increased the likelihood of a total loss on their investment. They had mansions to maintain, trade agreements to keep up, fishing fleets to oversee, rental property to look after. Sebastian's missing father and brothers were but one of their business ventures. And Sebastian was old enough and wise enough to know that in business, some-times a failed investment had to be simply written off.

But Sebastian was not yet ready to write off his father and Sancio and Ludovico, and he hated the cold pragma-tism that Day represented. He held the door open as Day adjusted his coat around his shoulders. Awkwardly, Day moved toward the open door, his hat in his hands. As Sebastian started to close it behind him, he turned, and looked first at Mattea and then at Sebastian, as if uncer-tain what to say. His shifting eyes returned to Sebastian's mother, but something in her face troubled him; he did not hold her eyes for more than a few seconds.

"I'll be in touch," he said finally. "Thank you for the tea."

When he was gone, Sebastian went to his mother and put his arms around her. "I can guess what he came here to tell you," he said.

"I'm all right," Mattea said. But she allowed her son to hold her for a lingering moment before extricating herself from his embrace and smoothing down the front of her dress. Then she went to the table and cleared the teacups.

Sebastian followed her, picking up the ceramic teapot and carrying it to the kitchen. "Father's pension . . ."

Mattea grabbed the note from the tabletop and waved

it at him. "Here," she said. "Paid, for the last time, at least until he shows his face in Bristol again. And I got the impression that if he does return, it had better be with a load of spices, or gold, or something of value."

"Something to make the whole thing worth their while, in other words," Sebastian said.

"Exactly." She tucked the note into a clay jar and began mopping the table with a small cloth. Sebastian watched her, waiting for her to say more. When she finished with the table, she turned her attention to other surfaces around the small kitchen, wiping away imaginary dust, cleaning cabinet doors that did not need cleaning. Finally, her back to him, she said, "I know he's still alive out there, somewhere, Sebastian. I just know it."

He wished he shared his mother's confidence. All he felt was a desperate kind of hope, stretching thinner with every passing day. "Well, there is my job at least," he said. "We will not starve, in any event."

"Oh, there is plenty of money," his mother said, finding a spot and scrubbing it hard. "Your father's pension will hold us for another year, at least. And you have become a man in his absence. He would barely recognize you."

Sebastian felt his ears warm at his mother's words. For a year he had envisioned meeting the *Pandora* as she returned triumphant from the Western Ocean, guiding the great ship upriver as his father admired his piloting skill. He had grown to what would be his full height, and filled out, and the long hours on the water had tanned his skin like a sailor's. If his father could see him now, could observe how well he handled a boat, what would he think of the decision to leave him behind?

But it had been sixteen months now. And the men who had put up the money for his father's search for Asia were convinced that he was lost at sea.

"What did he say," Sebastian asked, "about sending out a ship to look for them?"

"That it is a big ocean," Mattea replied. "The chances of finding four lost ships in all that water . . ."

"They're not going to do it," Sebastian said.

"There will be other ships," his mother told him. "The land over there is not going to be forgotten; too much effort and money have been expended already. But it will take time to build and finance another fleet—perhaps a year or two. And when they sail, it will be in search of a passage to Asia, not your father."

"They have given up on him," Sebastian said.

"They are businessmen, Sebastian," Mattea reminded him. "Besides, your father may return before they set sail, and surprise us all with new knowledge of the world."

"But why has he not returned already?" Sebastian cried. "He carried provisions for one year. It has already been much longer than that. Perhaps that man, that man from the first ship, beaten back by the storm, was right. Perhaps they foundered and went down, and they have been lost to us for all this time."

"No!" His mother clenched her fists. "I cannot believe that, Sebastian. Four ships, all lost? With your father in command? He has been through storms before. And he has always come back alive."

Sebastian took her hands in his, uncurled her fingers. "I want to believe too, Mother," he said softly. "I really do. But with each day that goes by, more of Bristol believes him dead. And Sancio, and Ludovico. How I wish I had gone with them!"

"Don't say that, Sebastian," his mother said.

"It's true. Perhaps I would be lost at sea, or cast away on some deserted shore, or held prisoner by some Asian king. But at least there would not be this doubt, this waiting."

"At least I have one of my sons within the sight of my eyes," Mattea said. "The other two . . . I will just have to believe in my heart that I will see them again."

An awkward silence fell between them. Sebastian recalled the strange arrival of Miguel Corte-Real in Bristol that spring, the quick visit to Redcliffe Street, the furtive departure. Even then the merchants had been developing alternate plans should John Cabot fail to return. Anger welled within him.

"Did not the king grant letters patent to John Cabot and his sons?" he said. "As long as I am here, the right to explore the Western Ocean belongs to our family, not to bankers and businessmen!"

His mother took a step back from him. "Sebastian, don't even think it," she said. "You are sixteen years old."

"And how old was Father when he first sailed to Alexandria?"

"That's different," Mattea said.

"How?"

Mattea turned from him, walked the length of the room. "Your father was in the employ of an established trading company, sailing well-known routes to well-known lands, on ships with experienced captains who had sailed the same routes many times before. He did not wake up one morning at the age of sixteen and decide to set off across the ocean. It was the Mediterranean, Sebastian. Men have been sailing the Mediterranean since the time of Agamemnon and Odysseus."

"It is a new day," Sebastian replied. "The Spanish are

sending ships back and forth to their new colonies every year. And Sancio is younger than I am."

"Sancio is with his father," Mattea said.

"If they are still alive," Sebastian mumbled, not looking at his mother.

"You have to believe, Sebastian."

"*They* don't," he cried, flinging an arm out in a gesture intended to carry through the walls and all the way up to the opulent houses of the men who ran Bristol. "They don't care *who* finds the way to Asia, as long as they can profit from it. But it is our family's name on the contract from the king. They cannot just ignore that."

Mattea approached him and placed her hands on his shoulders. "I know what you are feeling," she said. "But Sebastian, you have never been to sea. You are young still. And it is dangerous out there."

Sebastian pulled away from her. "I am not a boy," he said.

"No, but you are still my son. And until your father brings the fleet back to Bristol, as I believe he will, you are the only son I have. Think what would happen if they let you sail off on one of their new ships. They would not make you captain simply by virtue of your name. You would have to endure the hardships of a sailor's life, and I would have to stay here, alone, with three sons and a husband somewhere over the horizon."

Sebastian scowled at the floor.

"And there is your job to consider," his mother added.

"My job," Sebastian said with contempt. "Up and down the river, never more than three leagues from Bristol, looking always to the west for any sign of them. I am so tired of waiting!"

"I know, Sebastian. But that is the lot of a sailor's family—to wait. Please, for my sake, wait with me a little longer."

"And what happens when the new ships set sail, and I am not on any of them? Will everything our family has done be forgotten? Will it all have been for nothing? Mother, you have moved, and moved again, lived among strangers in Spain and England, all to enable Father to chase his dream. I can't let the dream die, can I?"

"Sometimes a man must do the sensible thing, Sebastian—the practical thing. I know you are your father's son, and you do not want to hear that. But it's true."

"And the sensible thing, in my case, is to do nothing. Is that what you are telling me?"

"Oh, Sebastian!" His mother sighed, and suddenly looked ten years older. "You are a man now, and I cannot tell you what to do with your life. All I know is that it will break my heart if you go running off to sea. I need you here, at least until your father returns."

"And if he does not?"

"He will," Mattea said, looking out the open door. "God is merciful. He hears my prayers."

Sebastian wondered if God also heard the prayers of drowning men aboard a sinking ship. Had He heard the prayers of the Jews who were burned at the stake in Valencia, or the Spanish sailors Columbus had left on his new island? Did the natives pray when—if the stories were true—Columbus's men cut off their hands or heads for failing to produce a steady supply of gold? If God heard all prayers, Sebastian thought, he was stingy with his answers.

The next afternoon, after finishing his day's work on the river, Sebastian went to see the Venetian mapmaker Lorenzo Pasqualigo. His father's friend greeted him warmly. A new chart, half-completed, lay spread out on the drafting table. Pasqualigo caught Sebastian's glance at it.

"A new commission, from Mr. Abercrombie and his friends," he said. "They want my best guess as to what your father has found out there."

"But how can you know?" Sebastian asked. "How can anyone know, until my father returns?"

"Indeed." The mapmaker chuckled. "Yet in Lisbon there are charts that show an extended coastline to the north and east of Columbus's Indies. They can only have gotten their information from someone in Bristol—either someone who sailed with your father two summers ago, or someone in the consortium, who would have seen your father's logbooks and reports."

"Someone like John Day, you mean."

Lorenzo placed a cautionary finger against his lips. "I would not go making accusations without facts to back them up," he said.

"I don't like that man," Sebastian said.

"I daresay Mr. Abercrombie does not particularly care for him either. But he is useful to them."

"And useful, too, to those men from the Azores who want to take over my father's contract," Sebastian said. "He has the ear of the consortium and of the royal court. A spy could not be better placed."

"I would keep that to yourself, Sebastian, until such time as you are able to prove it. You may be John Cabot's son, but you are still a youth of sixteen. John Day is very well-connected."

"You are the second person in two days to remind me of my age," Sebastian said sourly. "The first was my mother."

"How is your mother?" Lorenzo asked. "I have been meaning to call on her."

"She has the patience of a saint," Sebastian said. He scowled at the floor, then looked back up at Lorenzo. "Nothing seems to bother her. Yesterday, Day came to the house to tell her that Father's pension is being stopped. She gave him tea."

"I can see why you hold a grudge against him," Lorenzo said. "But Sebastian, he is merely the messenger."

"Then why is he negotiating with the Portuguese?"

"Ocean voyaging is expensive," the mapmaker said. "These Azorean men have money; Abercrombie and his friends have money. And your father is, after all, missing."

"Do you think he will return, Lorenzo?" Sebastian said, in a low voice.

Lorenzo Pasqualigo put a hand on Sebastian's shoulder. "I have been a friend to your father for a long time. He is one of the most resourceful men I know. But the sea . . . the sea has a will of her own." Pasqualigo took his hand away and slapped the chart. "I *hope* he returns," he said. "His return would render all of this obsolete."

"There is the matter of my father's contract," Sebastian

said. "It grants to Father and his sons the right to explore the ocean to the north, east, and west in the name of the king of England. If Father fails to return, and Ludovico's ship is lost also, the contract would fall on me. Surely Abercrombie and his friends are aware of this."

Lorenzo smiled to take the sting out of his next words. "And they are aware, as I must again remind you, that you are sixteen. Try to see it from their point of view. They have lost money on your father, unless by chance he returns next week or next month in ships laden with Asian riches. Your father is an experienced sailor and trader. You are neither. It's a question of money, Sebastian, as it always is. I do not doubt that one day you will become as able a captain as your father. But right now, at your age, they do not see you as a good investment."

"But there is the contract," Sebastian protested.

"Contracts have been broken before," Lorenzo said. "History is littered with them."

Sebastian fell silent. He paced the small office. He would not look at the chart on the table. Finally, he said, "Will you back me, Lorenzo? If I take my case to the king?"

"Sebastian, I am your father's loyal ally. It was I who recommended that he move here. Of course I would back you. But I am telling you here that it would not do any good. I am a Venetian, as you are. We are foreigners. Once Venice ruled the world, or the part we think of as the world, anyway. But we are far from those days, in both time and distance. The Spanish and the Portuguese are the masters now, and King Henry is afraid of them. He will go for this Portuguese alliance, because it will give him a measure of protection against the Spanish. And he will not have to raid the royal treasury in order to do it."

Sebastian absorbed this in silence. He knew down deep that his father's friend was right. No one would take him seriously—not the rich men who worked the port of Bristol to their benefit, not the sailors who manned the fishing boats far out on the Western Ocean or the toughened convicts drafted for ocean voyages who cared little whether they lived or died, and not the king of England, who had other options. All Sebastian had was his name—his father's name—on a contract, a piece of paper.

He was too young—that was the nub of it. Had he a few more years, he would have been able to invoke his rights and sail out into the ocean in search of his father and brothers. But he was too young. He would have to wait. Like his mother, who seemed capable of waiting forever.

"I'm sorry, Sebastian," Lorenzo said. "But those are the

harsh realities of the modern world. You are old enough to hear them."

But not old enough to do anything about them, Sebastian thought. He thanked Lorenzo and started to leave.

"Let us keep hoping that your father returns," the mapmaker said.

"That is all we can do," Sebastian said, his voice hollow. "Keep hoping."

He walked slowly up the hill toward his family's house in the slanted, late-afternoon sunlight. To Sebastian it felt as though the rays of light passed through him without leaving any warmth—like a cold wind blowing through the hole in his heart.

CHAPTER 16

AMERIGO VESPUCCI TAPPED ON THE DOOR of his captain's cabin and waited for the grunt that granted admission. Under his arm was the bundle of letters the boy had given him. The belowdecks area of the ship dripped with condensation. Vespucci felt rivulets run down his sides beneath his shirt. The air was heavy, and thick with moisture.

Alonso de Hojeda looked up from his writing table as Vespucci opened the door and entered. For a moment, the two men stared at each other. Vespucci was tall, and held himself like the banker he was. There was something regal in his bearing, as though he was always looking down the bridge of his long, aristocratic nose. The Spaniard Hojeda, though not as tall, was a larger man, thick through the shoulders and chest. He had dark hair, coal pits for eyes, and a black beard that he kept neatly trimmed and that gave him the appearance of a pirate. And a pirate he was, Vespucci thought, an outlaw in a place where there was no law. Even before the fleet had left Spain, Hojeda had stolen a ship from the harbor at Palos, leaving behind a leaky caravel in its place. Vespucci had watched his commander ransack one native village after another, searching for gold, ordering his men to cut off the ears or the hands of any natives not quick enough to cooperate. They had been on this coast for four weeks now, and while Hojeda's efforts had produced only a trickle of gold, the flow of blood had been steady.

"Well?" Hojeda asked, his feather pen, ink-dipped, poised above the paper on the desk. "What did you find out?"

"I believe they are who they say they are," Vespucci said. "The Venetian known as John Cabot, his son Sancio, seven of their men. Englishmen, except for Cabot and his boy. I have spoken with the boy in his native language, though he seems to know many tongues."

"And how did they get here?" Hojeda demanded.

"Shipwrecked," Vespucci said. "Far to the north of here, apparently. They have been traveling in their longboat for months, looking for a European ship. Most of the crew is dead. These nine are all that are left."

"Englishmen." Hojeda twisted one end of his mustache, thinking. "The king and queen would be much displeased if they knew that a crew of Englishmen has turned up in the Indies."

"I don't think they came here by design," Vespucci said. "Their circumstances seem desperate." He paused, and looked his captain in the eye. "And I think we both know that these are not the Indies."

Hojeda grunted, acknowledging the point. Columbus had come along this shore a year ago, but turned north when he realized he had missed the settlement on Hispaniola. Hojeda's ships had continued to the west along the coast of what could only be an undiscovered continent. The land was low and covered with a tangle of tropical forest, like the islands they had seen, but they had also passed the mouths of two great rivers, and all that fresh water had to come from somewhere. The natives built their homes on stilts above the water, which had prompted the expedition's navigator, Juan de la Cosa, to name the place "Venezuela," or "Little Venice." The Venetian leader of the English, John Cabot, had smiled through bloodied lips when Vespucci told him that.

Hojeda nodded at the bundle underneath Vespucci's arm. "Anything in there that could be of use to us?"

Vespucci hesitated for the barest second before answering, long enough for suspicion to flash in Hojeda's dark eyes. "No," he said. "Mostly letters to his brother— sentimental stuff, how he misses his mother and so forth."

Hojeda cracked his knuckles above the table. "Nothing about where they have been and what they have seen? Nothing said about gold, or spices, or dyes?"

Vespucci shook his head. "They seem to have spent much of their time lost at sea," he said. "It is a wonder any of them are still alive."

"They will not be alive much longer if they cannot provide me with something of value," Hojeda growled. He smacked the table with a fist. "How are we to know that they are not spies, sent out from a ship that is concealed somewhere along the coast?"

"Would they have sent the captain and his son on such a mission?" Vespucci asked.

Hojeda considered this. "They must know that they are in Spanish waters," he said. "I find their story preposterous. It is just the kind of story one would make up when outnumbered in hostile territory."

Vespucci marveled at how his captain was always ready for a fight. The man lived for battle and plunder. Already the natives all along the coast were terrified of him. And no wonder. In just a few weeks, Hojeda had perpetrated more acts of random cruelty, including murder and torture, than Vespucci had witnessed in years of travel in Europe, beset as it was with religious and factional strife. If European colonization of these new lands was to be led by men like Hojeda, Vespucci reflected, then the future for these simple natives looked grim indeed.

"I do not think they have a ship nearby," Vespucci said. "They looked awfully ragged when we came upon them." And they looked more ragged now, he thought but did not say, after their initial treatment at the hands of Hojeda's men.

"They are trespassing in an area that belongs to the king and queen of Spain," Hojeda said. "You say they have come from the north?"

"That is what they claim, yes."

Hojeda smiled, like a cat with a cornered mouse, anticipating the kill. "And what would happen," he said, "if we gave them passage to Europe, so they could tell the world about their journey?"

"I would imagine that Cabot would get credit for discovering the lands they passed," Vespucci said.

"And Cabot's sponsor is . . ."

"The throne of England," Vespucci finished for him.

"Precisely!" Hojeda smacked the table again. "And do you think Ferdinand and Isabella would be happy to share their lands on this side of the ocean with the English?"

"I very much doubt it," Vespucci said.

"I very much doubt it!" Hojeda got up from the desk, his figure looming large in the small cabin. "I very much doubt it! My friend, you have a gift for understatement. They would strip me of my commission. They might even have me arrested for treason. All lands west of the treaty line belong to Spain—the Pope himself has decreed it. We see no Portuguese ships over here; we would sink them if we saw them. These renegade Englishmen, desperate though they may appear, are trespassing in our waters. And trespassing is a crime."

He is a fine one to speak of crimes, Vespucci thought, but he held his tongue. Hojeda's temper could inspire him to fits of lethal madness. Most of his victims had been helpless natives, but Vespucci had also seen him order a sailor flogged nearly to death for falling asleep on watch. And he had burned an entire native village to the ground in retribution for one arrow that had found its mark in the chest of a member of his crew. His rages were frightening, because they could vent themselves on any available target.

"That fool Columbus still has no idea what he has found over here," Hojeda went on. "But Cabot knows, and he will take that knowledge back to Bristol—if we allow him."

"What will you do with them?" Vespucci asked softly.

"What is always done with spies and criminals," Hojeda said. "They will be hanged."

Vespucci was careful not to show any outward reaction. "I should like to speak with the boy," he said. "About these." He patted the package of letters under his arm.

Hojeda narrowed his eyes. "I thought you said there was nothing of value in them," he said.

"He may know more than what he has written down," Vespucci said. "And he is quite adept with language. He has learned some of the native tongue. Perhaps he has learned things from them—the extent of the land, or the location of their cities, if indeed they have cities. The information in his head may yet prove valuable, Captain."

Hojeda grunted. "His father told me nothing, even under the lash," he said.

Vespucci struggled to conceal his disgust. Violence was Hojeda's answer to everything. "The boy may tell me more," he said.

Hojeda sat back down and shrugged. "Very well. But

when the sun rises on Monday morning, they all die. You have until then to find out what you wish to know."

"The boy too?" Vespucci asked.

"Yes, the boy too!" Hojeda snapped. "He is not so young that he would not seek to avenge his father." His dark eyes shifted. "How many members of our crew know who they are?"

Vespucci felt a cold finger of fear slide along his spine. It would not be beyond Hojeda to have his own sailors put to death in order to silence them. Even he was not entirely safe, although he had influential friends back in Europe who would investigate his disappearance. But men died on ocean voyages, and the circumstances of their deaths often remained mysterious. Distance from Spain meant that Hojeda could give free rein to his ruthlessness, and Vespucci knew that Hojeda knew this. He could have anyone killed, and the royal court would sort it out months and even years later, if at all.

"I daresay knowledge of them is wide but not deep," he replied. "Most of the men know that we have captured a handful of European sailors in a longboat, but I think they assume they are castoffs from one of Columbus's ships, or from one of ours. Only you and I and their guards have spoken with them."

"That is good," Hojeda said. "Go speak with the boy, then. While he can still speak."

Sancio slept fitfully, for it was hard to relax in a sitting position, his hands bound to the post behind him. They slept in a circle, around the edges of the tiny hut, each man's hands tied in the same position. Their feet touched if they extended their legs. During the day, the hut sweltered in the moist tropical heat, and the insects feasted on their arms and faces, for they could not swat them away. At night there were bugs also, but of the type that crawled on the ground. Twice each day a guard brought them water, passed among them in a single tin cup, and each man received a slab of stale bread and some foul-tasting gruel as his daily ration. Guards stood outside the hut at all hours of the day and night. Sancio and the others were forbidden to talk among themselves; they were reduced to communicating through nods and lip-reading and messages whispered from man to man around the circle.

There were only eight of them now. Stephen Conant had been shot three days ago, as an example to the others, for protesting the conditions of their captivity. And Sancio's father had been taken out of the hut each day, to return with fresh lacerations and bruises. Several of the others had likewise been taken out and beaten. When a hand on his shoulder shook him awake, Sancio assumed it was his turn.

Amerigo Vespucci put a finger to his lips as soon as Sancio's eyes opened. Sancio could hear the slow, regular breathing of the other prisoners. On the far side of the hut he heard his father snoring. His father had never snored before. But during one of the question-and-answer sessions he had sustained several blows to the face, and Sancio surmised that his nose was broken.

Sancio wanted to kill Alonso de Hojeda. He had never felt such hatred for anyone in his life. What a moment of joy it had been to spot the sails of Hojeda's three ships. They had been half-starved, beset by illness and unfriendly natives. Sancio's friend William Hennessey had been buried at sea after becoming delirious and vomiting up all the liquid in his body, and Gardiner Morse had died quietly in the night and been lowered into the depths as well. It had been a shock, then, to be shackled and taken prisoner by their rescuers. Later, ashore, they saw the piles of severed hands and the burned-out homes of the natives, and they watched Hojeda's men melt down artifacts of gold that they had stolen from them.

"Where is Columbus?" John Cabot had demanded on

that first day, whereupon Hojeda had stepped up to him and backhanded him across the face, sending him sprawl-ing. Sancio had lunged at him, but a large Spanish sailor had held him back.

"I am viceroy of these territories, and you will answer to me!" Hojeda had roared. "Columbus is of no concern to you."

"Columbus would never permit such an outrage," Cabot had said from the ground. Hojeda had nodded, and one of his henchmen had then kicked Sancio's father in the ribs.

The memory of that humiliation was fresh in Sancio's mind as Vespucci untied his hands and led him out into the night. And he remembered also his father's words, whispered two nights earlier through split lips: "We must look for any means of escape, each one of us. If we could steal one of their ships, we might sail it back to Europe. It is our best hope."

A slim hope, Sancio thought, with them on land under constant guard, and each ship several yards offshore, manned by crews that well outnumbered them. And how were they to sail a caravel with only eight men? Perhaps his father's plan was to surprise the crew, kidnap them, and force them to sail to Bristol. But Sancio thought this unlikely, given his father's condition.

"What?" Sancio whispered as soon as he and Vespucci were outside.

"Quiet," Vespucci said, giving away nothing. "Come with me."

They walked through the encampment down to the shore, where the boats were hauled up. In the light of the half-moon, Sancio saw several men guarding them. His heart sank. He realized that his father's plan to steal one of Hojeda's three caravels would never work—not with all these guards around. They would never even get to the water.

But Vespucci was not taking him out to one of the ships. He led Sancio along a thin, sandy beach a short distance away from the Spanish encampment. The trees grew right down to the water's edge; only because the tide was out could they walk along the shore. Vespucci found a low-hanging branch, sat on it, and invited Sancio to sit with him. The small waves of the bay lapped at the sand near their feet.

From under his arm Vespucci produced the packet containing Sancio's letters to his brother. "I need to talk with you about these," he said.

"You have read them?"

"Yes." Vespucci looked out at the three ships riding at

anchor. "I have an advantage over my commander, in that I can read Venetian and he cannot. It is tragic that you have come so far only to fall into the hands of a despot. He is a cruel man."

"What does he intend to do with us?" Sancio asked.

Vespucci continued looking out at the ships. "He plans to hang the lot of you, at dawn, the day after tomorrow," he said.

"Hang us?" Sancio cried. "All of us?"

Vespucci nodded. "I will try to spare you, if I can. Perhaps I can arrange an escape, smuggle you aboard ship when we leave for Hispaniola. But Hojeda will have you killed if he discovers you. In his mind you are all spies for the English." Vespucci looked at the sand. "I am sorry, I truly am. But I am not the commander of this fleet. He is."

"But what about Columbus?" Sancio protested. "He and Father know each other. They were boys together. It was Columbus we were looking for when we came upon your fleet. Surely he would not permit the murder of one of his old friends."

"I am afraid Ferdinand and Isabella have grown tired of Columbus's promises," Vespucci said. "It is unfortunate that they sent a man like Hojeda in his place; but again, that was their choice, not mine."

"Where is Columbus now?"

"He is over here somewhere, probably in Hispaniola. But he has made a mess of things there. He has produced little except discontent. And he has certainly not found a passage to Asia, nor is he likely to." Vespucci slapped the packet of letters. "You speak of coasting a continental landmass that runs for hundreds of leagues. It is continuous, from the far north down to here?"

Sancio nodded. "If there is a passage to Asia, it is well-concealed," he said.

"And a long way, I should think. Everyone knows that Columbus underestimated the size of the world. These writings contain the proof."

"They are for my brother, in England."

"Yes, but they will be of great value to whoever brings this knowledge back to Europe. Be thankful that Hojeda is unaware of their contents. He would likely claim your father's discoveries for himself."

"My father wanted only to find the way to Asia, ahead of Columbus," Sancio said.

"We have seen nothing resembling Asian civilization," Vespucci replied. "Instead, we have discovered a great landmass stretching to the south, and your letters tell of an equally large body of land lying to the north. It is like finding half a world of which we previously knew nothing. A new world, in fact."

"New only to us," Sancio said. "Your treatment of the natives fills me with horror and shame."

Vespucci bowed his head for a moment, then looked up and met Sancio's eyes. "The world is changing, my boy—here, now, under our feet. Hojeda may be a brutal man, I do not dispute that, but there are bound to be men like him in every human adventure—stupid, ambitious men, who think only of personal gain."

"There are many men in Spain like him. I have seen their handiwork up close."

Again Vespucci paused before he spoke. "And in Bristol, too."

Sancio's thoughts churned. How his father had been wronged by the Spanish—first in Valencia and now here, to die at their hands, beaten and hanged like a common criminal. Sancio was not inclined to forgive their excesses as the acts of a few greedy men, not when his life and his father's life hung in the balance. At that moment, he hated all Spaniards, and anyone who worked for them.

"Is there to be no trial?" Sancio said. "No chance for us to defend ourselves? He cannot just hang us without good reason."

Vespucci shook his head. "My boy, Hojeda can do whatever he wants, and make it stick, so long as his men do not rise up against him. Most of his men seem to enjoy killing and torturing the natives. It is profitable for them. Hojeda has promised them a share of the gold. He has told them he will make them rich. If he orders a hanging, they will not hesitate to carry it out."

"But we are Europeans, like himself!"

"You are in his way," Vespucci said. "You stand between him and fame, and glory, and wealth."

They were a short distance from the encampment, close enough to hear the shouts of men and to smell smoke. Vespucci turned his head.

"What's going on?" Sancio said.

"I do not know."

Vespucci stood up. Sancio saw a flame climb toward the sky.

"Come on." Vespucci was already moving down the beach, beckoning Sancio to follow him. "Stay with me," he said when Sancio caught up. "Hang back, out of sight. It would not do for anyone to see you."

There was a great commotion now. Men ran between the makeshift buildings, shouting in Spanish. Sancio made out the imperious shape of Hojeda, striding across the open area toward the source of the flames. He wished more than anything that he had a crossbow in his hands at this moment. He could feel the heat from the fire.

"One of the buildings is on fire," said Vespucci, quickening his steps. They could hear the flames now, mingled with the screams of men. Suddenly Vespucci stopped, and Sancio nearly crashed into him. "Oh God," Vespucci said. He put his hands on Sancio's shoulders and stared into his eyes.

Sancio stopped and stared back. "What?"

Vespucci's face was stone. "It is the house where you were being held. It's burning."

For a moment Sancio stood as if struck, his body waiting for its reaction to the blow.

"NO!" he cried. He rushed forward, but Vespucci grabbed him, and held him around the chest. Sancio flailed with his fists, kicked out with his legs. "NO!" he cried, over and over again. He saw flames lick the sky, saw the charred outline of the hut through them, and he knew that his father and the remaining members of their crew were dead.

He drove an elbow into Vespucci's ribs. The older man gasped but hung on. "Let me GO!" Sancio shouted.

"Think, Sancio," Vespucci panted, tightening his grip

around Sancio's middle. "If you show your face now, they will know you did not die in there. Hide yourself, and I can save you!"

Sancio stopped struggling. He twisted and looked Vespucci in the eye, their faces inches apart. "You knew," he said. "You *knew*. That's why you came for me tonight, is it not? There was to be no hanging! All your talk about sparing my life! You took me out so you could kill them now, as they slept!"

"Sancio, I swear that is not true," Vespucci said. "You must believe me!"

Sancio drew his head back as far as he could, and spat into the man's face.

"You lying, despicable coward," he cried.

"Sancio, listen to me!"

With a vicious twist, Sancio freed himself from Vespucci's grasp, and pushed him away. He looked at the burning hut and the men gathered around it. There was no hope—none—that anyone had gotten out alive.

"I should kill you now," he said to Vespucci.

"Sancio, I can help you!"

"Help me? After you have killed my father?"

"I had no idea, Sancio! I told you what Hojeda told me—there was to be a hanging Monday morning. If

Hojeda planned to have the fire set, he did not tell me!" Vespucci stopped to catch his breath, and to wipe Sancio's spittle off his face with the sleeve of his shirt.

"Why should I believe you?" Sancio said.

"Because I am your only hope now." Vespucci was panting, but he managed to keep his voice calm. "If you go out there now, Hojeda will realize that you were not in the hut, and he will have you killed. He thinks you are dead, burned with the others. I can smuggle you aboard ship."

Sancio looked at him with pure hatred. "I don't need your help," he said. "You have helped enough already."

"Sancio, listen to me!"

"See that my brother gets those letters," Sancio said, nodding at the packet under Vespucci's arm. "That's all I ask of you. Nothing more." And he turned away from Vespucci, away from the fire and the Spanish invaders, and took two steps down the beach, toward the tree where they had sat and talked mere minutes ago.

"Where are you going?" Vespucci called after him.

"Away from you," Sancio said, and kept walking.

"There is nothing in that direction but savages," Vespucci said.

"I'll take my chances with them." Sancio lengthened his steps. Vespucci stood in the sand, outlined in firelight.

Sancio heard a whoop from one of the men around the fire. He looked back once, saw Vespucci standing in the same spot, watching him. He looked away and kept walking. A moment later he began to run.

Vespucci found Hojeda in front of the burning building, watching the conflagration with a group of men around him and a smile on his lips. The fire had died back some, but the heat was still staggering. The hastily built structure had collapsed; flames licked at glowing timbers that had fallen haphazardly upon one another. There were no signs of the bodies of any of the prisoners, but the stench of burnt flesh filled Vespucci's nostrils.

"You said they were to be hanged," he said to his commander.

Hojeda's smile did not change. "An unfortunate accident," he said. "One of the guards kicked over a lantern."

"Convenient for you," Vespucci said, his voice full of contempt. "It spares you the need to justify their execution."

"I would hold my tongue, were I in your position, Señor Vespucci," Hojeda said. He was still smiling, but there was no mistaking the menace in his voice.

Vespucci took the packet containing Sancio's letters

from under his arm. At the moment, he was the only person in the world besides their author who knew what they contained. He glanced at his commander, and saw that Hojeda was mesmerized by the flames. Vespucci envisioned him presenting the letters to Ferdinand and Isabella, taking credit for the discovery of these vast new lands, winning a royal contract to subjugate them. The thought filled him with loathing.

Advancing as close to the flames as he could, he tossed the letters onto the fire. Then he stood back and watched them burn.

EPILOGUE

SEBASTIAN CABOT WATCHED FROM THE DECK AS THE last of his boats pulled out from the shore toward the ship. He counted the heads twice, and arrived at the same total each time: six. Four more men lost to this godforsaken jungle.

Sebastian had been on the coast of South America for nearly four years. His orders had been to follow the coast south to the passage Magellan had discovered ten years before, and to continue on into the Pacific, eventually returning to Spain via the Spice Islands. He had ignored those orders, and now he feared his crew was on the verge of ignoring his. They would have good reason, Sebastian reflected. He had already lost two ships and more than a hundred men. The "River of Silver" had yielded no riches. The forest was impenetrable, except to the Indians, who had exhibited considerable skill in making life miserable for the Spanish invaders.

He would be in trouble when he returned to Spain with what remained of his fleet. And it was clear that they could not stay here much longer. His men would not stand for it. He had kept them in line with promises of gold and silver mines to be raided, but in fact it was the Indians who had done most of the raiding. They had burned one ship to the waterline, surprising the men on watch and incinerating the crew, and they had lured another ship onto the rocks a few leagues north of here, picking off with poisoned arrows the men who tried to swim to shore. Sebastian had tried to negotiate a truce, but their language baffled him, and he found to his amazement that the Indians were as skilled in the European arts of deception and double cross as he was.

Sebastian knew that the natives must eventually succumb to the might of Spanish arms and technology, but they had been harassing Spanish ships along this coast for many years now, and nobody could figure out why they were so tenacious. Sebastian thought he had an idea. He had not lingered on this coast for four years because of rumored deposits of gold and silver.

The undermanned longboat drew closer. Sebastian watched it, feeling old. He was forty-seven. It was unlikely that he would get another chance to cross the ocean, even if he managed to avoid imprisonment in Europe. Perhaps ironically, fate had been kinder to his father. He had sailed off into the unknown, never to return, but his reputation had outlived him. John Cabot had been the first sailor from Europe to reach the continent now called North America. Columbus had been nowhere near Asia, as Sebastian's father had maintained all along, and as Magellan's surviving crew had proved, years after the elder Cabot had vanished. Then again, what a shame to be vindicated only in death.

The search for a sea route to Asia had led instead to the discovery of two savage continents, which men from Europe were now busy subduing. Sebastian had heard tales of great cities in which people paid tribute to pagan gods with the blood of thousands. He had seen ships filled with African slaves leave Spanish ports, bound for the islands Columbus had discovered, where the Spanish had killed the native population and built huge sugar planta-tions. He had seen Columbus's estimate of the size of the Earth proven ridiculously wrong. His mother, God rest her soul, had been prophetic: His was the first generation to map the world.

But as the mystery of what lay across the Western Ocean had come gradually into focus, the greater mystery in Sebastian's life remained unresolved: What had happened to his father, and Sancio and Ludovico? His mother had died stubbornly clinging to the hope that they would someday miraculously return. Sebastian did not believe in miracles. The Bristol-Azorean syndicate (which John Day had been instrumental in putting together) had managed to send a fleet to the New Found Land, and had found nothing. Only after his mother's death in 1507 did Sebastian receive permission from King Henry VII to try it himself.

The expedition was a disaster. Sebastian made landfall on a barren, rocky shore and followed it north until cathedral-size ice floes forced him to turn back. Not only was there no passage to Asia, there was nothing of value to European civilization in that treeless wilderness. If his father and brothers had died along that shore, theirs had been cold and lonely deaths.

Upon returning to England, Sebastian had received more bad news: The king was dead, and his son, Henry VIII, had assumed the throne. This Henry was uninterested in Atlantic exploration and unmoved by Sebastian's petition to explore the coast to the south. Henry VIII's marriage to Ferdinand and Isabella's daughter, Catherine, signaled the end of English rivalry with the Spanish in the South Atlantic. With his mother gone and his father's old friends in Bristol dropping off one by one, Sebastian soon found himself forgotten in England. In the meantime, the Spanish conquest of the Americas—named for Amerigo Vespucci, the first man to recognize the new continents for what they were—continued. Very well, then—if the new English king had no use for him, Sebastian would see what he could do for Spain.

The longboat drew alongside. The men looked ragged and half-starved. They had been gone for three weeks, and Sebastian could see right away that they had come back empty-handed. The leader of the shore party, a graying, once-powerful man named Pedro Zaranoza—whom a rigging mishap had deprived of three fingers on his right hand—glowered at Sebastian from the stern. The two men had clashed frequently as the tropical heat and its associated illnesses, the hostile natives, and Sebastian's refusal to move on had eaten away at the morale of the crew.

"Now, by God, we'll set sail for Spain!" Zaranoza declared.

Sebastian stiffened. "I give the orders on this ship, sir."

Zaranoza only stared back silently as his men climbed aboard. Sebastian stared back. Zaranoza could probably rally a majority of the crew to mutiny at this point, he knew. Sebastian waited until the longboat had been taken aboard and they were alone on deck before he asked about the missing men.

"Shot from ambush, every one of them, by those accursed Indians," Zaranoza answered.

Indians. Even here, in this subequatorial jungle, they were closer to Spain than to India. Yet the misnomer had stuck.

"Did you see their leader?" Sebastian asked.

"I didn't see *any* of the godless savages," Zaranoza said. "We never do."

But Sebastian had seen him—once, only once. And that brief glimpse had glued him to this coast these last three years, even as he was supposed to be sailing in the wake of Magellan.

Silver and gold—who had not heard the rumors of silver and gold? And in fact, some of those rumors were true. Others were not. Sometimes the natives told Sebastian's translators what they thought they wanted to hear. They also spoke of their leader, a man whose name meant Wanderer or World Traveler in their language. He had white skin, the Indians said, and a great bush of a beard, and he could speak many languages. He had come from far away, they said, across the sea on the back of a huge sea creature. It was this great white leader who organized the raids on the Spanish ships and the ambushes of Spanish men.

Sebastian had thought it nothing more than a heathen legend until that day, three years ago and a hundred leagues north of this place, when he had gone ashore with several of his men to fill water casks. The Indians had surprised them. Three of his men went down without a sound before any of them knew what was happening. Sebastian and his men had two rifles and a crossbow between them. They chased the Indians into the jungle. And in an open spot in the forest Sebastian had come face-to-face with a bearded man, dressed like the savages in little save paint and a necklace of shells, his skin bronzed by the sun, but still paler than that of the other Indians. Sebastian and the man were a long stone's throw apart. He had an arrow drawn back, pointed at Sebastian's throat.

Sebastian froze, and in that moment his eyes met the eyes of the man about to kill him. And Sebastian knew in that instant that the bearded man was no native. It was something in the eyes, some long-forgotten glint that he recognized, and in the second that their eyes met, he remembered his brother Sancio.

Then Sebastian ducked as the arrow thunked into a tree trunk beside him, and he did not look back once as he ran for the safety of the longboat.

Three years had passed since that day, and Sebastian still could not go to sleep without that bearded face rising over the horizon of his mind. It had not been an old face, despite the wild hair and beard. And the eyes had been full of something like mischief.

Sometimes at night, when he couldn't sleep, Sebastian tried to remember what his younger brother Sancio had once looked like, and what he would look like now—as a man Sebastian had not seen since boyhood. He couldn't do it.

More attacks followed, on his and other Spanish ships, all along the coast of South America, at widely spaced places. The Indians had inferior weapons and were inevitably driven off, and there had been harsh Spanish reprisals. But the Indians had stealth and local knowledge on their side, and they were well-organized. Sebastian's translators plied the Indians for more information on this white chief. Could it be his brother, alive after all these years? Sebastian told himself the thought was ludicrous. Even had Sancio survived, he could not possibly have traveled the length of the Americas, living at the mercy of the Indians. Sebastian had been staring down the shaft of an arrow. In the moment before his death, his mind had conjured up a pleasant memory. That was all.

Yet he kept pursuing the white chief, seeking out news of him, sending out parties of men, ostensibly to search for minerals but really to find him. There was news, but there was also violent, unexpected death. Sebastian knew his crew had had enough.

The sea was calm; only the gentle rolling of the tide at the river mouth rocked the ship. Sebastian gazed out into the vast flat greenness of the land in front of him. He thought of his last words to his brother, more than thirty years ago, and his soul filled with regret.

At the changing of the watch that evening, Sebastian called Pedro Zaranoza to his side. The sky over the land was streaked with red clouds. "If there is a fair wind tomorrow," he said, "we will run north for Pernambuco and then home."

Zaranoza did not even smile. "The men will be glad to hear it, sir."

I'm sure they will, Sebastian thought. He contemplated the prospect of returning to Europe, as he had from his first ocean voyage, with nothing—no gold, no silver, no new trade agreements or conquered lands. He thought of the age that was passing, and what was likely to come after he was gone. He thought of a world served up to the appetites of the warring kingdoms of Europe, and he wondered what would happen to the lands his father had discovered.

But most of all, he thought that he would not pass this way again. He would face charges in Spain of mismanaging his mission, and indeed nearly every man aboard, Zaranoza included, was prepared to testify that he had mismanaged it. Of that Sebastian had little doubt. He would be lucky to escape prison.

Sebastian sighed, and looked down into the water below the ship. "It is a cruel new world, Zaranoza," he said.

"That it is, sir."

The End

AUTHOR'S NOTE

Little is known about John Cabot's voyages, and even less about Giovanni Caboto himself, or his family. What *is* known is that Cabot reached the coast of what is now Atlantic Canada in 1497, and set out from Bristol again the following year. There is no record of this expedition returning to Europe. Cabot's son Sebastian made two later voyages to the New World. The rest is conjecture.

As this is a work of historical fiction, I have tried to tell an entertaining story within a framework of overall historical verisimilitude. Any errors of fact are mine alone.

For historical information on John Cabot and his family, and daily life in the Bristol of the late fifteenth century, I am particularly indebted to Peter Firstbrook's excellent book, *The Voyage of the* Matthew, published by BBC books in 1997 as a companion piece to the television series of the same name, which Firstbrook produced for the BBC.

For information on navigation, life at sea, Christopher Columbus, and the chronology of events leading up to and surrounding the discovery of the New World, two volumes by Samuel Eliot Morison—*Admiral of the Ocean Sea: A Life of Christopher Columbus* (1942, Little, Brown) and *The European Discovery of America: The Northern Voyages* (1971, Oxford)—were invaluable.

Sources for depictions of Europe in the late 1400s include: *A World Lit Only by Fire—The Medieval Mind and the Renaissance*, by William Manchester (Macmillan, 1992); *The Discoverers*, by Daniel Boorstin (Random House, 1983); and *The Way of the West—The Reorganization of Europe, 1300–1760*, by Arthur J. Slavin (Xerox, 1973). Howard S. Russell's *Indian New England Before the Mayflower* (University Press of New England, 1980) was helpful for the scenes of meetings between Cabot's crew and Native Americans.

A complete bibliography is available on my Web site: www.hwgarfield.com.

Thanks to everyone who read early drafts of all or parts of this work and offered feedback. Special thanks to Barbara Markowitz, Jack Driscoll, and Richard Jackson.

Extra special thanks to Elaine for her love and support.

GLOSSARY

Astrolabe: Small circular instrument used for measuring altitude of celestial objects.

Brasil: Legendary island in North Atlantic; possibly refers to early sightings of Newfoundland by Bristol sailors.

Caravel: Small, two- to three-masted sailing vessel with a relatively shallow draft; faster and more maneuverable than earlier ships, it was developed for coastal exploration by the Portuguese in the mid–1400s.

Cipangu: Island off the coast of Asia unknown to Europeans in 1498; probably refers to Japan.

Dogwatch: A two-hour watch inserted into the regular shipboard schedule of four-hour watches, so that sailors do not serve watches at the same time every day.

Flagon: A large bottle of wine.

Kolchab: Second-brightest star in Ursa Minor; used to tell time at sea because it describes a circle around Polaris every twenty-four hours.

Lateen Rig: A configuration of triangular sails, developed by the Arabs, enabling a ship to sail less than ninety degrees from the direction of the wind.

Lead, lead line: A mass of lead suspended by a line for measuring depth.

League: A unit of measure approximately equal to 3.1 nautical miles.

Letters Patent: Contract granting exploration rights in the name of a king or queen.

Polaris, Pole Star: Bright star in Ursa Minor; used in navigation because it marks the north celestial pole.

Pope's Line: Meridian set by Pope Alexander VI dividing Spanish and Portuguese claims to new lands in the Atlantic: Spanish to the west of the line, Portuguese to the east. Formalized by Treaty of Tordesillas in 1494 at approximately forty-six degrees west longitude.

Vega: Bright star in Lyra; prominent in summer in the northern hemisphere.

BIOGRAPHY

The following figures from history appear or are mentioned in this book:

John Cabot (Giovanni Caboto) (c.1450–1498?)

Ludovico (c.1480–?) and **Sancio Cabot** (c.1484–?)

Mattea Cabot (c.1450–?)

Sebastian Cabot (c.1483?–1557)

Catherine (c.1485–1536) Daughter of Ferdinand and Isabella; married Henry VIII of England

Christopher Columbus (Cristoforo Colombo) (c.1451–1506)

Gaspar and **Miguel Corte-Real** (?) Portuguese explorers

Bartholomeu Dias (c.1450–1500) Portuguese explorer; first to round África

Fernão Dulmo and **João Estreito** (?) Portuguese explorers who sailed west from Ázores in 1487

Eratosthenes (c.276–194 BC) Greek astronomer and scholar

Ferdinand (c.1452–1516) and **Isabella** (c.1451–1504) Rulers of Áragon and Castile

Vasco da Gama (c.1460–1524) Portuguese explorer; first to reach India by rounding África

Henry VII (c.1457–1509) King of England, ruled 1485–1509

Henry VIII (c.1491–1537) King of England, ruled 1509–1537

Alonso de Hojeda (d.1509) Spanish explorer

John II (c.1455–1495) King of Portugal, ruled 1481–1495

Manuel I (c.1469–1521) King of Portugal, ruled 1495–1521

Marco Polo (c.1254–1324) Venetian merchant and traveler

Pope Álexander VI (c.1431–1503)

Ptolemy (c.100–168) Greek astronomer and geographer

Luis de Santángel (d.1498) Purser to Ferdinand and Isabella

Paolo del Pozzo Toscanelli (c.1397–1482) Florentine cartographer

Tomás de Torquemada (c.1420–1498) Spanish inquisitor general

Amerigo Vespucci (c.1451–1512) Florentine banker and explorer for Spain

John Day and **Lorenzo Pasqualigo** were real people also, but their characters in this novel have been largely fictionalized. Áll other characters are the author's fabrications.